IMMACULATE HEART

ALSO BY CAMILLE DeANGELIS

Bones & All

Mary Modern

Petty Magic

CAMILLE DeANGELIS

IMMACULATE
HEART

ST. MARTIN'S PRESS ≋ NEW YORK

IMMACULATE HEART. Copyright © 2016 by Camille DeAngelis.
All rights reserved. Printed in the United States of America.
For information, address St. Martin's Press,
175 Fifth Avenue, New York, N.Y. 10010.

www.stmartins.com

The Library of Congress Cataloging-in-Publication Data is available upon request.

ISBN 978-1-250-04651-2 (hardcover)
ISBN 978-1-4668-4678-4 (e-book)

Our books may be purchased in bulk for promotional, educational, or business use. Please contact your local bookseller or the Macmillan Corporate and Premium Sales Department at 1-800-221-7945, extension 5442, or by e-mail at specialmarkets@ macmillan.com.

First Edition: March 2016

10 9 8 7 6 5 4 3 2 1

For Seanan,
my Old Shoe

ACKNOWLEDGMENTS

Many people have encouraged my love of Ireland, and I apologize to anyone I'm about to leave out.

So much love and gratitude to my grandmother's cousin Gene Murphy and his wonderful family for all their kindness and hospitality over the years: Betty, Sharon, Yvonne, and Justin, and to our cousin Dick Wahner (may he rest in peace) for putting us in touch to begin with. Love to my father for giving me that first map of Ireland to hang on my bedroom wall, and to my mother and grandmother for inspiring me with their commitment to their faith. (We may not agree on the particulars, but I *am* convinced there's a world beyond the five senses, and I suppose my Catholic upbringing provided the foundation for a belief system that fits me.)

Go raibh míle maith agat to Pádraig Ó Cearúil, my Irish teacher at NYU, and a shout-out to *mo chara* Jennifer "Ní Bhlathanna." Kristen Couse and Tom Haslow, thank you for helping me get to Ireland for the first time in the spring of 2000 to check out the sights and pubs and hostels so I could write about it all. Ditto to Grace Fujimoto and the folks at Avalon for giving me another opportunity with *Moon Ireland* in 2006.

Seanan McDonnell, your friendship is one of the greatest joys of my life, and this story is so much better for your insight and thoughtful suggestions. Bán, JP, Fergal, Pádraig, Cían, Ann, Bríd Tynan, and the McCulloughs—you've always made me feel like a part of your family, to the point that "thanks a million" feels woefully insufficient. I've made many more dear friends through the MA in writing at NUI Galway: Ailbhe Slevin and Christian O'Reilly, Deirdre Sullivan and Diarmuid O'Brien, Shelley Troupe and James Mullaney, Patrick Curley (who, with his lovely sister Tara and mother Breda, kept me well and happy on a recent visit to Sligo), and Brendan O'Brien and his parents Margaret and Joe, who were always so kind to me on my visits to Carrick-on-Suir. Adrian Frazier, Mike McCormack, and Sinead Mooney: thank you for all the knowledge and insight you shared during my MA year. Emily Goldstein and Vince Murphy, you are terrific. I am also grateful to Celine Kiernan for advising me as to the finer points of Irish slang as well as which brand of cold cream an Irishwoman would use in 1987.

To my old-as-in-longstanding friends Kelly Brown, Aravinda Seshadri, and Leah Smith, and my sister Kate: thanks for your company (not to mention hijinks) on Inis Mór and elsewhere. Love and thanks to McCormick Templeman, Nova Ren Suma, Mackenzi Lee, Elizabeth Duvivier, Olivia White, Kelly Turley, and Amiee Wright.

Kate Garrick, you are *the best*. Sara Goodman, thank you so much for your seemingly limitless patience during the revision process. I feel so blessed to have you for my editor! Thanks to all the other wonderful folks at St. Martin's Press: Alicia Clancy, George Witte, Joan Higgins, Brant Janeway, Angie Giammarino,

Angela Craft, Lisa Pompilio, and Lauren Hougen. And thank you, as always, to Brian DeFiore and Shaye Areheart.

In addition to plumbing my mother's shelves for prayer books, hagiographies, and (rather too enthusiastic) tracts on the nature of hell and purgatory, I learned a lot from the following books: Patrick Tracey's *Stalking Irish Madness,* Nancy Scheper-Hughes's *Saints, Scholars, and Schizophrenics,* Russell Shorto's *Saints and Madmen,* Nicola Gordon Bowe's *The Life and Work of Harry Clarke,* Lucy Costigan and Michael Cullen's *Strangest Genius,* and Michael Walsh's *The Apparition at Knock.* Síle quotes from Keats's poem "The Eve of St. Agnes" in chapter six, and the fairy story Tess tells in chapter eight is very much inspired by Susanna Clarke's *The Ladies of Grace Adieu* and *Jonathan Strange & Mr. Norrell.* I was reading John McGahern's *The Dark* while writing Síle's journal entries, and if they're the best writing in the book then perhaps I can't take any credit for it. I must also thank Dr. Brian Hatcher at Tufts University, who gave me so much to feed my imagination in his Intro to Hinduism course.

To Memory Risinger, Debka Colson, Mary Bonina, Alexander Danner, and my other friends at the Writers' Room of Boston: I am very grateful for your warm welcome. Thanks to the WROB I was able to finish the first draft of *Immaculate Heart* in record time, and I have the loveliest memories of drinking coffee and watching the snow fall from my cozy little cubicle whenever I resurfaced out of the story.

IMMACULATE HEART

"They say time happens all at once," the woman says. "Did you ever hear that?" She stands in the surf wearing a blue dress that billows in the wind. The dress looks like one my mom used to wear on Sundays until somebody spilled bleach on it.

I shake my head. "What did you do with your shoes?" I ask. There are so many families on the outing today that I can't tell at first whose parents are whose. But she isn't anybody's mother. I've worked that out now.

The sun is at her back, so her face is in shadow, but I can tell she's smiling. "Past, present, and future, all rolled in together," she goes on. "So it doesn't matter what you do, does it? It doesn't matter, sure it doesn't."

I don't know why this lady wants to talk to me. I don't understand why she's telling me this stuff, when I'm just some kid digging for sand crabs along the shoreline of a country I've never been to before. From somewhere—all the way down the far end of the beach, it sounds like—I can hear my sister laughing.

"You don't see it yet, but you will." The wind lifts the woman's long black hair and makes darting shapes with it in the bright air. "It's happened, it's done, and that means you can do anything you like."

I

NOVEMBER 5

"The widow let out a terrible shriek, and her husband's hand fell from her waist as he crumpled to the floor. Then there came a great confusion in the house, but when the neighbors took him by the wrist, they found him well and truly lifeless. And that," said the old man, "is how Jack Brennan came to dance at his own wake."

Leo slumped back against the worn red upholstery inside the snug as if the story had exhausted him, and for a minute or two we sipped our pints in silence. He had the most remarkable ears I'd ever seen: the tops were mottled red and purple, the gray thatch sprouting from his inner ear was so thick it was a wonder he could hear anything at all, and the lobes dribbled down the sides of his face like melted candle wax.

"You didn't tell it quite so well as John did," Paudie said at last. "But sure, that's a good story no matter how you tell it."

I vaguely remembered Paudie and Brona from my first trip to Ireland when I was twelve, and Uncle John from the handful of times he'd come to the U.S., but this was the first time I'd met Leo. He told me he'd spent almost forty years making shoelaces in Liverpool, and I was still trying to work out whether or not he was joking.

"Ye'll never hear that story the way that Johnny told it." Leo rubbed at his eyes with trembling fingers. "Ye'll never hear it again. Not the way he told it."

The sight of the old man's tremors threw me backward into the afternoon. Halfway to Ballymorris in the pissing rain (as Leo called it), a crow had flown into my windshield, and just sitting here remembering it brought back the juddering of the steering wheel, the shuddering sensation up and down my arms. The wipers had flung the bird onto the highway, and when I'd lifted my eyes to the rearview mirror, I saw it, wings a mess, twitching on the pavement. A second crow came down to land beside the first, peering closely at its comrade, and I'd wondered if birds knew what to say in those final seconds any more than humans did.

Brona sighed. "Can't we talk of something *other* than death and dying?" John was gone, but it wouldn't do anybody any good to brood over it. She reached over and patted my arm. "What about you? You must have loads of stories from all the traveling you do, chasin' after news."

Leo dismissed his friend's question with a wave of a crinkled hand. "We've plenty of time to hear about all that." He leaned in with a conspiratorial air, drumming the table with his fingers. "C'mere, now, tell us: d'you have a wife or a girlfriend or—"

"He hasn't got a wife!" Paudie cut in. "Can't you see he hasn't got a ring on?"

Leo was not to be denied. "Well then, how about a girlfriend?"

I hid my face in my pint and waited for the moment to pass, because your love life is the last thing you want to talk about when you've left a good woman crying in her underwear only two nights before. Right now Laurel was probably in the living room, subtracting her books from the collection she'd so happily merged two years ago. Maybe she was alone, or maybe she'd invited a friend over—one who'd never liked me to begin with—but either way, there'd be nothing left of hers by the time I got home. I hated this: the knowing you couldn't give someone what they wanted, and the wishing they'd stop wanting it so the two of you could carry on with the easy life you'd already laid out for yourselves.

At least the worst of it was happening while I was three thousand miles away.

Brona proved her wise heart by changing the subject. "And how long do we have you for? Don't tell us you're leaving tomorrow!"

"I had a bunch of vacation days saved up," I said. "I fly home on the sixteenth."

"Ah, that's a nice bit of time," Paudie replied with satisfaction. "We'll show you everything there is to see, and a good deal more besides." Brona slid him a doubtful look over the rim of her glass.

"I thought I might drive down to Galway for a night or two," I said. "Maybe see the Cliffs of Moher. I don't know if we went there the last time I was here."

"D'you recall how our car broke down on the way home from Sligo that day?" Paudie laughed. "You lads were all worn out from the long day of swimming, and we had to pile ourselves into Johnny's and the Gallaghers' cars for the rest of the trip home."

As he spoke, the day revisited itself upon me: squished into the backseat of an old sedan, sand itching in every crevice, the right side of my body pressed against the freckled contours of a ginger-haired girl. We'd played together; I remembered I'd liked her, but packed into the backseat of that car with the threadbare red-and-brown upholstery, no one spoke or laughed as we had on the beach. Probably just sunburnt and cranky after the long day.

I shrugged and gave him an apologetic smile. "I wish I could remember more from that time we were here." When conversations went this way, I tended to act as if I remembered less than I did, even if the memory in question seemed inconsequential on the surface. The past was the safest place to hide anything you couldn't make sense of.

"Ah, well," Paudie sighed. "'Twas a long time ago now."

Brona had opened her mouth to respond when someone caught her eye in the doorway behind me. I turned and recognized their faces from the wake that afternoon, and once Brona had accepted their reprised condolences, I had to nod and smile through another round of *Ethna's grandson, all the way from New York!* (And in Park Slope, someone else was saying, *What an asshole he turned out to be . . .*)

Brona was my grandmother's first cousin, her closest family left now that her brother was gone. When I arrived at the little row house where my great-uncle John had lived out his bachelor-hood, Brona had answered the door, clutched me by the lapels, and drawn my face down level with hers to plant a thick wet kiss on my cheek. "You're twice as tall as the last time I saw you," she'd said, and I remembered how she'd once offered me a box of candy and inside was a sad little clump of Turkish delight left over from a none-too-recent Christmas. I'd pried off a piece, and my jaw went sore from chewing. "I light a candle for your poor sister every Sunday," Brona told me as she took my coat, and I hadn't known what to say to that.

It was odd to see a light burning in a dead man's window, to knock on the door and find the front room full of strangers who already knew my name, but it was a relief that I could actually understand them this time. When I was a kid, it would take me a minute to figure out what people were saying—they might laugh at what they'd said before I even got it—and those hiccups in my comprehension had made me feel stupid. My grandmother had lost most of her accent after living so long in Pennsylvania.

On Uncle John's kitchen table there were sandwich fixings, five different brands of whiskey, and a slab of fruitcake on a paper doily. There was a sense that no one would use these plates and teacups again after tonight, and yet the wake had felt a little like a birthday party. The coziness of a good stiff drink, a crackling fire in the fireplace, amiable company, and even a bit of laughter here and there—it was easy to go on as if we weren't feeling anything different underneath. John had been a good man, but I still speculated about the things in his life, the dark things, that no one here would ever know the truth of.

Brona had informed me that she sometimes did food demos for the local supermarket as she assembled a plate for me. "Here's some Gortnamona goat's cheese for your sandwich. Lovely stuff. You've never tasted the like of it, not even in New York City." When they spoke of John, they made me wish I'd paid this visit years ago, that my grandmother and I had come back together when I was old enough to appreciate things like goat's cheese and old people's ghost stories.

And yet I'd felt in the rental car, hadn't I, that Mallory was coming back with me somehow? I'd been looking in the rearview at that crow lying in the roadway when something in the backseat had caught the light: the white of an eye perhaps, as if she were turning away in tears from the heap of feathers on the wet road. I'd looked again, my heart lodged in my throat, and seen only my duffel bag there on the seat.

Mallory had always cried over dead animals. She'd found the jawbone of a sheep in the sand that day. It was only a bone, but she'd been pretty much inconsolable.

I shook myself. No more of that, now. I could blame myself for other things, but it wasn't my fault she was dead.

It was so comforting, all the clamor and reek of the pub. Brona and the men had fallen into talking of other things with their friends and neighbors—wasn't so-and-so in hospital passing a kidney stone, and didn't Carmel Keane down the road have her front garden dug up with all the plumbing trouble—and I couldn't see the television above the bar from my seat, so I occupied myself with the pictures and bric-a-brac on the walls. There were drums with harps or Celtic knots painted on the front, and a yellowed broadsheet titled *Poblacht Na H-Eireann,* and a vintage advertisement with a blonde flashing her legs atop a head of stout. *There are only TWO things a man can't resist . . . a pint of Guinness and ANOTHER pint!*

Then I turned to my right, and found a newspaper article in a dusty metal frame: *More Visions for the Ballymorris Four.* In the accompanying photograph four teenagers stood beneath a statue of the Madonna in a grotto thick with ivy, and to the side I could make out a cement ledge lined with pillar candles. *The Blessed Virgin has appeared to local children with a message of love and repentance: Orla Gallagher (16), Declan Keaveney (17), Síle Gallagher (14), and Teresa McGowan (16).*

Each of the girls wore a school uniform with a pleated skirt, but the boy had on an old leather bomber that, coupled with a surly turn of the lip, made me dislike him right away. Guys like that hadn't shoved me around in high school, but they'd *smirked* at me, and that was worse. I studied their faces, and it hit me: I'd seen this photograph before.

The clipping had arrived in the mail one day while I was at my grandmother's house after school. It was two months after Mallory's accident, and even the scent of the shepherd's pie baking in the oven seemed horribly wrong. Gran sipped her tea as she read the letter from her brother, and then she'd slid the folded bit of newspaper across the kitchen table for me to read. She passed no comment on the miraculous happenings. All she said was, "You remember those girls, don't you?"

I did. I knew Tess, with her freckled face and her long red hair, and I knew her friend Orla, though none but the youngest—Síle—seemed particularly happy to be photographed that day. *Sheila*. That's how I'd seen her name in my head, back when we'd known each other.

"Is it for real?" I'd asked my grandmother, and she'd pursed her lips as she tucked the letter and newspaper clipping back into the envelope. "Who can say?" she'd sighed. "Ah, but I do worry for them."

Now I studied Síle's face in the article framed and hanging on the wall. Her dark hair fell loose and gleaming over her shoulders, and it was remarkable how her eyes could shine out of a pattern of tiny black dots. She and Mallory had played together on the beach that day, and because of her, apart from the sheep's bone anyway, my sister had acted like a completely different person. She'd been happier than I'd ever seen her, happier than I would ever see her again.

I glanced up at the header—*28 March 1988*—and felt something cold slither deep in my gut. That was the day of the accident. If I'd felt I needed to come back here, to finish something I couldn't quite remember starting, well . . . didn't that just clinch it?

The funeral crowd was filing out the door now. I shook my head to dislodge the memory of the bird convulsing in the road, the gleam of an eye in the backseat. Paudie leaned over and pointed to the last girl in the photograph. "That's Tess, my brother Eamonn's daughter." He gave me a sideways look. "D'you remember her?"

I squinted at her face as if I hadn't already recognized her. "Yeah," I said slowly. "She has red hair, right?"

Paudie seemed like a nice guy, but I couldn't help feeling as if I'd passed some sort of test. "She does, indeed," he replied.

I tapped on the glass inside the frame. "So there was really a . . . what do you call it . . . a 'Mary sighting' here?" At the time, of course, I'd been far too preoccupied with Mallory's absence to wonder much about any of it. *Visions of the Blessed Virgin.* Was it like one of those statues weeping in a church?

"The apparition happened a few years after you were here," Brona replied. "It went on for months."

"Turned all of Ballymorris on its head," Leo went on. "I was on my holidays that spring, so I can tell you. First there were the reporters from RTÉ, then the pilgrims poured in from all over. The old hotel reopened, and there were new restaurants, new shops. 'Twas the best thing to happen to this place in a hundred years."

Brona shot Leo a look. "'Twas a good thing for Ballymorris, in *some* ways," she amended.

"The apparition," I said. "Where was it?"

"Just outside town, at the grotto above the Sligo road," Brona replied. "The young ones used to go up there after school, if the day was clear."

"Hardly anyone goes there now, though," Leo put in. "Not even to pray."

I didn't think my grandmother had ever taken us up there; I guess there hadn't been much of a reason to before this thing happened. "Was it recognized? By the pope, I mean. That's the way it works, right?"

Paudie cleared his throat. "It wasn't, no."

"Most of them aren't," Brona said. "They're reported, and someone says they'll be looked into, and then they quietly fade away, to everyone but those who've seen her."

Seeing as Paudie was related to one of the people involved, I couldn't come out with the most obvious question: did they actually believe in it?

"How are Tess and the others?" I asked him. "What are they up to now?"

"Well, Tess is with the Sisters of Compassion here in town . . ."

I felt an unpleasant little jolt of surprise, as if someone had opened the bathroom door on me. "She's a nun?"

"A lay sister," Paudie said. "She's the director of the youth center over in Milk Lane."

Again I thought of her hip and thigh pressed against mine in the car that day. It was impossible to picture her grown up and given over to God. "And the others?"

"Orla is married and livin' up the road with her three young ones," Paudie replied, while Leo added in a stage whisper, "You'll know her from a mile away. She's gone permanently orange with all the self-tanner." Brona clucked her tongue and smacked him on the wrist.

"As for Declan," Paudie went on, "he left for Australia years ago, and I don't know that anyone's seen or heard much of him since."

"And what about Síle?"

"Síle?" Paudie hesitated. "Aye, she's still here."

"She lives nearby?"

"She's living in Sligo. North of town, past Rosses Point."

There was a silence here that felt awkward, though I didn't see why it should have. The three exchanged a look. "She's in a place," Leo said. "A home, like."

"A home?"

"She's not quite right, if you know what I mean. She's a lovely girl, you'd never see a lovelier girl in all your life, but—"

"She's troubled," Brona broke in gently.

"How so?"

"She was always different, Síle." Paudie tilted his pint so the final mouthful sloshed around the bottom of the glass. "Like some wild thing out of a fairy story."

Leo was nodding. "Like a selkie, aye. She didn't belong."

"She charmed everyone she met," Brona went on, "and yet she hadn't a friend in the world growing up. No one ever knew what to make of her, you see."

"She and my sister got along very well," I said. "I do remember that."

Brona regarded me sadly. "If only you hadn't lived so far away."

I looked back at the newspaper article on the wall. Fourteen-year-old Síle Gallagher smiled at me out of 1988, and I felt something whisper, *You let them think you came back here for a funeral, but that's not why.*

"I'd like to know more about this whole thing," I said. "Do you think I might be able to speak with the priest?"

Paudie shot me a squinty look. "Would you be thinking of writing about the apparition?"

I finished my Guinness and licked my lips. "Maybe."

Maybe meant *yes,* of course. Writing about the weird things that might have happened to them gave me a reason to see them again—Tess and Orla and Síle. Síle, too young to flirt, and she did it anyway.

There was another pause around the table before Paudie said, "You might want to talk to Tess first. I'll ring her in the morning and see can she speak to you." He made a valiant attempt at a smile. "Sure, you'll be wanting to see her again regardless. The two of ye were great friends that time you were here."

They didn't seem disapproving, exactly, but I caught their uneasiness flickering like a subliminal message on a movie screen. Leo glanced at me as he lifted his glass, and quickly looked away.

Then they fell into talking of other things, and I got up to buy another round. At one time the pub had done double duty as a grocery, and a shelf behind the bar was lined with tins of "coffee whitener" that looked older than Paudie and Brona and Leo put together. Napper Tandy's was their local, through and through—I gathered they never drank anywhere else.

I shouldn't have ordered that last pint. Sometimes I caught an anecdote and chuckled along, and other times I almost forgot where I was. I was too tired to be good company, but they forgave me.

Brona set me up in her spare room, but even with a space heater there was a dankness and a mildewy smell clinging to the bedding and towels. I almost felt as if I were entombed in this little room where the brown floral bedspread matched the draperies, and yet I was as unencumbered by my own life as I could possibly be: the uncertainty of my position at the magazine, the certainty of Laurel. The light had never gone out of her eyes, not even on that last night when I'd left to sleep on a friend's couch. Maybe she was still hoping I could be the man she'd mistaken me for.

I got into bed and turned out the lamp, but I was too restless to sleep. There were basic things about that childhood visit I genuinely couldn't remember. Had we stayed here or at John's house, and what had we eaten besides Turkish delight, and had John played any card games with us? Had we seen any ring forts or castles? How had we occupied ourselves when it rained?

And yet the most ordinary moments had never lost their clarity: Mallory throwing a pebble at me on the beach, Mallory asking our grandmother if our parents were getting a divorce, Mallory crawling behind a sofa in search of Gran's gaudy fake-gold clip-on earring. Maybe the memories of Mallory were clearest only because there would never be any more of them.

The silence weighed on me in that damp little room. I was alone, and yet there was a weird air of expectancy, the way it is when you're in the midst of a difficult conversation and you're just sitting there, fool that you are, waiting on the other person to speak.

2

The mattress was worn, the springs digging into my ribs whenever I surfaced out of a dream, but I told Brona I'd slept well. The narrow bathroom still smelled of her husband's aftershave, and the electric shower yielded little more than a trickle.

After breakfast I drove out to "Apparition Hill," where a brown sign marked GROTTO led up a gravel track from the main road. The level ground at the top was punctuated by a crag wreathed in thorny brush, into which the shrine was set. It hadn't changed much since the newspaper photograph: in her niche the Virgin clasped her hands, eyes rolled heavenward in that signature expression of vacant serenity, and bouquets of faded synthetic flowers and pillar candles brimming with rainwater lined the cement ledges on either side. There was even a crutch propped against the ledge—but only one, as if the Mother of God had started on a miracle before changing her mind. I was pretty sure my grandmother hadn't brought us up here.

I parked my rented Micra behind a bench scored with the

testimony of ancient teenage romances. From here you could see the little town laid out like a forgotten game of checkers, beyond it a muted green patchwork receding into hills and fog. The grass was strewn with potato chip bags, crumpled cider cans, and empty packs of cigarettes.

On the far end of the lot, I found a little white truck with a counter along one side, facing the grotto to keep the wind out. Rosaries and prayer cards spilled out of the window on hooks and display racks. I came a few steps closer and saw someone hunched inside—closer still, and I found a gaunt little lady I guessed to be nearly ninety, if not past it. Her skin was crinkled like twice-used tissue paper, and her jutting chin gave her the air of a witch in a fairy tale. I could tell before she opened her mouth that she had dentures, and also that she wasn't wearing them.

"Good morning," I said.

She stared at me, then remembering herself, fumbled for a jar on a shelf by her elbow. "Beg pardon," she said as she plucked her teeth out of the container and fitted them in. "I'd a pain in me jaw."

"Toothache?"

She rolled her eyes and clucked her tongue. "If you live long enough, you'll have none of yours, either."

I replied with a smile as I looked around at her inventory. A fluorescent light buzzed and flickered overhead. The old woman drummed her yellow fingernails on the counter, inspecting my face through her dusty bifocals. "Now, what is it that brings a nice lad like you up here on such a filthy morning?"

I picked up a prayer card, gave it a glance without reading any of it, and put it back. "Fresh air," I replied. "You get much business up here?"

She shrugged. "Enough."

I looked at her, and she parted her lips in a gummy grin. She knew I knew she was lying. "You've heard the stories?" she asked.

"About the apparition?"

The old woman nodded, and leaned forward on her stool as if she were about to divulge something juicy. "Did they tell you about the miracle?"

"What miracle? I thought the church decided the apparition wasn't real."

"Oh, aye, they always do. Doesn't mean it wasn't."

"You think it *was* real?"

"If it was or it wasn't, what *I* think makes no difference a'tall."

I laughed. "There's a slippery answer."

The lady gave me a sideways look as she pointed to a rack of cross pendants and religious medals in what passed for gold and silver. "Now, you'll be wanting a souvenir from your time here. Something for your gran?"

"Why?" I asked. "Do you know my gran?"

"I know everybody's gran that was born in Ballymorris, and that's a promise." Again she seemed to be sizing me up. "I remember you, lad. You came back with her, ah, let's see, 'twas a good few years back." She nodded to herself with a weirdly satisfied look on her face. "You came in the summertime."

I laughed. "You can't possibly remember me. That was twenty-five years ago, and we were only here a week."

The old woman stared at me in mock contempt. "Sure, you're only sayin' so because *you* don't remember *me*."

She had me there.

"Let's see here," she went on, "I've Saint Anthony, Saint Patrick, Saint Joseph—ah!—and I've this miraculous medal as well—that's the Blessed Virgin, y'see—now wouldn't this make a lovely wee gift for your granny?" She plucked another box from the rack. "Saint Christopher, here's the one you'll be wanting, for he's the patron saint of travelers. This one's forty, but I'll give it to you for thirty-five, so."

"I did make it across the Atlantic without any help from Saint Christopher," I pointed out.

"Ah, but who's to say what might happen on the return journey?"

I raised an eyebrow, and she answered with another shameless grin.

"I'll take my chances," I said.

"These rosaries have been blessed by the bishop," she went on, running a crooked finger along the rows of plastic beads. "I've rosaries from Medjugorje and Fatima and Lourdes, and I've holy water all the way from Rome as well as Saint Brigid's Well just down the road. What about a bottle of holy water to bring home to your gran?"

"No, thank you."

Then she saw me glancing over her tiny army of statuettes. "This one's my bestseller," she said as she thrust a five-inch image of the Virgin into my hand. "Wait and see. She glows in the dark."

I couldn't imagine she sold enough of anything up here to have a bestseller. I replaced the statuette on the counter, and she pressed another laminated prayer card into my hand. *Save a dozen souls in the time it takes to boil an egg.* The prescribed prayer followed in small print. "I think you'll find this one very useful."

"One down, eleven to go," I said, and this time I decided to humor her. She sold me the card for a euro fifty, and I tucked it in my wallet. "Now that you've made your sale, will you answer my question?"

The old woman looked up at me, her pale eyes wide and mocking. "And what question would that be?"

"Do you actually believe in all this?"

"You might ask Martina McGowan," the old woman replied. "Sure, weren't the doctors about to take her leg above the knee before the Blessed Mother healed it, and with the waters of this very well?" She jabbed a finger toward the row of little plastic bottles of holy water.

"Is that true?"

"Course it's true."

"Nobody mentioned it to me before. I feel like that's the sort of thing they'd have told me."

"Who's 'they'?" she asked, suddenly sharp. "Who told you?"

"Paudie, who owns the bookstore on Shop Street, and Leo, and my cousin Brona."

"Ahhh," she said slowly. "They don't speak of it, y'see. 'Twas Martina's own daughter, Paudie's niece, who took part in the visions." She cocked her head, and I saw a brightness in her eyes that hadn't been there before. "'Twas Síle did the healing. She saw things none o' the rest o' them could see."

It was beginning to rain. "And how would you know that?" I asked.

"Ask the girl—if you can," said the old woman, just before she pulled out her teeth and redeposited them in the jar by her elbow. "They say she doesn't know what's real, but *I* knew her better than most. I've a notion they don't like what she saw, and they've hidden her away for it."

"Paudie rang a wee while ago," Brona said when I came back from the hill. "He says Tess has agreed to meet with you, but he'd like to speak with you before you ring her."

I had borrowed John's old cell phone, and found Paudie's number in his contacts while Brona fixed us tea and sandwiches for lunch. "She'll meet with you tomorrow morning, if that suits," Paudie said. "And have you any plans for the afternoon?" When I told him I wanted to go to the library to read up on the apparition in some of the old newspapers, he said, "No need for the library, lad. Joan, my wife, she kept a scrapbook of all the news articles from that time. It's still here somewhere. I'll have it ready for you by the time you call over."

I told him I'd stop by the bookshop after lunch. Then I called Tess—I found her number, too, already in my phone. "Paudie mentioned you were coming back," she said. "I saw you at the funeral, but there were so many people I thought perhaps I should give you my condolences another time."

I couldn't hide my surprise. "You mean . . . you remember me?"

She paused. "I do, of course. We'd a lovely day together at the beach."

"Yeah," I said. "I do remember that."

Something shifted on the line, and when Tess spoke again, her tone was friendly but brisk. "Paudie says you wanted to speak to me about the visitation. I don't know that I have much to say at this stage, but you're welcome to call round for a cup of tea." We arranged for me to come to her office at the youth center the following morning, and she hung up.

McGowan's bookshop was only three doors down from Napper Tandy's pub, and though both signs were missing apostrophes, I doubted there was much overlap in the clientele. The two rooms, front and back, offered that crammed and cozy feeling a shop can have only when it's as old as it looks, with the proprietor living upstairs. Paudie put the kettle on in the tiny kitchenette off the back room, its only window looking out onto a muddy yard, and I had a quick browse while he made the tea.

NEW OLD AND RARE read the hand-painted sign outside, but it seemed the only new books were corralled on a small table near the entryway. I pulled down a clothbound hardcover called *Permissive Society in Ireland* and caught a hint of pipe tobacco as I opened it, taking one more sniff from the gutter before putting it back on the shelf. This was the best thing about secondhand shops, coming upon proof of lives that would never intersect with mine apart from this one simple object.

Paudie drew up another stool for me behind the counter, poured the tea, and began rummaging through a pile of newspapers and magazines on the shelf beneath the cash register.

"I went up to the hill this morning," I said as he frowned at the clutter. "You know the woman up there who runs that little shop out of a truck?"

"Ah, that would be Margaret O'Grady. Old Mag, they call her." I watched his eyes light up as he produced his wife's scrapbook from the bottom of the stack. "Now! Here we are. Knew it was here someplace."

"She said something about Tess's mom having her leg cured," I went on. "She was supposed to have it amputated?"

Paudie laid the scrapbook on the counter and seated himself on his stool before answering, and he didn't meet my eye as he spoke. "Aye, that's so—my brother's wife, Martina. 'Twas a miracle, by all accounts."

I was watching his face. "Why do you say it like that?"

The old man ran his fingers over his dead wife's handwriting. *The Ballymorris Visions, 1987–1988.* "Discomfort in the face of the great mystery, I suppose. You want to believe, but it never sits easy with you."

"How does Martina feel about it?"

Again Paudie hesitated. "She was very grateful, of course. It renewed their faith." There was something awkward in all this miracle business. He was talking around it, but I've gotten pretty good at knowing when to bide my time.

He opened the binder and we paged through it together, Paudie patiently sipping his tea as I read each article and jotted down names and details in my pocket notebook. The apparition headlines didn't vary much from one day to the next—*Blessed Virgin Appears to Ballymorris Teens; Messages of Love and Hope from Ballymorris to the World*—nor did the content of the articles themselves, though they appeared in the *Connaught Daily* almost every day in February and March, 1988. Each article was clipped and pasted onto its own page, complete with header and date. "Your wife was very neat," I said. "She must have been a big help to you here."

"She was—ah, she was!" When Paudie sighed, I sensed a hole in the stillness of the shop, a vacancy that hadn't been there until the moment we spoke of her. "Do you remember my Joan, lad? She made the sandwiches for the picnic that day. Helped you choose a novel for your summer reading."

"I think I remember that," I said, because I wanted to please him. The ham-and-cheese sandwich recalled itself with greater clarity than the book selection.

"We met at the library at UCD. I found herself behind the reference desk, pestered her with every question I could think of while I gathered the courage to ask her out to lunch." He cocked his head, glancing around at his bookshelves. "'Twas her idea to come home again and open this shop. Not *her* home," he amended. "She was from Wexford, only she hadn't much family left to go back to." Paudie seemed half sad and half content, which I suppose was the only way you *could* feel after a long and happy life with someone you loved.

They say you can't possibly know the shape of your own future, but that's not true. Sometimes you do. And I would never know anything close to what Paudie was feeling now, not for anyone, not ever.

I turned the page and found the article accompanying that picture on the wall at Napper Tandy's: *More Visions for the Ballymorris Four.*

An apparition of the Blessed Virgin Mary has appeared to four local teenagers. The young people, Orla Gallagher (16), Síle Gallagher (14), Teresa McGowan (16), and Declan Keaveney (17), attend secondary school at St. Brigid's College in Ballymorris. The apparition initially appeared on the first of November, and has continued to reveal Herself most afternoons at the same time and location.

"It was an ordinary day," Miss McGowan explained. "We like to go up to the hill above the Sligo road for the view, so that's where we were. It's hard to describe what happened. It was like the air around us changed."

Miss Síle Gallagher elaborated: "Declan was telling a story, but all of a sudden his voice sounded very far away. The air felt thick, like we were in the middle of a great rolling fog, but there was no fog; and all the lines and colours around us softened, and there she was."

The Blessed Virgin offered a message of forgiveness, repentance, and universal love. The teens agree that whilst they did not hear Her speak aloud, Her words were clearly felt, and that the message was the same for each of them. The Blessed Virgin also asked that they share Her words with all the world's faithful. "We'll begin with Ballymorris, and continue from here," said Miss McGowan.

The pastor of St. Brigid's Church, Father Michael Dowd, has interviewed each of the four youths, and is currently compiling a report for Bishop Scanlon of the Diocese of Ardagh. "These young people are all from very devout Christian families, and very earnest in speaking with me as to what they saw," Father Dowd said. "I cannot doubt their sincerity."

The four friends agree that the experience has strengthened their bond, and that they now feel more inclined to prayer and reflection. "We believe She has chosen us for a reason," said Miss Orla Gallagher. "Not because we are the most devout, but because we could be."

Her younger sister, Miss Síle Gallagher, went on to explain that the apparition took solid form. At one point she felt the Blessed Virgin's hand, warm and soft, on her own. "It was as real as when my mam used to come in to kiss me good night," she said.

I shivered a little, and looked over at Paudie. "Did Tess ever talk to you about what she experienced?"

"From time to time, she would tell me a bit. She hasn't spoken of it in years now, so don't be surprised if she says very little to you when you see her."

"She did agree to meet with me," I pointed out. We'd known each other a long time ago, but not well enough to justify any sort of reunion. Not really.

"So she did," Paudie said.

A little while later, we came to the end of the scrapbook. I'd expected to find an interview with Martina McGowan about the "miracle," but in the later articles, it was only ever mentioned in passing, as if the writers had taken the whole business for undeniable fact. Yet another opportunity wasted through lazy journalism— and, as had happened to me on more than one occasion, I felt spurred on by someone else's failure. *Someone* had to tell the story properly, and I knew it should be me. This place was in my blood, after all.

"I'll only ask you the one thing." Paudie closed the scrapbook and laid his palm on it as if he were about to swear on a Bible. "Whatever Tess tells you, I'd like to read your piece before you publish it. Can you promise me that?"

"Of course," I said. I'd reneged on this sort of thing before, but I'd worry about that when the time came.

The old man nodded. "Good lad."

I rose from my stool to help him with the tea things. No one had come into the shop in the hour I'd been there, but if Paudie noticed, he gave no sign.

Late that afternoon, Brona drove me out to a place called Gurteen to see the tumbledown stone cottage where my grandmother's father was born, and the quiet little churchyard where the rest of our ancestors were buried. Paudie and Leo came along and provided a running commentary from the backseat. They pointed out what looked like an old milking shed and said that was where their parents had gone set dancing back in the day. "That place, there." Paudie tapped on the foggy glass. "That was Jack Brennan's house. The man who danced at his own wake." The rain eased to a drizzle but never let up entirely, and as we passed building after ruined building, I began to understand why my grandmother had been so desperate to leave.

"Sometimes I get a bit lonely for the old days," Leo sighed. "Before there was anything more to build and all the Poles showed up."

"Leo!" Brona gasped, and I laughed.

"If he's going to be xenophobic," I said, "at least he has the decency to be upfront about it."

We came to the ruined church and got out of the car. The building wasn't *that* dilapidated, actually—it still had a roof—and we waited behind Brona as she fitted the key she'd borrowed from the parish secretary into the padlock on the side gate.

"This is the old Protestant church," said Paudie as we passed into the graveyard. "If you travel round, you'll find the Catholic churches are all on the new side, owing to the suppression of the faith up to the time of Daniel O'Connell."

"Oh, don't bore the lad with all that!" Leo replied breezily.

Paudie sniffed. "I was only after givin' him a bit of historical context."

"Tell me about your gran," Leo asked. "Is she happy?"

It was a simple question, but it still struck me as a bit odd. "She seems happy," I ventured. "She likes living in Florida. She stays busy."

"Oh? And how does she keep busy?"

"She volunteers at the library, she's part of a bridge circle, stuff like that. I guess you could say it keeps her young."

"She'll always be young to me," he said as we passed onto the uneven ground of the graveyard.

I had no idea what it felt like to know that you'd never see an old friend again—even if you were both still alive and well on opposite sides of the ocean—and I hoped I never would. "I guess it's been a long time since you last saw her."

"Sixty years," Leo replied, and there was more emotion in those two words than I'd seen in him so far.

Beyond the churchyard wall stretched a crooked grid of fields. Everything was green, but nothing was growing. "Were you very close friends growing up?"

"Oh, aye. Johnny and Paudie and Colum and Brona. And myself and Ethna," he added. "Did she tell you about me? Before you came?"

I laughed. "If you're asking if she remembers you, Leo, I'd say forgetting you was never an option."

He gave an impatient wave of his hand. "But did she mention me a'tall?" He faltered on a sunken patch of earth, and I reached out and gripped him under the elbow.

"She told me about you, yeah." Brona was leading us down to the Donegan family plot. I couldn't have cared less, but she didn't need to know that.

"And what did she say? Your gran?"

"She said you were a troublemaker."

He chuckled, but I could see he didn't find it as funny as he was making out to. "That's Ethna," he said, and then we arrived at the old gravesite.

We watched as Brona cleared away the dead leaves from the base of the marker, then got down on her knees and crossed herself as she murmured a prayer. The stone was speckled gray and green with lichen, the list of names meaningless beyond the simple fact of genetic inheritance. This was an old graveyard, but the burials had continued until recently. There were plaques full of platitudes headed MOTHER or SISTER, waterlogged plastic globes with fake flowers inside. Paudie stood with his hands thrust in his coat pockets, looking up at the trees and the sky as if he might find what he was looking for above our heads rather than beneath our feet.

After a minute or two, Leo and I started back to the car. "Did ya know your granddad?" he asked.

"He died when I was a kid," I said. "I wish I'd had more time with him."

"Was he a good man?"

"Everyone says he was."

"Aye, but how do *you* remember him?"

A memory welled up, Christmastime in midtown Manhattan. Mallory was only a baby.

My grandparents had taken me up to the city for the day to see the Rockettes, and while my grandmother was off shopping in one of the department stores, my grandfather snuck me into a tobacconist's. The place was crowded, the men in the lounge area towering over me in a haze of smoke. "Don't you ever take up smoking, son," my grandfather told me as the man behind the counter handed him a package of pipe tobacco. "It's a nasty habit, but I can't seem to help myself." That had been his second-to-last Christmas.

"He was kind," I said. "Yeah. I do remember him that way."

I glanced at Leo and found him already looking at me. The old man nodded gravely. "Then he was worthy."

"I counted twelve pubs on the ride back," I said as Paudie delivered the first round that night. "Why do you always go to the same one?"

"Ah, we've been comin' here since we were each of us in nappies," Leo replied as he took his first sip. "Why go anywhere else, when here's the next best thing to your own sitting room?"

"And that's no exaggeration," Brona put in. "Paudie's uncle used to own this place, long before it was known as Napper Tandy's, and all the family would come out for the Sunday carvery."

"They don't do the carvery anymore," Leo said gloomily. "Now, that I don't like. They'd do very well to start it up again, but sure, no one listens to an old man."

"The Sunday carvery," Brona sighed. "We took you once, when you were here. You and your sister. Do you remember that?"

I'd eaten all the roast beef on Mallory's plate. She hadn't wanted it. But I shook my head. "I don't. I'm sorry."

"When you go home, ask your gran if she remembers the carvery lunch at McGowan's pub, and how afterwards we'd play conkers in the yard."

"I'll ask her," I said.

For a minute we drank in silence. "And what's your plan for tomorrow, once you've met with Tess?" Paudie asked.

"Hopefully I'll get to talk to Father Lynch," I said. "And if there's time in the afternoon I'll drive up to Sligo to see Síle."

"Look at this one, all free and easy!" Leo's laugh made me think of opening a soda can that's been shaken. He was fizzing over. "From all that they tell me, lad, you'll have an easier time gettin' in to see the queen of the Shee."

3

I found St. Brigid's Youth Centre around the corner from the church in an old row house, sunflowers and butterflies painted on the façade by childish hands. There was no sidewalk, so I was pretty much standing in the road as I waited for Tess McGowan to come to the door. The houses were two-storied, but there was a smallness to them that made me feel I could reach up and tap on an upstairs windowpane. Every other house on the street was done in some desiccated color, gray or beige or yellow like old teeth. Smoke rose from the chimneys of several houses along the lane, the scent in the air rich and earthy, though Brona had told me hardly anyone burned real peat anymore, only peat briquettes from the corner shop. The smell of peat I remembered from the last trip, even though we'd come in the middle of July. It was ten o'clock in the morning, and nothing stirred the lace curtains in every front window.

When she opened the door, her freckles were the first thing I saw: bright and abundant on her pale skin, as if she were still a ten-year-old tomboy. She'd pulled her burnished red hair back from her face with the sort of clip my mother had worn in the eighties, and a gold cross pendant dangled below the neckline of a plain gray pullover. She greeted me with a firm handshake and a cautious smile, laughing out loud when I called her Teresa.

"Call me Tess." Her eyes roved over my face. "You've hardly changed."

"Neither have you," I said cheerfully, but I didn't like how it made me feel, replying as if we'd known each other better than we had.

Today was Wednesday, but when we passed the front sitting room, a pair of teenage boys glanced up from the television. In that second, I took in their knobby throats, spotted cheeks, and worn-out band shirts, the black vinyl couch and the Nintendo controllers clenched in their skinny fingers, the open bags of potato chips and overturned soda cans on the shag carpet at their feet.

"Shouldn't they be in school?" I whispered as Tess led me up the stairs.

"If they're going to mitch, I'd much rather see them here," she replied as she closed her office door behind me. "I want this to be a safe place for them to grow out of all that." She went to a sideboard and picked up an electric kettle. "I've just boiled water for tea. Will you have a cup?"

"Yes, please." Her desk looked out over the narrow street. Settling myself in the thrift-store chair beside it felt a little like taking a seat in a confession box.

Tess dropped tea bags in a pair of mugs and poured the water. "So Brona passed you Johnny's phone, did she? It gave me a fright yesterday when his name showed up on the caller ID."

I was taking in the walls, the cracks in the plaster carefully patched. There were years' worth of photographs of teenagers dressed like pirates and witches and aliens; strumming guitars on a makeshift stage with their hair in their eyes; standing outside the youth center with their arms slung casually around Tess's shoulders; holding up their paintings for the camera while trying not to look quite so proud as they felt. There were posters too, JESUS IS MY FAVOURITE ROCKSTAR and WE LOVE BECAUSE HE LOVED US FIRST. I turned back to face her. "Sorry about that. It's just easier for while I'm here. The roaming charges on my iPhone are crazy."

She cast me a wry smile—*Johnny wouldn't mind*—as she carried the mugs to the desk. I watched her remove the tea bag and stir a spoonful of sugar into her cup. "How long have you worked here?" I asked.

She cocked her head, forming a mental tally. "Seven years? Eight? Closer to eight, I suppose."

"Paudie says you run this place single-handedly."

She shrugged. "That makes it sound like work. I've never seen it that way."

I drank my tea. "I guess you're doing what you're meant to be doing, then."

Tess smiled, and the smile was her answer. She would have been attractive if she weren't dressed like a nun—but then, she *was* a nun, or near enough to it.

She cleared her throat. "Well, then. I suppose we'd better get to the purpose of your visit. You want to write an article about the apparition, is that right?"

"I'm not sure yet. I guess I should start by telling you I don't have any preconceived ideas about what you experienced, and I'm not looking for an answer as to whether or not you actually saw what you think you saw. I may be a journalist, but I also know that some questions truly don't have answers." She raised her fingers to the cross around her neck and smiled faintly in agreement. "I'm interested in the social context," I went on. "Leo was telling me that the visitations brought the town a great deal of money and attention, and I want to understand how and why it changed this place." I gave her my most affable smile. "So what do you say, Tess? Is it all right if I ask you a few questions?"

She gave me a look I couldn't interpret. "You're one of those people who're never not working, aren't you?"

I grinned. "I'll admit to it if you will."

She let out a soft little laugh. "Fair enough."

"If I'm being too pushy, will you tell me?"

She hesitated.

"Tess?"

"It's only . . . it's only that it's a bit strange to have you back here after all this time. To know you and *not* know you at the same time, and to have you . . ." She drew a breath. "To have you here, asking after the one thing I never talk about."

"Look," I said. "I'll be perfectly honest. I *want* to remember that trip in 1982 a whole lot better than I actually do. I remember we went to the beach that day, and of course I remember you . . ." From the way she was looking at me now I could tell I'd hurt her feelings, though she was making an effort to mask it. "I'm sorry," I said. "I really wish I could remember more. I know I liked you—I know we got along well that day. Could we . . . could we maybe start there?"

She nodded and gave me half a smile. "I'll tell you whatever you'd like to know. It's just that I haven't discussed it in so long. I haven't given an interview since that time."

"Really? Not in twenty years?"

She picked a speck of lint off her jeans. "I try not to speak or think of it, if I can help it."

Tess seemed like a practical, down-to-earth sort of woman—not at all a religious nut who'd stake her life's work on a hallucination, or make up elaborate stories for the attention they'd temporarily afford her. We would come around to the apparition itself; I just wasn't sure yet how the conversation would carry us there.

"We can just talk about the town, if you prefer." I drew my digital recorder out of my jacket pocket. "May I?" She nodded, and I turned it on and laid it on the desk between us. I began the recording with her name, the date, and our location. "Can you tell me a little bit about what life was like for you growing up in Bally-morris?" I asked. "Did you like it here?"

She laughed. "Don't tell me you haven't noticed it's the sort of place everyone dreams of running away from!"

"And yet you're still here." I smiled. "Presumably long-term?"

Tess nodded, then remembered the recorder. "Long-term, yes."

"You grew up here—and did you go away to college?"

"I went to university in Galway. And afterwards I went abroad, for the better part of my twenties."

"Some sort of missionary work?"

"I was a volunteer. I lived and worked in orphanages in Kenya and Nepal. There were several other projects I was involved in over the years, but those were the ones nearest to my heart."

"So what brought you back to Ballymorris?"

I watched her face as she gathered her answer. "Wasn't there ever a time in your life when you realized you had to face your fate—that there wasn't any sense putting it off?"

"Every morning," I replied, and she smiled.

"Ah, but I mean it," she said. "The real work is here. I've trav-eled quite a bit, through Africa and Asia and South America, but I always knew I'd come home again."

"And are you happy here now?"

"I'm happy when I'm useful," she replied. "So yes, I am happy."

I couldn't help smirking a little. "That's a bit of a nonanswer, don't you think?"

"Why?" she asked. "Are *you* happy?"

"I'm sitting in a comfortable chair with a hot cup of tea, having a lively conversation with an old friend," I said. "Sure, I'm happy." It wasn't a lie, really—this trip was the best sort of distraction from how rotten things were back in New York.

Tess gave me a searching look, but I kept smiling. "Fair enough," she said.

"Paudie tells me you're a member of a lay order of nuns. How did you decide on the religious life?"

"It isn't something you decide on," she replied. "I suppose you could say it chooses you."

Something chilled me in the way she said this. "That's an interesting way of putting it. How do you know when it's 'chosen' you?"

"There's no mystery to it. How do you know when you're angry, or tired? How do you know you're attracted to women?"

We looked at each other, and it came back to me in a flash of light and color: Tess in a blue-and-white-striped bathing suit, the sand stuck to our wet skin, my lips pressed to hers. *Jesus.* I was such an idiot.

Tess looked out the window as if something down in the street had caught her interest. "And how old were you when you realized it?" I managed to ask. "Was it linked with the apparition in any way?"

"Of course," she said quietly. "It had everything to do with the apparition."

"And yet you give me the distinct impression it was somehow unpleasant for you. Not a spiritual experience, at least not in hindsight. Something else, maybe." I was reaching, but it felt right.

Tess took a deep breath, drawing it out to buy herself a bit more time. "I don't speak of it," she said finally.

"You keep saying that."

"I keep saying it because I *need* to speak of it, only there hasn't been anybody I could tell it to. Everybody already has their notions about what really happened in that time."

"Yeah," I said. "That makes sense." We looked at each other. "Would you like me to turn off the recorder?"

She hesitated. "Doesn't that mean you can't use what I'm saying?"

I nodded.

"All right," she said.

"All right?"

"All right."

"Okay." I switched off the recorder. "There were four of you who saw it, right?"

"Four of us, aye. It was myself, Orla and her younger sister, Síle—you might remember, we were all at the beach together that day—and our classmate Declan."

"You and Orla were best friends," I said. It was Orla who'd called her away. Tess had looked back at me as if we might have another moment like the one we'd just had, but we never did.

Tess nodded. "She and I were thick as thieves in those days, always over at each other's houses. So much so that her mother would always set an extra place at the table for me. It was different, of course, when she and Declan started up, but—"

"She and Declan were dating?"

"For, ah, eight months or so, before he left for Australia. But they were careful to include me, at least in the beginning."

"So the day it happened—the day it first happened—you were all hanging out up there on the hill?"

"The three of us, and Síle. Síle had a bit of a crush on Declan. Truth be told, everybody did. It aggravated Orla to no end, but

Síle would have gone home and made a fuss if she'd resisted, so it was just easier to let her stay with us."

"It was after school?"

Tess nodded. "We'd sit on the wall, drinking Fanta and talking nonsense, and Declan would roll two cigarettes—one to smoke and one to tuck behind his ear for later—and tell us about all the places he was going to go. Bali, Malaysia. Said he wanted to walk the Great Wall of China." She laughed. "I told him he'd better lay off the fags. I never thought he'd actually leave—not that I didn't like him, but he did talk a lot. I was wrong, though, and I'll give him that." She paused. "I would have remembered that day regardless. He asked her if she'd come with him, and she said she would."

"That was before the apparition, I take it."

Tess nodded, her eyes on the desk between our mugs. "The weather was fickle that day."

"Isn't it always?"

She smiled. "Even more so, on that day."

"How did it begin?"

"Síle saw it first. We thought she was having some sort of fit. She fell on her knees, and I was frightened when I saw her eyes—they'd gone all glassy, like marbles. She looked . . ." Tess cleared her throat. "She looked possessed.

"Still, I could see she was *looking* at something. So I turned round, towards the statue of the Virgin that used to be in that grotto at the edge of the car park, and . . ." She took a breath, raised the mug to her lips, and took a long drink. I opened my mouth to ask if the statue in the grotto now wasn't the original, but she went on. "I do hope you'll forgive me. It was a long time ago, and I've spent most of that time trying to forget it."

"Why?"

"Why." She laughed quietly to herself. "I wish I could give you everything I remember, and let you see it for yourself, and feel what I felt then, and what I felt afterwards. This is why I don't speak of it—because nobody else can understand."

"What about your friends? Even if you found it an unpleasant experience, surely you could take some comfort in the fact that you experienced it together?"

Tess shook her head. "It wasn't like that. Afterwards we would talk about it, and we could never agree. I don't mean small details either. It was as if she were saying something completely different to each of us. And when we each tried to draw her, well . . . we may as well have sketched four women we'd met in the street."

"I read some of the newspaper articles from that time," I said, as gently as I could. "That's not what you told the reporters."

She sighed. "In the beginning it was different. We felt called—we felt blessed. It was only afterwards that we realized just how differently we were each experiencing it."

"What did she look like to *you*, then?"

"Not like any of the pictures or statues I'd ever seen. Her face was plain; she had thin lips and wide eyes, and I remember she looked at me almost as if I were the one who'd surprised *her*, and not the other way round."

"But you knew who she was?"

Tess nodded. "I knew she was the Blessed Virgin. Her head was covered by the blue mantle, that much was as you'd expect, and she seemed too serene to be anyone but."

"And how did she appear? Did she look . . . I don't know, ghostly? Or was she more solid looking?"

"She had a bit of a glow about her, but she seemed solid enough." Tess put down her mug and began to draw one fingertip along the palm of her other hand, as if she were telling her own fortune. "On other occasions, later on, she actually touched me."

"You felt it? Like it was a real person touching you?"

She nodded. "A real person. A real hand. Soft but callused, and smelling of Pond's."

"Pond's?"

"It's a brand of cold cream."

"Ah."

The Mother of God, washing her face like an ordinary woman? Really? But I held my tongue. "And she spoke to you?"

Tess stifled a laugh. "Oh, she spoke to me! In the beginning— the first two or three times she appeared to us—she told me she had a message for me and me alone."

"And how did that make you feel?"

"It was a queer sort of thrill. You can just imagine. But when she gave me the message, I was disappointed."

"What was it?"

"Love. That was her 'message.' She said . . ." Now Tess laid her hands palms down on the desk, staring at them as if they belonged to someone else. "She said I found it easier to love the poor and afflicted on a distant continent than the people I professed to love in my own home." Then she gripped her mug and took another long drink, though the tea must have gone cold in the meantime. "I'm sorry, this is harder than I thought it would be. Is it all right if we end it here, for now?"

Damn. I'd wanted to ask her about her mother and the "miracle" with the well water. I tucked the digital recorder back in my pocket. "Of course."

"I just need to gather my thoughts," she said absently as she rose from the table.

"Look, Tess—the last thing I want to do is pressure you," I said to her back as she busied herself tidying up. "We don't have to discuss it again if you don't want to."

"No, no," she said. "But it may take me a few days. How long did you say you were staying?"

Tess agreed to introduce me to the parish secretary, and I followed her up the tiny street and into the church through a side door. It felt colder inside than out. A notice on a small bulletin board in the entryway read VISIONS OF HEAVEN, VISIONS OF HELL: JOIN US FOR A WEEKLY REVELATIONS STUDY GROUP, WEDNESDAYS AT 7 PM IN THE PARISH HALL. ONLY THROUGH YOUR OWN FAITH AND PRAYERS CAN THE DEVIL BE OVERCOME. Another notice read THINKING ABOUT THE PRIESTHOOD? WHY NOT! as if the commitment were one night only instead of the rest of your life.

Holy effigies looked down from the stained-glass windows, their faces competently rendered, though blank and uninspired, and the statues of the Virgin and Saint Patrick spooked me as if I were seeing them for the first time. They were cast in plaster, painted in flat colors, and wreathed in synthetic flowers, and underneath the statues, rows of red plastic votives imitated the flicker of real candles. Another coffin rested under a white cloth on a sort of wheeled trolley in front of the altar. There was a remoteness to the place—as if you'd actually drifted farther away from God by stepping inside—and a dampness that felt like it would never leave you, not even after a piping-hot cup of tea by a roaring fire.

Through a series of doors out of the sacristy, we made our way into the rectory, where the air was warmer and more human. Tess introduced me to Louise, the secretary, but hesitated when it came time to excuse herself. "Would you like to come to Mass with me?"

"Next Sunday?"

"Tomorrow," she said. "There's Mass every day, though it isn't particularly well attended." Out of the corner of my eye, I saw Louise smiling to herself in agreement; clearly she had a healthy sense of humor about her job. "You might learn something," Tess went on. She read my face and said, with a wry twist of the lip, "You never know."

I had a feeling there might not be enough time to drive up to Sligo today, so I wanted to leave tomorrow open. "Okay," I said. "I'll come. I made plans for tomorrow morning, but what about the day after?"

"That would be fine," she said. "I'll see you here Friday at eight, so."

With his buzz cut and guarded demeanor, Father Lynch seemed more like a cop than a priest, and he was probably only a few years older than I was. Another priest, a white-haired man who must have been nearing retirement, had said John's funeral mass.

The young priest greeted me by name, pumping my hand and offering his condolences as he invited me into his office. "Now," he said as he settled himself behind the desk. "Louise tells me you've a few questions about the history of Ballymorris. The apparition, is it?"

I nodded. "But I imagine it was well before your time, Father."

"Right you are," he replied with a cordial smile. "The purported visitation took place in Father Dowd's time. He was my predecessor."

The purported visitation. "Is Father Dowd the priest who said my uncle's funeral mass?"

"Ah, that would be Father Pat. No, I'm afraid Father Dowd passed away seven or eight years ago now."

"Oh," I said. "I'm sorry to hear that."

"He would have been the one to speak to. I'm told Father Dowd conducted quite a thorough investigation of his own before reporting the case to the Church authorities."

"Do you have any of his records?"

Father Lynch hesitated, his eyes on his old-fashioned ink blotter. "Now, that I couldn't say. I'll ask Louise does she know where they are. Louise!" he called through the half-open office door. "Have we the records of the visitation, do you know?"

I heard the creak of a chair as the secretary rose and came into the doorway. "Not anymore, Father. We gave them to Tess to hold on to after Father Dowd passed."

"Ah, right." The priest turned back to me and said, "Would you believe you're the first person to ask for them, in all my time here?"

"That *is* surprising. It sounds like a dramatic story, by all accounts."

"Dramatic, sure. And it was quite a boon for the town, for a good year or two, anyway."

"Lots of pilgrims?"

"Aye, and from all over Europe, too." The priest gave me what felt like a look of appraisal. "Louise tells me you're a journalist. Now, if you don't mind my asking, what particular aspect of the visitations would you be thinkin' of writing about?"

I had to answer him carefully. "The story I'm considering writing has everything to do with the social context. As you said, the visitations brought the town a great deal of money and attention, and I'd like to explore how and why it may have changed this place. A portrait of small-town Ireland, if you will. American readers are very interested in anything to do with life in Ireland, even those of us without Irish ancestry." I smiled. "Maybe you know my grandmother left Ballymorris when she was a very young woman. This is my second time here—she brought me over when

I was a kid." I cleared my throat. "That was about five years before the . . . visitation."

"I see," he said. "I see."

I didn't like the way he was saying that, so I went on: "I don't want to take up too much of your time, Father, but I was wondering if you could share your impressions of the four young people who saw her." I only allowed him a second's pause before I added, "I've only spoken with Tess so far."

"Aye," he said. "Louise mentioned it was Tess who brought you round."

I'd had a feeling her name was currency, and I was right. I took out my voice recorder and notebook. "Like I said, Father, I know you're busy, and I really want to respect your time. But if you could spare maybe fifteen or twenty minutes, no more than twenty, I'd be very grateful to you."

He nodded. "Louise?" he called again over my shoulder. "Could you put the kettle on?"

"I'm makin' the tea now, Father," she called.

"Ah, bless you!" Father Lynch turned back to me and rubbed his hands together. "They say a good secretary knows what you need before you do. Did you ever hear that?"

I shook my head. "I've never had one."

"Ah, sure. You take your own notes." He gave me a genuinely friendly smile. "We'll just leave the door open till she brings in the tea."

We spoke of the rotten weather, Gaelic football, and my uncle John being the local postmaster until Louise carried in the tea tray with a plate of store-bought cookies. "Ginger bickies!" Father Lynch exclaimed with satisfaction—"They're a local delicacy for all they come out of a package"—and Louise closed the door softly behind her.

The priest took a sip from his steaming teacup as I reached

forward and pressed the RECORD button. "Now," he began, "to be perfectly frank with you, most of what I can tell you I learned through the local gossip. I wasn't born in this parish—I'm from Meath originally—so of course when I arrived here, I picked up bits and pieces about the local history as time went on."

"The Marian apparition being one of the more colorful chapters in that history?"

"Oh, aye. And by now I'm sure you've noticed that we don't see many people from other parts. I've no doubt your visit is the talk of the town at the minute. So you can just imagine what it would've been like with the reporters and pilgrims running around. There were all sorts of new shops opening along the high street, and every widow from here to Carrick opening her doors for B and B."

"Everyone saw an opportunity," I said.

"And who could blame them, when the history of Ireland was a history of leaving?" He sighed. "Anything to keep the young ones here at home where they belonged, all the new jobs—they could only be good for this community."

I couldn't let myself ask the most obvious follow-up—not yet, anyway. "So there were four people who said they saw the apparition?"

"Aye, there were four involved: the Gallagher sisters, Síle and Orla, and Declan Keaveney, and Tess, whom you know. I'll tell you I was surprised when Louise said you'd talked with her. Seems to me she goes out of her way not to speak of it."

"Why do you think that is?"

"Tess is terribly hard on herself. Always has been, for all the years I've known her. It's what drives her to do all the good she's done for this town, but it also drives her to doubt."

"You think she doubts what she saw?"

"Now, that's a question you'd have to ask her." The priest gave me a hard look. "If you haven't already."

"We're working up to that." I responded, with what I hoped was a disarming smile. "I've heard and read about the miracle, too."

Father Lynch shook his head. "I wouldn't be able to speak to that, now."

"It's powerful stuff, though, isn't it?" I asked. "Wasn't Mrs. McGowan scheduled to have her leg amputated the next day?"

"It's a powerful story, aye," he replied. "But I wouldn't be able to speak to that."

I made a mental note to reframe the question later on in the interview. "Tess says she and Orla were close friends growing up. Do you know Orla at all?"

"I do. I see her every Sunday."

"She's still quite devout, then?"

"More so than most. She occasionally volunteers her time as a teacher's aide in the Sunday school, which isn't easy to do, I imagine, having the three wee ones at home to care for."

"Do you know her well, then?"

The priest glanced out the window beside his desk. "Not well, no."

"Tess tells me Orla and Declan were dating at the time of the apparitions."

"Is that so? I never heard that, now."

"Tess said he was on his way to Australia, so I imagine you've never met him."

"You'd be right about that," he sighed. "I know his mother quite well, poor lady—very devout, in the second pew at Mass each and every morning, you know the way—but as I say, all I can tell you is the bits and pieces I've heard over time."

"What kind of bits and pieces?"

"By all accounts, the boy was a bad influence. Sucking down

the Buckfast, rolling his own cigarettes from the age of nine, marijuana, and who knows what else." The priest shook his head. "Your typical waster, so they tell me."

"What about his father? Is he still around?"

"He left when Declan was small. It happened quite often among the men of that generation, and the one before it: they left for work in England and never returned."

I thought of Leo, with no one to come home for—but he'd returned just the same. "Was Declan's father from Ballymorris?"

The priest shook his head. "He wasn't, no. They say he was a Dublin man. Who knows what brought him here? I don't suppose even Mrs. Keaveney could tell us now, poor woman."

"You speak of Mrs. Keaveney as if she were—"

He caught my meaning, and nodded. "Mrs. Keaveney, it pains me to say, goes about her days under the tragic misapprehension that Declan is coming home any day now. Sometimes it's tomorrow, she tells me, and other times it's sure to be next week. He's a very busy man, she says. Up to something important down in Australia, something so important that he hasn't yet found the time to come home and visit his poor old mam, not once in twenty years.

"But then," he sighed, "mothers can never be brought to think ill of their sons. If only they could, then perhaps the boys would behave better."

I felt my mother's arms like a lead weight around my neck, murmuring words like *kind* and *sweet* as if they applied to me, and I reminded myself that the priest was speaking only of Declan. "It must surprise you, then, to hear that he and Orla were dating."

Father Lynch shrugged as he drained his cup. "Sure, people change." Then something occurred to him. "It's a strange thing, though: in all these years, I've never met Orla's husband."

I tapped my pen on my open notebook. "What about her sister?"

"Síle?" He looked almost startled. "Surely Tess told you about Síle."

"I heard she's living in a home. Do you know what's wrong with her?"

"Now, that would be something you'd have to talk to the family about."

"Do you know her at all?"

"I've never met her, no, though I do know the Gallaghers quite well."

"How did they react when their daughters told them about the apparition?"

"Oh, I suppose it's safe to say they were concerned. But they'd known Tess all her life, and as I say, Tess has always been the sort of lass you can set your faith in. If Tess saw it, then no one could've been telling tales."

"So you think the apparition was real?"

I thought we'd geared up for this, but I'd miscalculated. The priest leaned back in his chair and eyed me coolly. "I believe Tess saw what she claimed to have seen."

"Ah, but Father," I said, "that's not the same thing. Was it real?"

He crossed his arms and glanced at the calendar on the wall to his right. "Now, that is a question I can't answer."

I reached over and switched off the recorder. "Can't, or won't?"

"Won't," he conceded. "Surely you understand. I couldn't have my parishioners reading in your magazine that I believe their children were seeing things, or healing an ailment that may never have been there to begin with."

"But you've just admitted that's what you think."

The priest gave me a grim smile. "You can't print it if I haven't said it." He sighed. "Look, I'm not trying to give you the run-around here. No one was playing tricks or telling tales. I understand your interest; I just don't see how any good can come of encouraging it."

Then, all too conveniently, there came a gentle knock on the office door. "Father?" Louise called. "Mrs. Moloney is here."

"It seems your twenty minutes are up, young man," the priest said dryly.

John's phone beeped as I was leaving the rectory. It was a text message from Tess. *Louise tells me you were asking for the tapes,* she wrote. *I'll leave them with Paudie at the shop, so you can listen to them before we speak next.*

It was early afternoon by the time I finished with Father Lynch, and Brona had promised me dinner at six, so I decided to get some work done and save Sligo for the following day. I didn't want to feel rushed when I went to visit Síle.

I typed out everything I could recall from the unrecorded portions of that morning's interviews, taking pride in setting the gems down pretty much verbatim. *She said I found it easier to love the poor and afflicted on a distant continent than the people I professed to love in my own home.* I wanted to show the town as it was and the people as I found them, and a line like that would add just the right tenor, subtly unnerving. I needed this to be the best thing I'd ever done.

Afterward I put in a couple hours on a story I had due at the end of the month, and then I powered down my laptop and went out. It wasn't raining, but Shop Street was deserted apart from a few people coming in and out of the SuperValu. Through the bookstore window, I spotted Paudie behind the counter with a cup of tea and his nose in a hardcover. I drew out my pocket notebook, ducking into vacant entryways to jot down my thoughts as they occurred to me.

Manorview Hotel shut since 1992. Redevelopment notice looks almost as old. Carvery menu (roast beef & turkey, baked sole in lemon & white wine sauce, banoffee pie—?) still posted in front window.

Get numbers on towns near other main apparition sites (Bosnia, et al). Numbers for Ballymorris early 1988–c. 1993?

Town's economic fortunes hinged on Rome's stamp of approval. Mysticism meets Church politics/bureaucracy (& commerce) = inevitable paradox. Play up "purity" of visionaries' initial experience. Faith of Irish Catholics—quaint, peculiar—how they see the world & their place in it. Compare/contrast with American Catholicism.

Web search: pilgrims (from Ireland & elsewhere) who may have written about their experiences here. Any international press?

"Hartigan's House of Devotions"—dust on window is an inch thick. Front door padlocked, but someone got inside to write "Owen is a wanker" backward to be read from the street. Through cleared parts, can see there is still some stock on the shelves (including 4-foot toddler Jesus with scepter, mantle & crown). Same sort of junk as Old Mag's. Have Paudie introduce me to Hartigan & other former shopkeepers if they're still around.

I reached the intersection of Shop Street and Milk Lane, and thought of Tess.

Find someone at hospital who might talk to me? Nurses/orderlies?
(The more devout they are, the more they'll be willing to talk?)

Then I remembered the look on Tess's face as she said, "I need to gather my thoughts." Maybe not.

After dinner we met Paudie and Leo at Napper Tandy's for the third night running. "Did you have anything for supper, Leo?" Brona was saying as I laid the first round on the table and took my seat in the snug.

The old man shrugged as he brought the pint to his lips. "Sure, I've a meal in a glass."

Brona clucked her tongue. "He's lucky to be alive, that one," she said to me out of the corner of her mouth.

"You've been a busy man, I hear," Leo said blithely, ignoring what was perfectly audible to all. "Spoke to Father Jack, did you?"

"I didn't realize we're allowed to call him Father Jack."

"Not to his face." Leo laughed. "He's a clever one, that Father Jack. No time for nicknames when you've an eye on the bishop's chair."

Paudie turned to me and patted an old black shoebox on the seat beside him. "I've a package for you, lad."

"Thanks for bringing it over. And for setting it up so Tess and I could talk."

Paudie fiddled with his beer mat. "She rang me after you left today."

I braced myself. "Oh?"

The old folks traded a three-way look. "I'm beginning to think you've a certain effect on people," Paudie ventured. "She was livelier than I've heard her in a long while."

"What do you mean by 'lively'?"

"She isn't the sort to open up to strangers, Tess." Paudie sighed. "She never has been."

I'd found a fossil on the beach, and we'd pretended to examine it, but it was just an excuse to come closer. *Like a ghost trapped in stone,* she'd said, and that was when I'd kissed her.

"But she spoke to you today?" Brona asked.

"She started to. I'm hoping she'll let me interview her again at some point before I leave."

"Ah, she will," Leo replied. "Twenty years is a long time to be keepin' your own counsel."

"Does she have friends?" I asked. "Maybe that's a weird question, but I don't know if lay nuns are supposed to refrain from, you know, 'earthly attachments' or whatever."

"I don't know that there's a rule about that, as such," Paudie mused. "Tess is well loved. She's a friend to everyone, if you know what I mean."

"So there's no one she'd confide in," I said.

"Not really, no."

"And did you get up to see Síle?" Leo asked teasingly.

"I didn't think I'd have time," I said. "I'll go tomorrow. I'd like to talk to Orla, too."

"She's only up the road," Brona said.

"Good luck gettin' Orla to speak wit'cha," Leo retorted.

"Why don't you think she'd talk to me?"

"If Tess *wants* to forget, Orla's already forgotten," Paudie replied. "She's changed."

"Sure, we're none of us the people we used to be," Brona said sagely.

Leo lifted his fingers to what little remained of his hair. "And more's the pity." The others smiled ruefully into their drinking glasses. "They say Madden is a shadow man," Leo went on under his breath. "That Orla made him up. Would lead you to wonder where the babbies came from, if it were true!" Leo threw back his head and laughed uproariously.

"Anyhow," Brona continued, "that's how seldom anyone sees him. Must be quite an important job he's got up in Dublin, to be gone so much of the week."

I'd see about Orla in the morning, but in the meantime, I wanted to talk about her sister. "I put in a call to Ardmeen House after I talked to Father Lynch," I said. "I'm waiting for the director to call me back."

"And you'll go on waiting," Leo replied. "It's up to yourself, but if I were you, I'd go on and make the drive up there."

"I don't know," I said, though I'd be taking his advice no matter what happened tomorrow. "I don't want to presume they'll let me in and not be able to see her because they think I'm too pushy. I don't even know how I'll explain myself."

"It'll take you an hour and a quarter to get there," said Brona. "An hour and a half at most."

"Don't tell them why you want to see her," Paudie put in, "or they'll never let you. The apparition is part of the reason she's in there."

I paused with my pint glass halfway to my lips. "How can that be, when she isn't the only one who saw it?"

"I said *part* of the reason," Paudie replied. "You'll find out the rest for yourself."

"Sure, you couldn't make it up." Leo clucked his tongue. "C'mere, now. Did ya ever think of writin' a book?"

My grandmother was always asking me the same question, and it never got any easier to answer. Nobody likes to be reminded of all he *hasn't* accomplished, and likely never will. "Maybe someday," I replied. "I guess I'm still looking for the right subject."

"You could write a book about anythin', anythin' a'tall," Leo said, "and if the story's good, they'll all be wanting to read it."

"Listen to him," Paudie sniffed. "This one hasn't cracked a book since 1955!"

"I read that book you gave to me that time!" Leo protested. "The mystery. Yer man from Galway."

"That was a Christmas gift nearly ten years back!" Paudie laughed.

"What about a screenplay?" Leo asked. "Didja ever think of writin' a script? They say there's piles of money to be made in scripts, if you've any luck a'tall."

I hid my face in my pint to conceal my irritation. I'd tried to write a screenplay once.

"Sure, if it were that easy, we'd all be makin' fillums," Paudie said.

We had two more rounds, but my heart wasn't in it after that. I kept thinking about those tapes, looking forward to the time when I could lock myself in Brona's spare room and listen to them undisturbed.

They were labeled by date. It seemed Father Dowd had interviewed Tess first, then Declan, then Orla, and finally Síle over a two-month period from January into early March of 1988.

Brona scrounged up her husband's old Walkman and left me in peace. I put on the headphones and pressed the PLAY button, and when the dead man began to speak, I couldn't help writing the screenplay version in my head.

```
FADE IN:
INT. - SIMPLY FURNISHED RECTORY OFFICE—DAY.


FATHER DOWD, a priest on the late side of middle
age, clears his throat and taps his pencil softly on
```

the ink blotter. A crucifix hangs on the wall above
his head. The girl, TERESA, sits across the desk from
him, wide-eyed and eager to cooperate.

> FATHER DOWD
>
> Today is the eleventh of January, 1988. This
> recording is an interview with Teresa Mc-
> Gowan, who is sixteen years of age and a
> sixth-year student at St. Brigid's College,
> Ballymorris. Let it also be noted that I have
> known Teresa from the time of her birth. I
> baptized her myself.

I pictured the priest with a red nose and a full head of white
hair. I wanted him to look like one of the jovial old gents I'd
met in the pub. He had to seem kind and dependable, because
Tess would've trusted him; it was, after all, the most important
secret of her life, and he would have to know the wisest way to
reveal it.

> FATHER DOWD (CONT'D)
>
> Now, Teresa. You came to me today to make an
> extraordinary statement. Do you agree that
> we must record your experiences for the ben-
> efit of all the faithful?

> TERESA
>
> I do, Father.

A glance passes between the priest and the young
girl; he leans forward, silently urging her to
continue.

TERESA (CONT'D)

I believe that myself and my friends have seen an apparition of the Blessed Virgin.

FATHER DOWD

And do you recall the occasion of the first apparition?

TERESA

It was at the beginning of November, Father.

FATHER DOWD

And why did you not come to me immediately after the first visitation?

TERESA

We weren't sure of what we were seeing. We . . . we wanted too badly for it to be real, for *her* to be real, so we prayed first for clarity.

FATHER DOWD
(more gently)

You must tell us everything you remember, Tess. As clearly as you can. Begin by stating the names of your friends.

TERESA

Orla Gallagher, her sister Síle, and Declan Keaveney. Sometimes on a clear day we go up to the grotto on the Sligo road after school.

FATHER DOWD

And how do you generally pass the time you're
at the grotto?

TERESA

Just talking, Father.

With a wheeling hand motion, the priest urges her to
elaborate.

TERESA (CONT'D)

We talk about school, our classmates and
teachers. What we intend to do when we're
grown.

FATHER DOWD

You don't go up to the grotto to pray?

The girl fidgets in her seat, her eyes on the desk
between them.

TERESA

Not really, Father, no.

FATHER DOWD

Not to worry, Teresa. I appreciate your can-
dor. Now tell us what happened on the afternoon of the first of November.

TERESA

We were sitting on the bench, just talking,
and suddenly everything felt strange.

(draws an audible breath)

Everyone else seemed very far away. Declan was telling a story, but it was like he was a thousand miles away and I could only hear the echo of an echo of what he'd been saying.

FATHER DOWD

Go on.

TERESA

Everything went very silent, and when I saw someone moving out of the corner of my eye, it felt like it took forever just to move my head to see what was happening.

FATHER DOWD

And what *was* happening? What did you see?

TERESA

I saw Síle. She was kneeling on the pavement, looking up towards the statue in the grotto. At first I couldn't see her face, but I knew something was happening. I came closer, and she had a queer look in her eyes.

FATHER DOWD

And did you see the statue of the Blessed Virgin?

TERESA

It wasn't there, Father. There was only a bright light. It was so bright it felt like

the daylight was fading into night behind me.
Darkness behind me, and the bright light
ahead.

FATHER DOWD

As if . . . you'd been given a choice?

TERESA
(after a pause)
Aye, Father. So I looked into the light, and
she was there.

FATHER DOWD

Tell us what she looked like.

TERESA

She was smiling. Beaming down at me. That was
the first thing I noticed about her. And she
wore the blue mantle.

FATHER DOWD

Did she carry the Christ child?

TERESA

No, Father.

FATHER DOWD

And did she speak to you?

TERESA

Not at first. To begin with, she only smiled,
and I felt nothing but her love for me.

> (pauses)
> I might have been kneeling there for hours,
> I've no idea. It was like everything else in
> the world fell away, and there was no such
> thing as time. It fell from us, all of it: the
> sky above and the ground below. Even my own
> name.

I had to stop the recording just to take that in. There was something familiar about this description, as if Tess had explained it all to me once before, a long time ago.

As if she could have.

> FATHER DOWD
> But she did eventually speak?

> TERESA
> She did, Father. She said, "Do you know who
> I am?" and I said yes, that I had always
> known. I had . . . I suppose I had the sense
> that this was meant to happen.

> FATHER DOWD
> Tell me, what did she sound like? Her voice?

> TERESA
> 'Twas high, and clear, and sweet.
> (smiling)
> She'd a voice for radio, you might say.

The priest offers her a brief, tight-lipped smile.

FATHER DOWD

And *how* did she speak? Had she any accent a'tall?

TERESA

I don't know that she did, Father. I don't ever remember noticing that.

FATHER DOWD
(with a smile in his voice)
So the Blessed Virgin isn't a Connaught lass?

TERESA
(earnestly)
No, Father.
(hesitating)
It was like we were speaking without words. Her lips never moved.

FATHER DOWD

Ah! Our Lady spoke directly to your heart.
(pausing)
Then what did she say?

TERESA

She told me . . . told *us* . . . she had a message for the world, and she wanted us to spread it.

FATHER DOWD

And did you ask why she'd chosen you?

TERESA

I did, Father. She said that we four needed
to follow the message just as diligently and
faithfully as anyone else in the world. We
weren't meant to be special in any way.

FATHER DOWD

And did that give you a certain comfort?

TERESA

(nodding)

My pride is my greatest fault. I know that.

FATHER DOWD

And what did she say to you next?

TERESA

She said we must live our lives with love,
no matter how trying the circumstances, and
show compassion even to those we feel aren't
worthy of it. *Especially* to those we feel
aren't worthy.

FATHER DOWD

She was asking ye to be more Christlike. To
honor your faith by living it.

TERESA

Aye, Father. I told her I would try harder to
be a good Christian. To show love even when
it was most difficult to be loving, and to be

humble when I felt tempted to set myself
above others.

                    FATHER DOWD
                 (nodding approvingly)
And were you aware of your friends around
you? Did you hear their replies?

                    TERESA
I didn't, Father. I almost forgot they were
there. But then, they each felt the same way,
as if she were speaking to them alone.

                    FATHER DOWD
Aye, and I'll be recording what each of them
has to say in turn.

                    TERESA
And what happens after that, Father? Have I
to speak to the bishop?

                    FATHER DOWD
You needn't worry, child. I'll be the one to
speak to him.

The girl hesitates, clearly needing more in the way
of reassurance, so the priest goes on.

                FATHER DOWD (CONT'D)
I've informed Bishop Scanlon of these extraordinary circumstances, and if I am satisfied

with the results of the preliminary interviews, he will then appoint a Commission of
Inquiry, formed by myself and two colleagues.
Together we'll speak to the four of you—one
at a time, just as I'm doing now—only in
greater depth. And then, if we are agreed on
the nature of what you have experienced, we
will formally present the case to the bishop.

                    TERESA
Will they listen to these recordings before
they speak to us?

                 FATHER DOWD
    They will.

After a pause, the priest gathers himself to resume
the interview.

               FATHER DOWD (CONT'D)
    Now, Teresa. What happened next?

The girl doesn't answer at first, and in that silence, a door slams somewhere down the rectory corridor. When she speaks again, her voice is brimming
with emotion.

                    TERESA
    She asked if I was . . . if I was ready to see.

                 FATHER DOWD
    To see?

                    TERESA
              (in an unsteady voice)
She clasped her hands in front of her . . .
her bosom . . . and when she opened them
again she . . . she was showing me . . .
she showed me her heart.

From the look on his face, we can tell the priest is
moved beyond words. For a while, neither of them
speaks, and when the light changes inside the little
office, neither of them can say if it's the sun coming
out or something even more astonishing.

                  FATHER DOWD
And how did that make you feel?

                    TERESA
                 (sniffling)
I couldn't say, Father.

                  FATHER DOWD
Now, Tess. If we're to present this case to
the bishop, as I've explained, you must answer each and every question posed to you.

The girl draws a clean handkerchief out of her pocket
and presses it to her eyes.

                    TERESA
                  (muffled)
Sometimes I just don't know how to answer,
Father. I can't see what's the right answer.

FATHER DOWD

There isn't any right answer. What you feel can't ever be wrong.

The girl is silent. He tries a different tack.

FATHER DOWD (CONT'D)

Let Our Lady guide you. Always remember: that's why she's come to you in the first place. Hold to your faith, and you'll always speak the truth.

The girl takes a deep breath, and when she opens her mouth, she speaks shakily.

TERESA

I don't know that I can speak to anyone. Anyone apart from you, Father. I don't know if I can.

FATHER DOWD

Don't worry yourself, Tess. You're a good girl; it's your very reluctance that speaks the world of you. I know you've nothing to hide.

TERESA

It's not that. I'm sorry, Father. I don't know that I can speak about this any more today.

That was the end of the first recording. For a few minutes, I just sat there—the old mattress springs digging into my ass—mulling over everything I'd heard. She'd put him off midway through her story, and yet that much-younger Tess had answered questions she hadn't wanted me to ask.

That day at the beach was coming into clearer focus now: the adults unpacking their picnic baskets and mold-speckled beach chairs, passing a thermos of tea down the line of white limbs and red noses; that strange woman walking alone down the length of the beach, who had spoken to me as if she'd mistaken me for someone she knew; Tess and Orla diving into the surf, Mallory and Síle laughing over their shoulders as if they'd been talking about me. I was outnumbered four to one, but it wasn't long before Tess called after me, wanting to know how old I was and had I ever been to Disneyland.

That I had known her once, years before any of this had happened to her—it gave me the willies.

4

I was up too late listening to Tess's interview tape, but I dragged myself out of bed for breakfast with Brona. Afterward I reached for Johnny's cell phone. "Hello, am I speaking with Orla Madden?"

A baby wailed in the background. "This is Orla."

I gave her my name and said I was in town for Johnny Donegan's funeral. "I don't know if you remember that day we went to the beach? When we were kids?" Reading the silence that followed, it was clear she didn't. "Síle was quite good friends with my sister Mallory . . . ?"

"Right," she said cautiously, drawing out the word like a piece of taffy.

"So I'm back for the next week, and Brona and some of the others have been telling me about the visitation you experienced. I'm a journalist for an American magazine, and I have to say, it's one of the most compelling stories I've come across. I was wondering if you'd be willing to have a chat with me."

Orla cleared her throat. "I really don't feel comfortable speaking to any members of the press about something that happened twenty years ago."

"I understand, and I'm sorry if I've intruded on your privacy. It's just that I talked to Tess McGowan yesterday, and I guess it didn't occur to me that you might feel differently about being interviewed."

Another silence on the line. Currency, to a different purpose. "You've spoken with Tess?"

"Yes, I have."

"And you're a cousin of Brona Tuohy's, is that right?"

"I am, yes."

"Well . . . ," she murmured, and I knew she was going to agree, I *knew* it. Finally she said, "I suppose I could speak with you, for a little while." I let the smile of satisfaction linger on my face for only a second, or else she'd hear it in my voice. "Ordinarily I'd suggest meeting you someplace in town," she went on, "but given the subject, it might be best if you call round to the house."

I rubbed the last of the smile away with the back of my hand before I spoke. "That's fine. When works for you?"

"I've an hour right now, if now suits you?"

Orla lived only a ten-minute walk from Brona's place, but at some point on Kilbride Road, I passed into the Celtic Tiger section of town, where the houses were big and new and exactly alike, apart from different-colored front doors. I found the right house number and passed a silver Lexus parked in the driveway.

When Orla opened the door, I saw right away why Leo made fun of her—the woman's skin was almost as orange as the Oompa Loompas out of *Willie Wonka & the Chocolate Factory*. Her dark hair was pulled into a high ponytail, and she wore pink velour pants and a clingy white T-shirt that rode up at the midriff, which was tinted to match the rest of her.

Of the three Irish girls on that beach outing, my memories of Orla were the haziest. We hadn't talked much, hadn't bonded over something cool or unusual like Tess and I had, so I was surprised at how much she seemed to remember.

"Yeah," she said slowly when she opened the door. "I do know you, now you're here. Síle dropped her chips on the floor, and you gave her the rest of yours." Her laugh had an edge to it. "I was grateful to you. Saved me having to give her mine to shut her up. You probably remember how she would carry on."

I did remember that, now that she mentioned it: not Síle making a scene, but sliding my paper boat of french fries across the table, and how she cooed with delight. "Thanks for making the time to meet with me," I said as Orla took my jacket. Through the sitting-room doorway I could see a pair of sleek leather couches and a glass-topped coffee table, strange choice of furniture for a family with young children.

"It's no bother," she said. "My daughters are at the crèche until two, and I just put my son down for a nap." As I followed her into the kitchen, I noticed a certain tautness in her muscles and movements. A human dynamo, never still—but I guessed stillness was an impossible luxury when you had three little kids and a husband working long hours. "Would you like a cup of tea?" she asked over her shoulder.

I watched her fill the kettle and draw a new package of digestive biscuits out of a cabinet. "I have to say, I'm a little surprised at the welcome," I said as she opened the package and carefully laid out the cookies on a plate. "You seemed hesitant over the phone."

Orla sighed. "It's not a chapter in my life I ever wanted to revisit."

"I understand."

As she pulled out the box of Barry's, she gave me a look over her shoulder—*How* can *you?*

"I mean, I know I can't understand," I said. "But I'd like to try to."

"Which magazine did you say you work for?"

I told her, and she lifted her eyebrows. "And you think *they'd* be interested in a story about 'the Virgin of Ballymorris'?"

I had yet to pitch the story to my editor, but I nodded anyway. "Like I told you, I spoke with Tess yesterday, and then she introduced me to Father Lynch . . ."

Orla's back was turned as she poured the boiling water into the teapot, but I could see her stiffen. After twenty years, they were still cringing at the mention of each other's names.

She brought the teapot and mugs to the table. I drew my digital recorder out of my pocket, and she nodded when I held it up for her to see. "But before we go any further, I want to hear everything Tess told you. What did she say about me?"

"Only that you were best friends growing up. But I got the sense that the apparition was the beginning of the end of your friendship."

"Did she say that?"

I shook my head. "She didn't have to."

"I'll be perfectly honest with you: if you find me uncooperative, it's because I've blocked it completely. I don't remember anything about it. Even my memories of school and home in those days are hazy at best."

"You think you wanted to forget?"

"Oh, I've no doubt it's my own doing," she replied. "I'll never be able to say for certain whether or not I saw anything. But I tend to think not."

"Are you saying you imagined it—that you all imagined it?"

I watched her face as I spoke. "Or is there some other explanation I haven't considered?"

She hesitated. "Look, would you mind turning off the recorder?"

I reached over and switched it off.

"Thank you."

I waited. "What was it you wanted to say . . . ?"

"Right, well. If I saw it—and I'm not saying I did, because I truly can't remember—I suspect it was only some part of me trying to cover for Síle. What I mean is, if she was the only one to see it, then there could very well be something wrong with her, but that wouldn't hold if we saw it together."

"What about Tess?"

"Knowing Tess was seeing it too made me think it was real, at least at the time," she replied as she poured the tea. "Tess was always the sensible one. She was also the most devout of all of us, but she'd be the last person ever to say she'd seen something just so people would pay attention to her."

I took the implication out of the silence and made it plain: "Unlike your sister?"

Orla sighed. "Mam and Dad took her to a psychologist a few years after this happened, and he gave her a diagnosis. Hysterical personality disorder. I thought she might have been schizophrenic. You know how they hear voices? See things, even people who aren't there?" She stirred in the sugar and milk, and I followed suit. "But there was a name for what she had—*has*," she corrected herself—"though it wasn't something to be medicated so much as managed. And that was well before everyone started pill popping, anyway."

"So is that diagnosis why you thought afterward that you might have made it up?"

"Not only that." She stared down at the table between us, her mug poised at her mouth. "There are lots of reasons."

"Pick one," I said. "Whichever is easiest to talk about."

Orla let out a sharp little laugh. "The first doesn't have much to do with us, personally. It's to do with Ballymorris. Suddenly people had money again, and even those who didn't had something to gab about—and all because of what we'd seen, and because we went to the priest with it. Everyone wanted so badly for it to be real, which makes me think even more now that it wasn't."

"I get it," I said. "That makes sense." I watched her sip her tea. "What's another reason?"

She sighed. "The other reason *is* personal. Our lives were never the same after the apparition, not even after it stopped."

"When was that? Tess told me they started in November of eighty-seven and continued through the winter . . . ?"

"It continued through the beginning of May. Then Declan took off for Australia, Tess moved to Galway, and I went to UCD. Síle was still here at home, of course."

"Did you have any plans to follow Declan to Australia?"

"Did Tess tell you that?" Orla was still staring through the table, sour at the lips. "I was never going to follow him. He knew it, and I knew it, and Tess ought to have known it, too."

"But you did talk about going at the time?"

She shrugged. "You hatch all sorts of plans when you think you're in love."

And that, unfortunately, reminded me of Laurel. *You hatch all sorts of plans when she thinks you're in love.* Here I was, undoing them all in absentia. "How did you know you'd never go with him?" I asked. "You didn't want to travel?"

"Not the way Declan did, no. My husband, Joe, and I go to Malaga on holidays, and that's always been enough travel for me."

"Did you keep in touch?"

"He wrote me a letter, but I never replied to it."

"Have you had any contact with him since?"

She let out a derisive little laugh. "Never."

"Ever hear about him?"

"Just what his mother tells people—but between you and me, I'm not sure she isn't only making it up to console herself. Declan was never what you'd call a devoted son."

"Father Lynch told me as much," I said. "So can you tell me what changed for you? You'd said your lives were never the same afterward. Not for the better, I take it."

Orla shot me a hard look. "You're right about that."

"Tell me how your life was different?"

"As I say, I can't remember much, but when I try to think back on those days, I do remember the confusion. Nothing was clear to me, and none of the things that had made me happy in the old days could cut through the fog. The feeling only worsened when I got to Dublin, and at some point it occurred to me . . ." She gazed vaguely around her immaculate kitchen as if trying to recall the one small thing she'd neglected to do.

"What occurred to you?"

"That if I'd seen her—if we'd *really* seen her—everything should have felt clearer than it had before. Not the other way round."

"That makes sense." I reached for a ginger biscuit and took a bite. "How did you manage to move past that period of your life?"

"I didn't." Orla set down her mug and looked at me. "It faded over time, but it's never truly left me."

I didn't know what to say to that. The cookie turned to cardboard in my mouth.

"As for my sister, you could say it was the beginning of her unraveling. It happened slowly. The first breakdown happened after she got to university. Ended up in hospital and everything.

Mam and Dad thought it best if she came back to Ballymorris, but with her home, things only got worse. She waited tables for a while, but apart from that, she hardly bothered looking for a job. She'd either stay up all night painting her canvases or go out with guys who'd turned into even bigger tossers than they'd been at school. She fought constantly with our parents, so much so that I dreaded coming home at the weekend. So I usually found excuses not to.

"Finally, when she was twenty-two or so, she had a massive row with our mam and dad. Smashing glasses, 'I wish ye were dead,' and that. I remember it because I'd come home that weekend, and regretted it the minute I walked in the door. I remember thinking, 'I wish we could put her in a room somewhere, lock the door, and let her sort out the demons in her head instead of letting her unleash them on everybody else.'" Orla sighed, passing me a mildly embarrassed look over the rim of her mug. "Of course, now that I have what I asked for, I still can't say I feel much better about the situation."

"But she left to travel at some point, is that right?"

Orla nodded. "She took off in the middle of the night soon after that. Left a note on the kitchen table just saying she was leaving and not to worry." Orla snorted, and it was not a pleasant sound. "Can you imagine! To this day, I haven't the faintest notion where she got the money for that plane ticket. She claimed later that she'd saved it, and that she supported herself doing odd jobs wherever she happened to be—but as I said, Síle was never much of a worker."

"People change," I said, and she snorted again.

"You sound like an only child."

I thought of my sister's face in the white casket, the gash on her forehead showing through the mortuary makeup, her hands folded primly over her heart.

"Shit." Orla hid her mouth with her hand. "I'm so sorry. They told me, years ago, when it happened. I forgot."

"It's okay," I said.

Orla looked at me. Somehow she knew to leave it. "So there Síle was," she went on, "living out of her rucksack on the far side of the world, free as you please. She hardly ever rang home—maybe once or twice a year, that was it. Never came back for Christmas, not once in six years. When she did ring, she told Mam and Dad all sorts of tales. Always on the move, always having adventures as if she were the only person who ever did anything worth doing." Her eyes were hard, glittering with the anger she'd never been able to let go of. "It wasn't a secret that she believed she was meant to do bigger and better things than any of the rest of us. Síle always believed that, even when she was small."

"I guess you could say that about most people with an artistic temperament," I remarked, and Orla huffed in agreement.

"And anyway, I don't know that she got to quite so many places as she liked to say she had. But all the while, she'd be sendin' things home for birthdays and Christmas, things Mam would never need or want."

"So what finally brought her home?"

The look she gave me was the sharpest yet. "*I* did. She wound up in hospital again—someone found her passed out on the side of the road someplace in India. A complete mystery as to how it happened, of course. I told our mam and dad I'd go to her—somebody had to, and it wasn't as if Síle had any real friends—and swearin' all the time it was the last thing I'd ever do for her." She paused for breath, as if to remind herself that it was long since over and done with. "I spent a fortnight in a place called Madurai before she was well enough to fly home. Longest two weeks of my life."

"So when you brought her back, after India—was that when she went to live in Sligo?"

Orla shook her head. "She spent a couple years in Dublin and Galway, trying to make a living with her painting. Síle always thought she was a great artist—or at least she was *going* to be a great artist. I don't know much about art myself, but even I could tell you she's mediocre." She sighed. "I suppose none of us did her any favors by not telling her so. Not that she would have listened."

Mediocre? I wanted to say. *Have you looked at your life lately?*

"Then came another breakdown," Orla was saying, "the worst one yet—and that's when Mam and Dad put her at Ardmeen House."

I swallowed that irrational little blip of indignation so I could ask, "What kind of a place is it?"

"It's a big old house by the sea. It's like she's on a holiday that never ends."

"So it's not like a—"

Orla laughed. "A madhouse? Not entirely, though I suppose some in town think that's the sort of place it is. She can't come and go as she pleases, but that's for her own good." She sighed. "Síle is sick, there's no denying she's sick, and Ardmeen is a safe place. She may not be happy, but at least she's safe. And it really is lovely up there."

In truth, Orla seemed more concerned about everyone *else's* so-called safety. I gave her a look. "A very pretty view through the bars on the windows?"

She sighed. "It pains our mam and dad, having her hidden away like that, but we can't risk her having another meltdown somewhere it would take us ages to get to. I've had three children since the last time; I can't be leavin' them to go and rescue her again."

I dipped another biscuit in my lukewarm tea. "It sounds like you and Síle still don't have much of a relationship."

"We have *no* relationship. I don't speak to her, I don't visit her. I must seem awfully cold to you, but perhaps you'll understand: all I wanted was a happy family life, a peaceful home for my children. I needed a life that had nothing to do with what I was meant to have seen on the hill—no illusions, no superstitions, no phantoms—no more of that interminable selfish drama." She gestured toward the only remotely untidy thing in the room, a laundry basket of brightly colored children's clothing on a kitchen chair. "And in the end, I got what I wanted, believe me—more dirty nappies than I know what to do with." She laughed softly, and as if on cue, I heard her baby cry out from upstairs.

Orla rose from the table, and I caught another glimpse of her ridiculous orange midriff. "Now," she said, "that should give you plenty to work with. Only don't go writin' down anything I said about Síle. Our parents have been through enough."

I drove northwest out of Ballymorris, past Sligo town and the churchyard where William Butler Yeats was buried, arriving at Ardmeen House around one o'clock. The building was more or less as Orla had described: a large Georgian perched on a hill above the north Atlantic. Beyond the high brick wall, I imagined, the back garden stretched all the way down to the dunes. From a distance, the building had looked like a deluxe bed-and-breakfast, and then I drew close enough to see the grilles on the windows. The parking lot afforded a decent view, so I sat in the driver's seat staring out at the sea as I scarfed down a bacon and mayonnaise sandwich out of a triangular box. The beach they'd taken us to was long and sandy, like this one. Paudie's car had broken down a few miles into the return trip, and we'd had to consolidate three carloads of people into two before stopping in Sligo town for fish and chips.

I rang the bell at the front door, and a young woman in cartoon-print scrubs showed me to the director's office. When Dr. Kiely appeared after a five-minute interval, she did little to conceal her irritation. "You really ought to have rung first."

"I did," I said. "I called yesterday morning. You didn't get my message?"

"You ought to have waited."

I folded my hands in my lap. "I apologize." I could submit when the situation called for it. "Will it be possible for me to speak with Miss Gallagher?"

The doctor narrowed her eyes. "What is your connection with Síle, exactly?"

"We have a mutual friend, who asked me to pass on some news best relayed in person." Dr. Kiely looked at me askance, as if a person in a mental home couldn't possibly *have* any friends. "A mutual friend, is it?"

"Mishka Beatty-Harkins," I said. "A childhood friend of mine. She and Síle met in India." The name Mishka had been a stroke of inspiration, and a double-barreled surname would sound too complex to be invented on the fly. I wish I could say I'm a terrible liar, but there it is.

"All right," she said. "I'll allow you to see her for a short while, but if she shows any sign of distress—"

"Distress?" I cut in. "She isn't a danger to herself, is she? I was under the impression that Síle isn't too far removed from being able to live independently."

"I'm afraid that assessment is rather too optimistic." The director gestured to a young man in blue scrubs who'd just appeared in the doorway. "If Síle becomes overwhelmed at any point, Martin will escort you back to my office."

Dr. Kiely watched with a bored look on her face as the attendant patted me down and turned out my pockets, telling me he'd return my Swiss army knife at the end of my visit. On our way down the hall to the stairs, Martin said, in not so many words, that Síle had always been his favorite. I hadn't laid eyes on her since 1982, but I wasn't surprised.

Síle was at her easel when Martin showed me in, and she did not turn to greet me until he'd closed the door behind him. Everywhere there were canvases of all sizes, easels, a drafting desk at the window, and another table covered with brushes in glass jars of murky water, palettes spattered with the rainbow, squeezed-up tubes of oil paint, and tins of turpentine. The figure and portrait sketches pinned to the walls certainly seemed better than mediocre to me. Two tall iron-barred windows looked out over the back garden, the ocean visible beyond a jagged stone wall. I watched the muscles in Síle's pale, slender arm tense beneath her skin as she laid down one more brushstroke.

"So you're a friend of Mishka's?" She turned to face me then, and I held my breath as the unmade bed taunted me out of the corner of my eye. I wanted to grab her by the shoulders and fling her onto it. "Dear old Mishka," she said. "We whispered obscene things round the dome of the Gol Gumbaz at Bijapur—all of which echoed eleven times, as legend promises—and afterwards we were marched to the police station before an angry mob. Did Mishka ever tell you that?"

She wanted to entertain me, and for a second, I forgot I'd invented Mishka myself. I shook my head, smiling, and offered my hand. Síle clasped it—I noticed then that she was left-handed—and I caught the scent of sweet musky soap under the nose-curling odor of turpentine.

"May I ask you something?" she asked.

"Anything," I said.

"Who is Mishka, anyway?"

I tried to keep a serious look on my face as I replied, "I don't know, but she asked me to give you her best."

She sighed, smiling. "Dear old Mishka."

I looked at the aquamarine paint on the tip of the brush she held between slender blue-streaked fingers, and the glistening strokes along the canvas on the easel. "I'm sorry," I said. "I've interrupted your work."

"I suppose you have." She dropped the brush in a jar of turpentine and looked at me intently as she wiped her hands with a rag. "But I've all the time in the world to finish it."

I couldn't wait any longer. "You don't remember me, do you?"

"Of course I do. You came to Ballymorris that summer. They took us out for an afternoon by the sea." She applied the rag to a fingernail caked with blue paint. "But you haven't come here to reminisce about our childhoods."

My pulse switched to double time. "I haven't?"

"You haven't," she said. "I know why you're here."

"Oh?" I tried to sound casual. "Who told you?"

"Some things nobody needs to tell you." She turned back to her canvas and gave it one last appraising glance. "You're here about *Her*, aren't you?"

"That's one way of putting it." We locked eyes, and I lost my nerve completely. I took a breath and turned to the wall. "May I have a look around?"

"Of course." She moved like a cat to a sink by the door, washed her hands, and began filling an electric kettle at the faucet. "You'll have tea?"

"Yes—please—thanks."

The charcoal portraits were pinned to the walls all the way up to the molding, half a dozen variations per model: a young man in owlish eyeglasses with his hands always touching his face, an old man with a beard best described as epic, a woman with a long nose and eyes bulging like a frog's, her unbuttoned blouse thrown off the shoulder to reveal one glass-cutting nipple. Other people who lived here? They had to be.

"I've lots of different kinds. Assam, Ceylon, or Darjeeling?"

"Whatever you're having," I said. I didn't know much about art, but I did know more than Orla: everything about Síle's work exuded professional confidence. She could have sold any of these pictures quite easily. "You're very good," I said.

"I'll keep at it," she said dryly, and I laughed.

I pointed to a signature at the bottom right of one of the paintings: *Síle Ní Ghallchobhair.* "Is that the Gaelic version of your name?"

She nodded. "Irish, not Gaelic."

"Sorry."

She smiled as she rinsed out a metal teapot. "Keep saying 'sorry,' and you'll fit right in."

"Did you go to art school?"

"For a time." Síle drew a couple of bags out of a tin as the water came to a boil. "It didn't agree with me."

"Maybe you didn't need it." I watched her pour the water into the teapot and place two mugs, a ceramic sugar pot, and a package of ginger biscuits—the same brand her sister had offered me that morning—on a plain wooden tray.

"I don't drink cow's milk," she said. "I hope you don't mind."

I shrugged. "Have you had many journalists visiting you here?"

"I've lived here nearly four years, and you're the first. Most people have long since forgotten about it, and I suppose that's for the best." She brought the tray over to a narrow table beside her bed, and we sat down opposite one another.

"Best . . . for you?" I asked.

"Now, that I couldn't say." Síle flicked me a sardonic look. "They tell me I'm the last person to know what's best for me." She poured the tea and nudged the sugar pot toward me with the back of her hand.

It was too soon to be asking any more questions along that line. I turned to look out the iron-barred window. To the left the sea was dark and roiling, and to the right I could see a strange knob of a mountain in the distance. "You're right on the Atlantic," I said.

"Pity the weather's so foul. I'd love to go for a walk on the strand." She smiled deviously. "Like old times, you might say."

"It's the same beach?"

"The very one."

I tried to picture us running along the sandy strip between the water and the rocks, but with the weather this bad, it was impossible to imagine. The irony of her living here now—trapped in an old house overlooking a place where she'd once been as free as children ever get. It made me shudder.

"We'll go out the next time you come," Síle said.

Again my pulse quickened, and a little voice behind my ear said, *You can't even remember why you came here.* "Would they let us do that?"

She shrugged. "I can do what I like."

"It seems like you're happy enough," I said as I glanced at the drawings on the walls. "Like you're making the best of it."

"Which is what I'd still be doing, were I anywhere else." Síle smiled as she brought her steaming mug to her lips. "They're spending massive amounts of money to keep me here. Have you any notion what a place like Ardmeen House costs?"

"No idea."

"What do you reckon? 'Ballpark,' as you Americans say."

"Two hundred a day?"

She laughed, knowing I'd aim much too low. "Nearer to eight hundred." I gasped and muttered a four-letter word. "Insurance covers most of it, and my mam and dad pay the rest. When I first got here, it kept me awake nights, the feeling burdensome, but I don't worry about that anymore. It's for their peace of mind that I stay here, so I don't feel guilty for saving the money I make from my paintings."

"Where do you sell them?"

"There's a gallery in Sligo," she said. "I've sold some there, and at a couple other places in Derry and Athlone. And there are a few cafés in Donegal that sometimes hang my pictures as well. The owners come to visit me here, and they choose what they like. I don't make a lot, but it's a much more useful thing to do than just sitting in a corner carving up the insides of my arms." I winced. "Sorry," she said. "Sometimes I go too far."

"Does your family visit you?"

She smirked to herself as she topped up our mugs. "More often than I'd like."

"How often is too often?"

"Once a month. Always on a Sunday."

"I met your sister this morning."

She lifted her brows, but I could tell she wasn't surprised. "Did you?"

"You're very different."

Síle laughed. "How is Orla?"

"All right, I guess." I paused. "She told me she never visits you."

"I did speak to her on the phone there the other week. But she never comes; she tells our mam and dad she's too busy with the wee ones. It's easier for both of us that she doesn't, although I do wish I could meet the babbies. But she'll never let me—not before they're grown, at any rate."

I knew then, somehow knew for certain, that Orla had blocked everything she'd seen and heard and felt. I didn't see why one sister should be free and "normal" and the other in a mental home when they'd had the very same experience. It was bad enough to live like a bird in a cage, but it was an even bigger shame for a bird so lovely.

"A lot of things have happened to me in the meantime," Síle said gently. "Orla was afraid. She's always been afraid. Better not to see it, she thinks. Better not to feel it. In some ways, I'm much freer in here than she'll ever be."

There was such truth in what she'd said that I could practically feel it humming in the walls. "Síle?"

"Hmm?"

"Why are you here?"

"Because they say I'll never be cured. Cured of what, though, nobody seems to know—or at least they won't tell me. There used to be a name for it, but they've since taken it out of the book."

I looked at her. I had to put one hand on top of the other to keep from reaching out to run my thumb along her lower lip.

"I could leave," she said softly. "I could behave exactly as they're asking me to, and after a time, they'd let me leave. Whatever the doctor's told you, we're none of us a danger to ourselves or each other. But if I were to go out—find a flat, find a job—and then things got too confusing again, I'd only end up back where I started."

Now I reached out and touched her lightly on the knee. "You're the sanest person I've met since I got here."

She flashed me a sad little smile. "That's kind of you to say."

"I mean it."

"Do you want to know what it's like? To be mad, I mean." I nodded, and she said, "You have people round you who profess to love you, but then they go and twist every word you say to make you look like you don't know which way is up." Síle sighed. "No— that isn't fair of me. They don't do it purposefully. They've no idea they're doing it."

"Everybody does that," I said.

"Don't they, though?" She leaned forward and moved the tea tray to the floor. "I want to do something for you," she said as she reached for my hand. "I'm going to read your palm." She pressed my fingers open and gently squeezed the base of my thumb. "Tell me something."

"Anything."

"D'you have a girlfriend?"

I'd known this would come up somehow, but I still couldn't answer without hesitation. "No," I said.

She traced her forefinger along my life line, and considered it. "Did you love her?"

What kind of man would I be, if I said no? "I think so."

"Then you did the right thing."

"Are you reading that off my hand?"

We looked up from my palm at the same time. "I don't have to," she said, and we kept looking. I couldn't remember the last time I'd wanted someone like this.

"Next time you come," she went on, "you can tell me everything Tess and Orla told you. Then I'll tell you my part."

"We don't have to," I said. "Not unless you want to."

"It's the reason you came, isn't it?"

I'd all but forgotten why I was here, and she knew it. I gave in to the urge to paper it over. "They said you saw her first," I said.

"They do say that."

"Do you remember it? The first time it happened?"

"I do," she said. "I remember it well."

"Can you tell me about it?"

Síle looked beyond me now, as if the past were reconfiguring itself just over my right shoulder. "They wanted people to think that I was the one who saw Her the clearest and that maybe I'd even convinced them of things that weren't there. But I wasn't the only one to see Her," she said softly. "I wasn't, and I'll tell you how I know. After a certain point, Tess started going up to the hill by herself. She thought none of us knew, and I don't know, maybe Orla never guessed. They were drifting, by that point."

"She didn't tell me she went up by herself," I said. I liked Tess—had always liked her. I didn't want to think of her misleading me.

When Síle refocused her eyes, it was like she could read my thoughts scrolling across my forehead. "I wouldn't think any less of her. Haven't you ever forgotten anything on purpose?"

We just looked at each other. "Maybe I have," I said.

She rose to her feet. "You don't have much time."

"Is that on my palm, too?"

She laughed. "I meant time left in your visit. He'll be knocking in a minute."

"Will they let me come again?"

"Oh, Martin and I have an understanding," she replied airily. "Dr. Kiely never lets on, but she lets him do as he thinks best." Síle smiled then, a luminous smile, as if she'd swallowed the moon for breakfast. She'd flashed me that smile many times before.

"I'm sorry about your sister," she said softly. "I've been wanting to say it since you first walked in, but I just couldn't bring myself to it." Síle reached out a pale hand as if to touch my chest, but she didn't. "Sometimes I pretend she's alive as ever, and I can't see her only because we've gone our separate ways."

I looked at the floorboards. "Thanks," I said. "That's . . . very kind of you. To think of her."

"I remember that day so clearly. I've always remembered her. How we laughed and laughed together. How I wished she lived here, so I could have her for a real friend." Brona's words came back to me: *no one ever knew what to make of her.*

"That might have been the happiest day of her life," I said, and the truth of it set my skin to prickling. "The happiest day, thanks to you." Another smile shone out of that lovely face, and I let it eclipse the memory of Mallory in the little white casket, Mallory in the dark.

Then there came the knock at the door, and Síle put her hand to my cheek in the second before it opened.

Brona decided not to come down with me to the pub that night, and it was just as well. "So you met Síle Gallagher," Leo said musingly. "Fair play to ya, lad! Some led me to believe they defend that place with swords and cannon fire." He drained his pint glass and smacked his lips. "What didja tell them?"

"Said I was an old friend."

"Sure, that's true enough," Paudie said.

"And when you went in to see her—what did you say?" Leo asked.

"We talked about a lot of things. She's very . . . playful," I said lamely. "She knows how to put a person at ease."

Leo tittered like a nine-year-old girl. "And what sort of things did ye talk about?"

"Her adventures in India. Her artwork. Her family. That sort of thing."

"You didn't ask her about the apparition?" Paudie asked.

"There wasn't time."

I didn't look up from my pint, but I could feel Leo smirking at me. "You got there and forgot why you'd come, isn't that it?"

I tried to suppress a grin, and failed. "Pretty much."

"She's the sort makes you forget yer own name," he said. "I may be an old man, but I'm young enough yet."

Paudie rolled his eyes. "Will you be seein' her again?"

The old men looked at me. Leo tossed back his head and laughed.

The next tape was labeled *Declan Keaveney, 8 February 1988*. In that room in my mind, the boy in the black-and-white newspaper photographs came to life: the surly turn of the lip and the anywhere-but-here posture, his hair in greasy black spikes, handsome and callow. I saw him dressed in a thermal shirt, army boots, and the leather bomber, and he tapped his foot on the hardwood floor and settled and resettled himself in the chair as if fidgeting could get him out of the interview any faster. Father Dowd asked him the same basic questions about the apparition, and his answers essentially matched Tess's, though they were not so willingly given. When the priest asked him to interpret what he'd seen, he became even less cooperative.

```
                    FATHER DOWD
        Do you feel blessed?



                      DECLAN
        I don't. I don't feel any different.



                    FATHER DOWD
        You saw a vision of the Blessed Virgin Mary,
        and you don't feel any different?
```

                    DECLAN
        (irritated at having to repeat himself)
    I don't feel any different.

                    FATHER DOWD
    Don't you see? This is a chance to do some
    good in the world, lad. To *be* somebody.

The young man rolls his eyes as the priest is talking.

                    DECLAN
    I'm already somebody.

                    FATHER DOWD
    And are you *already* doing good in the world?

                    DECLAN
    Probably not by your standards, Father.

The priest heaves a sigh, and just then he looks at
least ten years older.

                    FATHER DOWD
                    (sternly)
    If we're to see this through, we need your
    cooperation.

                    DECLAN
    How do ya mean, "see it through"?

                    FATHER DOWD
    Why, bringing Our Lady's message to the world.

The priest pauses, for emphasis. But it's like the boy's bricked an invisible wall across his desk and nothing can get through it.

FATHER DOWD (CONT'D)
You have been called, Declan.

DECLAN
It was Tess who told you. Not me.
(smiles mockingly)
You can say it, Father: you're surprised she appeared to me at all. That I'm the dodgy one, the one who wasn't supposed to be there.

FATHER DOWD
I can say this much, Declan: I'd never presume to know what's going on up in that mind of yours.

DECLAN
You're not denying it, Father.

FATHER DOWD
Remember Our Lady, Declan. Remember her message. It goes beyond all our petty opinions and hopes and wishes for ourselves.

DECLAN
Look, Father. If you want to tell the men in Rome or whatever that I was a part of this, I don't care. You can tell them what I saw, as long as *I* don't have to tell them.

The boy taps his boot on the floor and runs the
sleeve of his thermal shirt under his nose. His eyes
rove all over the room, anywhere but at the priest.
When he speaks again, his tone is less resentful than
matter of fact.

                    DECLAN (CONT'D)
      You're right about one thing. I may have seen
      her, and maybe I'll keep on seeing her when
      we go up the hill sometimes, but beyond that,
      I've no part to play in all this.

The recording ended abruptly, as if Father Dowd had finally
lost his patience and brought his finger down hard on the STOP
button. I saw the boy rise from his seat, nodding to his inquisitor
only to keep from shaming his poor pious mother entirely; and
after he'd gone, the priest sat looking out the narrow window into
the yard behind the rectory, so mired in his infuriated thoughts
that his secretary had to ask three times if he wanted any tea.

5

I walked into the church expecting that Tess and I would be the only people there under the age of eighty, apart from the priest, but I was wrong. There were maybe a dozen parishioners assembled in the first few pews, and most of them were in their forties or fifties. Tess went down on her knees, clasped her hands, and bent her head. I just sat there waiting for the service to start, staring up at the half-size crucifix suspended above the altar and feeling awkward.

Once it began, though, the Mass passed with surprising briskness. Everyone spoke the prayers at a different pace, so that there was a sort of discordant murmuring going on throughout the church. A woman in the pew behind us had apparently memorized the entire Mass, even the priest's parts, though she uttered them so mechanically that she couldn't have put any thought into them at all. There was no music and only two readings, and Father Lynch delivered his homily as if there were someone at the back of the church holding up a stopwatch. I looked over and saw Tess mouthing the Our Father with her eyes closed and her palms open at her sides, as if she were expecting a rather sizable gift. She didn't seem to care that I didn't rise for Communion.

It was over in twenty-five minutes. On our way out of the church, we approached a middle-aged woman already deep in conversation with Father Lynch. As we came near, she looked up at us with pale startled eyes, as if she'd only just realized she hadn't been the only person at Mass.

"That's Mrs. Keaveney," Tess whispered after we'd nodded to Father Lynch and passed into the vestibule. I stopped short and looked over my shoulder. "Only don't speak to her now. 'Twould be best if you called round to her house later on."

I walked with Tess to the youth center, and it was still only "half eight," as the Irish say. "It's a bit early to be starting your workday, isn't it?" I asked. "We could go for coffee at that place up the street?"

"I've plenty of tea and coffee in the office. You're more than welcome to join me."

I followed her upstairs and took the same seat beside her desk as Tess filled the electric kettle. "Have you much on the agenda today?" She spoke wryly, so I guessed she was still puzzled over why I wasn't just sightseeing like any other tourist.

"Not too much," I said. "Yesterday was busier. I drove up to Sligo to see Síle—"

"Did you!" Tess smiled as she drew two tea bags out of the Barry's box. "How is she?"

"She seems to be doing well to me. The doctor acted like she was seriously disturbed, but I'd say she doesn't belong in there at all."

Tess gave me a pensive look as she poured the milk. "Perhaps you're right."

We looked at each other, and I wondered what she was really thinking.

"Now," she said as she brought the mugs to her desk, "think of how good it would feel to begin every day the way we've started this one."

"Do you feel virtuous?" I asked, and suddenly she looked stricken. "Relax," I said, trying to laugh. "I was kidding."

Tess looked at me doubtfully as she took her first sip of tea. "So," she said, "in all seriousness. What did you think of the Mass?"

I shrugged and tried to smile. "It was tolerable," I said. "I was raised Catholic, but I guess we were always just going through the motions, you know?"

"I know," she said, a little sadly.

"And I think about all the same stuff on the rare occasions when I do go to church. Like, if Jesus died for our sins, then how come the world is just as full of evil and suffering as it was before? I mean, what was the point of that stuff with the crucifixion and everything? What difference did it actually make?"

"Just think of the state we'd be in if he *hadn't* come," Tess replied, and I had to smile.

"Okay, here's the most basic point," I said. "God does terrible things in the Old Testament, right? Really terrible things. He's angry and jealous and vengeful, like some ordinary jerk with a serious case of road rage. He's definitely not behaving like the creator of the universe. An angry God makes even less sense to me than no God at all."

"I see what you're saying," Tess replied. "I've wondered about these things myself."

"And did you come to any conclusions?"

"I *can't* know God," she said softly. "I can devote my whole life to reading the Scripture, to prayer and contemplation, and I still won't understand why He does what He does." She drew a breath. "When I think of it this way, it makes sense to me. I'm only me, you know? My understanding is limited by my human brain, my human emotions. My human perceptions and limitations. The same is true of those who put the Bible together. God is too vast to be comprehensible to anyone, in the end. If He were, He'd be a much smaller god than any of us could give Him credit for."

For a minute or two, we sipped our tea in silence, and I mulled over what she'd said. There was a poignant sort of sense to it.

"Would you like to hear what else I did yesterday?" I asked finally, and Tess nodded. "I talked to Orla."

I watched her face fall, as I'd known it would. She cleared her throat. "And what did she have to say?"

"She says she doesn't think she saw what she said she saw."

"Aye," Tess said softly. "Didn't I tell you as much?" I nodded, and she sighed. "It may have seemed to anyone else like an experience we were all of us sharing, but underneath it, we weren't, not really. Much of the time I felt that Síle and I were the ones who wanted to see her, that Orla and Declan were being carried along despite their will. There was always a reluctance with them." I watched a smile bloom faintly on her lips, and fade away a moment later. "Síle and I, we never spoke of it outright, but there was an affection there between us. We were accepting of the blessing and the responsibility; we were always together in that."

"I can hear it in your voice," I said. "Whenever we speak of her, you still feel that fondness for her."

Tess gave me another sad smile. "You say you don't think Síle belongs in there, and I want to believe you're right." She hesitated.

"How do I put this? Síle used to have these . . . well, Orla called them fits, but I never wanted to think of them that way. It wasn't fair to call them fits, because she wasn't possessed—or if she was, I dunno, it seemed like it was the Holy Spirit filling her up, rather than something dark. That's how it seemed to me because of how watching her made me feel. It felt good to watch her. I wasn't afraid at all. And there was the difference. Does that make sense?" She looked to me for confirmation.

"It makes a lot of sense," I said.

The phone rang, and Tess reached for it with an apologetic smile. "St. Brigid's Youth Centre, Tess speaking," she said, and listened. "Ah, sure. Of course, of course. I'll be over to you shortly."

"I'm so sorry," she said as she put the receiver down. "I've got to begin work now. Next time I see you . . ." She took a deep breath. "Next time I see you, we'll have a proper chat."

I went back to Brona's, loaded the next interview tape (*Orla Gallagher, 13 February 1988*) into the Walkman, and brought it with me. The sun didn't seem to be going anywhere for once, so I decided to go for a drive. Paudie had mentioned a passage tomb in a field three or four miles northwest of town, and I wasted half an hour trying to extract the Micra from a series of muddy country lanes before giving up looking for it.

The light withdrew suddenly on my way back to Ballymorris, and as the downpour started, I found myself taking the turn for the grotto. Mag O'Grady's little white truck was there, sure enough, but this time I didn't get out of the car. I put on the old-fashioned earphones, and when I pressed the PLAY button, I saw Orla sitting before the priest twenty years younger, her cheeks still full with lingering baby fat and her skin as pale as it ought to be.

> ORLA
>
> She was so beautiful I could hardly look Her in the face, Father. I told Her . . . I told Her I didn't feel worthy.

The priest reacts more skeptically than he did with Teresa. There is no hostility, as with Declan, but the sense of rapport between questioned and questioner is noticeably lacking.

> FATHER DOWD
>
> And what did she say to you?

> ORLA
>
> She blessed me and said She knew that from now on I would *try* to be worthy, and that was all She could ever ask of me.

> FATHER DOWD
>
> What about Declan? D'you reckon he feels unworthy, too? I spoke with him last week, as you know, and I can't say he was as coopera-tive as you and Teresa have been.

> ORLA
>
> He means well, Father, he really does. He just doesn't know how to feel easy about any of it. He's so used to everyone givin' him a hard time for how he looks.

FATHER DOWD

You'll understand when you're older, Orla, that "givin' a hard time" to a young person is all to a purpose. With every word you speak, every gesture, every impulse you give in to without reflection, you're building your character. At the end of your life, your character is all you have to show for yourself. Do you see that?

The girl's manner is still respectful, but she crosses her arms and sits taller in her chair.

ORLA

I see, Father. But I don't believe that when two people don't see eye to eye, one of them has to be wrong for the other to be right.

FATHER DOWD
(sighing)

Someday, when he's much older, Declan may look in the mirror, and he won't like the man he sees. And by then it will be too late.

ORLA

I don't see that, Father. Declan wants a different sort of life for himself, and I don't see how that's wrong.

FATHER DOWD

You don't see it *yet*.

An icy note enters into the girl's voice for the first time, and if the priest notices, he doesn't follow suit.

                    ORLA
I thought we were meant to be talking about Our Lady.

                FATHER DOWD
It's all of a piece, child. Why d'you suppose she came to ye, and not to me?

                    ORLA
I don't know, Father.

                FATHER DOWD
I don't pretend to know, either. But I *can* say she's asked a great deal of ye, and ye must try your very best to be worthy of the blessing, as you yourself have said.

The priest grows animated, gesticulating with both hands.

            FATHER DOWD (CONT'D)
Ye are the messengers! The bringers of peace in our own time! Do you see that?

The priest's fervor rises to the point where the girl has to lean back in her chair to keep from being overwhelmed by it.

FATHER DOWD (CONT'D)

This is what Declan must grow to understand:
now isn't the time to turn in on yourselves.
Your friends and schoolmates may behave as
they like, but ye haven't that luxury now.
Ye've been called, and the call must be answered.

ORLA

I don't know, Father. I'm not sure of what I
saw, and if I can't be sure, then it wouldn't
feel right to go out into the world and talk
about it.

The priest stares at her, shocked by the sudden
about-face, and when he speaks again, there's a sub-
tle note of panic in his voice.

FATHER DOWD

How d'you mean, you're not sure? Didn't
you say you saw her? Didn't you say she was
the most beautiful woman you ever laid
eyes on?

ORLA

If I really saw what I thought I saw, I think
I would feel differently about it. I would
want to go out and speak of it.

FATHER DOWD

A heart in doubt: that *is* a sign, Orla. So is

reluctance, and the not feeling worthy. Tess feels it, and I can see you feel it, too. It means you understand deep down that this glory, the glory ye must speak of and spread to anyone who is ready to listen: 'tis God's glory, not yours. 'Tis a beautiful thing, to understand that.

                    ORLA

That's not what I mean, Father. I know this isn't about me.
                  (pauses)
I don't know if it was real. That's the simple truth of it.

                 FATHER DOWD

If you don't think you saw Our Lady . . . what do you think you saw?

                    ORLA

Nothing. I . . . I think I made myself see something so that . . .

The girl draws a trembling breath. She can't look the priest in the eye.

                ORLA (CONT'D)

I don't think I saw it. I think I only made myself see it.

                 FATHER DOWD

But why? Why would you think that?

ORLA

For Síle. So *she* wouldn't be seeing things,
Father. That's why.

FATHER DOWD

Now, Orla. I have interviewed each of you on
your own, and you have each described Our
Lady in terms that would lead any reasonable
person to conclude that you were experiencing the same phenomenon. I have asked certain questions of each of you, and both you
and your friend Tess have answered them in a
fashion which would satisfy any skeptic. Did
Tess tell you the questions I'd asked her in
strictest confidence? Did ye take the opportunity to agree upon your answers beforehand?

The girl's reaction is too shocked to be anything
but the honest truth.

ORLA

No, Father!

FATHER DOWD

Was there any drink involved?

ORLA

No, Father! I never drink except when my dad
offers it at Christmastime.

The priest shoots her a doubtful look, and a flash
of contempt passes across Orla's face ("This is just

what I was talking about. You see I'm with Declan, and you make assumptions.")

FATHER DOWD

Then explain to me how you could be misled by your own eyes.

ORLA
(hesitatingly)

It seemed so clear at the time. I accepted it. It felt real. But now I don't know, and Declan doesn't know either, and I don't know what to think.

FATHER DOWD

It seems to me that when the two of ye speak of the visitation ye've only been confusing each other.

ORLA

But it's not as if I could somehow make myself sure again. I wish I could be sure of everything, one way or the other.

The priest is well and truly exasperated now, but he's making a visible attempt to suppress it.

FATHER DOWD

What about Tess? Do you believe she saw Our Lady?

                    ORLA

Tess is the most honest person I know.

                 FATHER DOWD

I would say so, too. Tess has a strong character. When Tess opens her mouth to speak,
you can be sure the words that come out are
the truth.

                    ORLA

I know, Father.

                 FATHER DOWD

And Tess knows what she saw. She has perfect
conviction.
                   (pauses)
So if your sister were seeing things that
weren't there, then Teresa would have to be
seeing them, too.

                    ORLA

Aye, Father. I've thought of that.

                 FATHER DOWD

Sometimes the most extraordinary explanation
also happens to be the correct one, Orla.

I guess they don't teach Occam's razor at the seminary, I thought
as the tape clicked off. If people used their own common sense,
then what would they need the priests for?

A flutter of movement near the grotto drew me away from my

notebook. A lanky figure in a black hooded sweatshirt stood with a hand on that ledge lined with all the pillar candles and glow-in-the-dark Virgins, and when the boy turned to look at my car, I recognized him by the size of his Adam's apple.

I rolled down the window. "Hey," I called. "Didn't I see you down at the youth center the other day?" The boy looked at me blankly, so I added, "With Tess?"

The sound of her name seemed to soften him, just as it had everyone else. "You a friend of hers?" the boy asked.

"Yeah, I am. I'm in town for my uncle's funeral."

"Who's your uncle?"

"Johnny Donegan?" I don't know why I said his name as if it were a question, or why I even felt the need to talk to this kid.

He nodded. "Sorry for your loss."

"Yeah, well." I coughed. "He was a nice man, but I hadn't seen him since I was a kid." I flipped up my hood and got out of the car. "What are you doing up here, anyway? It's nasty out."

The boy shrugged, and I glanced back at the tchotchke truck. The light was on, but I couldn't see the little old woman inside.

"Were you asking Tess about the apparition?"

I turned back to him, caught off guard, and he stifled a smirk. "I didn't think it was something she talked about," I said.

The boy shot me a pointed look. "Then that makes two of us."

We both turned to the water-stained statue of the Virgin in her cement niche. "Is she why you're up here?" I asked, burying my hands deeper into my pockets and hunching my shoulders against the wind. "I didn't think anybody really believed in this stuff anymore." Certainly nobody young enough to know better. Then again, what was *I* doing here?

There was a gawkiness to him that some boys never grow out of, and I suspected he'd be one of them. "Tess believes," he said.

I quirked a brow. "Do you?" She'd come up here by herself,

Síle had said. Had the apparition come to her then? What had it said to her?

The boy turned to the statue with an unreadable look on his face. There was an awkwardly protracted pause, and it hit me that he was *listening* to something. I cleared my throat. "Hey. Are you okay?"

The boy turned back to me then, but he wasn't entirely there. He nodded vaguely.

"You need a ride back to town?"

"Nah," he said, and in another beat, he'd come back to himself. "I'll be all right."

Casting me one last wary glance, the boy turned and stalked down the hill toward town, and I looked up at the blank-faced statue with the unnerving sense that I'd been excluded.

I walked over to the tchotchke truck. Tiny old Mag O'Grady had propped herself against the back wall of her shop, snoring softly as her toothless jaw went up and down, up and down, like she was dreaming of dinner.

I had my laptop with me, but I got blank looks in cafés and pubs whenever I asked about the Wi-Fi. I had to go down to the library to dash off an e-mail to Andy, my editor at the magazine. *It's along the lines of weeping statues, minus the religious nuts,* I wrote. *I'm talking to the women who saw it when they were teenagers. Social and economic angle as well. Mysticism and the Celtic Tiger.* The next time I signed on, I'd find a reply from Andy, cautiously approving, and then I'd go ahead and draft the piece. Every time my thoughts wandered back to the boy on the hill, I brushed them away again. If religious visions were as common as that, Mag O'Grady would be raking it in. Síle would sketch and paint in a studio without bars.

At lunch I told Brona I'd booked a room at Mrs. Halloran's B and B for the rest of my stay in Ballymorris. "Take it up with my grandmother," I told her when she protested. "She's the one who says fish and houseguests stink after three days, and I've already been here five."

"She didn't mean your own family!" Brona cried, but I wouldn't let her sway me. It felt too good to know she didn't want me to leave.

"And how did you find the Mass this morning?" she asked, once she'd resigned herself.

"It was over in less than a half hour," I said. "There were more people there than I thought there'd be. And I saw Mrs. Keaveney. Tess pointed her out to me."

Brona replied with that automatic click of the tongue. "The poor dear!"

I gulped down the last of my toasted cheese sandwich before I spoke again. "Can you tell me where she lives?"

Brona cast me a squinty look. "Why d'you ask?"

"I thought I might speak with her, if she's willing."

"Oh, she'll speak to you," she sighed. "As for whether she'll speak any sense, that's another matter altogether."

"Father Lynch did say she's not . . ."

"Not quite right?" Brona took a sip of tea, and sighed again. "I'm afraid so. She's convinced Declan's coming home any day now. She's been sayin' it for years, and he never comes."

"So you think I shouldn't try to see her, then?" I don't know why I bothered asking, when I was going regardless.

"Sure, you can speak to her. I just can't see what you'll gain by it." Brona shook her head. "Poor Peggy Keaveney. There's some of us who're worn down by the business of life. The falseness. First the husband, then the son."

"Are you sure they left her? You hear about people having

accidents sometimes and no one ever finds out what really happened."

As she cleared our plates, Brona gave me an eloquent look. For all their reputation for chattiness and storytelling, the Irish I knew were so skillful with words there was sometimes no need for them at all.

She gave in, though, and it turned out Mrs. Keaveney lived just around the corner. From the outside, the house seemed better kept than I'd've expected, the hedge under the front window neatly pruned. I knocked a second and third time, and only then did I notice there wasn't any smoke coming out of the chimney. Next door a very old man stuck his head out his front door and said, "She'll be havin' a kip right about now." I opened my mouth to ask what a kip was, but he went on: "You're Johnny Donegan's nephew, aren't you?"

I nodded, and he nodded back. "Come back later this afternoon," he said gravely, as if he'd put a considerable degree of thought into it. "'Twould be a good time to come, right about four o'clock. Will I tell herself you called?"

I thanked him but said no, that wouldn't be necessary. When I turned to leave, he said, "I remember you, lad. It's a long time since you were here, but I remember you."

"That was twenty-five years ago," I said, laughing a little. "You couldn't possibly!"

"Ah, but I do. Johnny brought you round to the parish picnic, and your gran told us all about you," he replied, and then he called me by a nickname I hadn't heard since I was fourteen.

I shivered as I turned the corner for Brona's. I couldn't help feeling again as if I were being watched.

————

It was turning into a wasted sort of day, but there was no use fighting it. I walked back to Brona's in the rain and told her I was going up for a "kip" myself, but when I drew the curtains and got into bed, the Walkman—and the piece of Síle inside it—beckoned to me from the dresser.

The young girl sits demurely in the chair opposite the priest, her hands folded in her lap, a serious expression on her lovely face as she answers his questions. For his part, the priest looks more stern than we have yet seen him.

FATHER DOWD
Now, Síle. We'll start from the beginning, and with no embellishments.

SÍLE
I don't know what I've done to make every-one think I'm lyin' about what I've seen, Father.

FATHER DOWD
Let me put it to you this way, child: do you feel that the Blessed Virgin has singled you out? Has she given you a special mission? A calling no one else can answer?

The girl looks down at her hands.

SÍLE
I don't feel I'm special in any way.

FATHER DOWD

That's the truth, is it?

Síle looks up, her pale face suddenly alight with righteous indignation.

SÍLE

I don't mean to be thick wit'cha, Father, but you're askin' questions you think you already know the answers to.

FATHER DOWD

You're right, Síle. You *are* being thick with me.

SÍLE

If you think I'm no good, then why am I here? Why did you ask me here if you think I'm makin' it all up for the attention?

FATHER DOWD

I know you're not "makin' it up." Tess saw her, too. And your sister. And Declan.

SÍLE

But you wouldn't be takin' us seriously if it weren't for Tess.

FATHER DOWD
(sighing)

From the beginning, Síle. From the very beginning. Why were you up on the hill that day?

> SÍLE

We go up there to talk. There's space up there, and the air is fresh.

> FATHER DOWD

You're younger than the others. How does your sister like you tagging along with them at the end of the school day?

> SÍLE

I'm not taggin' along, Father.

The two exchange a look. She's a smart girl; she knows he'll only humor her, but she still has to let him.

> FATHER DOWD

All right. Would you say you and your sister are friends?

> SÍLE

I'd say we are.

> FATHER DOWD

But would she have something else to say about it?

Síle replies with a defiant lift of the chin.

> SÍLE

Someday we'll be better friends than we are now.

FATHER DOWD

I hope that's so. And tell me, are you friendly
with Tess?

SÍLE

Oh, aye. Tess is a friend. She's always been
kind to me.

FATHER DOWD

Tess is kind to everyone.
                (after a pause)
And as for Declan?

SÍLE

What about him?

FATHER DOWD

They tell me he and your sister are going
out.

SÍLE

I suppose they are. Once or twice I've seen
them snoggin' behind the garage. But they
don't hold hands or anythin' whilst we're all
together.

The priest responds with a look of distaste. He might
be able to supervise the school dances, but he holds
no jurisdiction behind the family garage.

FATHER DOWD

Do you get on with him?

SÍLE

Declan? He's grand.

FATHER DOWD

He's nice to you?

SÍLE

He gives me the second Snack bar when Orla
doesn't want it.

FATHER DOWD

It sounds like you get on better with your
sister's friends than you do with Orla herself.

SÍLE
(defensively)
I love my sister.
(pauses)
But most of the time, whatever I say, it's
the wrong thing.

FATHER DOWD

Has the vision changed things a'tall? Between
the two of ye?

SÍLE

Sometimes I think it has. Other times we're
just as we were, and she walks by me like I'm
a piece of the furniture.

FATHER DOWD

Have you spoken with her about what the
Blessed Mother said to each of ye?

SÍLE

Orla agrees we're meant to take Our Lady's
message into the world.
                    (desolately)
When we talk about the messages, she forgets
that I'm a pest.

FATHER DOWD

Tell me how it began, and do your best to
recall the details. You went up to the hill
after school, as usual? Do you remember what
the four of ye were talking about?

SÍLE

Declan was tellin' us about a man he met who
worked on a cargo ship and that's how he got
to see the world.

FATHER DOWD
                    (scoffing)
And how would Declan meet such a man?

SÍLE
                    (wryly)
I couldn't say, Father. He was about to tell
us, and Our Lady broke in.

FATHER DOWD

None of that cheek, now. Tell us how it
started.

SÍLE

Declan was talkin', but all of a sudden he
sounded far away, like I had a ringin' in me
ears, only there wasn't any ringin'. It was
very quiet, and there'd been a wind before but
it died away all sudden-like. I found myself
lookin' up toward the statue in the grotto,
but it wasn't there anymore, and that's when
the light started.

FATHER DOWD

Tell us about the light.

SÍLE

It was so warm and lovely. Better than a hot
cup of tea when you've just come in out of
the rain. That's what Her love feels like.

FATHER DOWD

Our Lady's love for the world?

SÍLE

Her love for *me*.
                    (pauses)
And for the world.

Here is another opportunity to put the girl in her
place, and the priest pounces on it.

FATHER DOWD

Remember, Síle. This isn't about you.

SÍLE

No, Father. But She doesn't love us all the same. She loves us equal, but She doesn't love us the same.

FATHER DOWD

She said that, did she?

SÍLE

She did. She said God made each of us in a new mold, and no mold is any more perfect than the others.

FATHER DOWD

But what did she say, in the very beginning? When you saw her in the light?

SÍLE

She said, "Do you know me, child?" And I said, "I do. You're the Queen of Heaven," and She smiled, and when She smiled, She just lit the whole world up. Everywhere was brightness.

FATHER DOWD
(softening)

That must have made you feel very happy.

The girl's eyes fill with tears.

                    SÍLE

I was never happier in all my life.

                FATHER DOWD

And what did Our Lady look like?

                    SÍLE

                 (sniffling)

Not like She looks in the paintings and statues. She had a real face, like a real woman.

                FATHER DOWD

What do you mean, "a real face"?

                    SÍLE

In the books and paintings and statues, the
Blessed Mother always looks like a mannequin
in a shop window. Haven't you ever noticed
that, Father? The *real* Mary looks like somebody's mam.

A wry little smile plays on the priest's lips, but he
quickly suppresses it.

                FATHER DOWD

Now there's an apt description . . . though
not a particularly reverent one.

                    SÍLE

She had long black hair, and She was wearin'
Her blue mantle, but I could still see it

flowed down to Her waist. And She had dark eyes. Smilin' brown eyes, like She had a story She couldn't wait to tell me. And Her hands were long and pale and She had them laid over Her heart, and all of Her was aglow, even Her toes. Her feet were bare, Father.

FATHER DOWD

What did she say to you?

SÍLE

She said, "I need your help. Will you carry my words out into the wide world?" And we said we would.

FATHER DOWD

You heard the others give their assent?

SÍLE

I did, Father. There were times She called me by name, but I knew She was saying the same thing to each of us.

FATHER DOWD

Did you ask her why she'd chosen you?

SÍLE

I didn't, Father. It didn't occur to me.

FATHER DOWD

It occurred to Tess.

SÍLE

Maybe She only came to the rest of us because of Tess.

FATHER DOWD

I can see you don't believe that.

SÍLE

No, Father.

FATHER DOWD

You believe you were chosen.

SÍLE

We *were* chosen. I look back on all the
months we'd been going up there to the
grotto, and I see it now. I see why we were
drawn there.

FATHER DOWD

Now, hold on a minute. You've admitted the
four of ye only went up there to gossip.

SÍLE

We went up and spoke of ordinary things,
that's true. But She was *calling* us there.
Waiting for the day when we'd be ready to
hear Her.

FATHER DOWD

What changed? What was different about the
first of November?

SÍLE

I don't know, Father.

FATHER DOWD

All right. What happened next? Did she give
you her first message?

SÍLE

She did, Father. She said we weren't meant to
suffer.

The priest is visibly taken aback.

FATHER DOWD

She can't have said that. Life *is* suffering,
child.

SÍLE

She did say it. She said we'd built this world
of suffering, and if we'd made it, we could
unmake it . . . and build a new world.

FATHER DOWD
(contemptuously)

And just how do you propose to build this
new world?

SÍLE

'Tisn't as grand as it sounds, Father. She
says we must build the new world out of the
things we can't touch or see. Love will be
the new currency, She says. The only currency
from now on.

FATHER DOWD
(sneering)
That's very poetical.

SÍLE
I didn't make it up. That was exactly how the
Blessed Mother said it.

FATHER DOWD
And what had she to say of sin, and repentance, and forgiveness?

SÍLE
She didn't speak of sin, Father.

FATHER DOWD
Tess told me she had quite a bit to say on
the subject.

SÍLE
I remember what She said to me. I remember
it clearly.

FATHER DOWD
I'm sure you do.

SÍLE
Maybe She had different messages for each of us.

FATHER DOWD
That's not what you told me to begin with.
You said she spoke the same to each of you.

SÍLE

I thought She had, Father.

FATHER DOWD

(with a huff of frustration)

How am I to tease out what's actually occurred here?

SÍLE

I know what She said to me, Father. It may
be the same or it may be different from what
the others heard, but I know what I heard Her
say.

FATHER DOWD

Right. So she'd nothing to say of sin. Then
what did she say to you?

SÍLE

She told me to pray. First I should pray for
my own sake, for it's only after I've offered
up my secrets that I'll be free to pray that
everyone else might do the same.

FATHER DOWD

Aye, that's true, child. That's why you must
come to confession. You see, Síle: She spoke
of sin after all.

SÍLE

Still, it wasn't like how you speak of it in
your homilies, Father. She made it sound

as simple as washin' your hands before
dinner.

FATHER DOWD
It's easy to sin. It's the recognizing you've
done wrong and asking the Lord for forgiveness that's the hard part. Didn't Our Lady
tell you that?

SÍLE
She never used the word "sin."

FATHER DOWD
You mean to say she actually spoke of "offering up your secrets"?

SÍLE
I don't remember the words She used when She
said that part. But I remember Her meaning.

FATHER DOWD
What did she say next?

SÍLE
You're not going to like it, Father. I didn't
want to tell you before because you were already so—

FATHER DOWD
(sighs)
Out with it, Síle.

SÍLE

She said to remind you of the sixth beatitude.

The priest stares at the girl. He can't even fathom
her audacity.

FATHER DOWD

Remind . . . remind *me*?

SÍLE

I told Her you'd think I was being cheeky,
but She said I shouldn't mind. "Blessed are
the pure of heart, for they shall see God."

FATHER DOWD
(explosively)

I well remember the sixth beatitude, Síle!

SÍLE

I was only sayin'.

FATHER DOWD

"How shall the young remain sinless? By obey-
ing Your Word." That's from the Psalms. You
said before that the Blessed Mother told you
your heart *wasn't* pure.

SÍLE
(pensively)

Sometimes I feel like I've done something

terrible and I'm the only one who can't remember it.

FATHER DOWD

No one's implying you've lied to your mother
or cheated on an exam. But it's terribly
easy to congratulate ourselves for leading
fine upstanding lives when we harbor unkind
thoughts and fantasies, and when we hold
ourselves above others even if we pretend not
to. *Those* are the secrets Our Lady spoke to
you about.

SÍLE

But I don't have unkind thoughts or fantasies.

FATHER DOWD

Everyone has unkind thoughts.

SÍLE

Even you, Father?

FATHER DOWD

Even I.
                    (clearing his throat)
Now tell me what happened when the Blessed
Mother took her leave. What did she say to
you then?

SÍLE

She said She would come to us again, and that

She loved us all very much, and that I should
keep a record of our conversations. A diary,
like.

FATHER DOWD
She didn't say that you should devote yourself to the catechism?

SÍLE
No, Father. Then She just sort of melted into
the air, like a mist, only it was the light
that went away. The world seemed so *dim* to us
after that.

FATHER DOWD
(thoughtfully but firmly)
I believe Our Lady left it to me to guide you
in your devotions. You and Orla must come to
Mass. No more having a lie-in on a Sunday.
And I'd like ye to come to study group on the
Tuesday evening.

SÍLE
Aye, Father. We will.

FATHER DOWD
And I'd like to see that diary from time to
time.

SÍLE
Oh, but I couldn't, Father. There are some
things She says you aren't ready to hear.

Father Dowd grows even more red in the face. (She's
making it up, all of it. It doesn't matter what Teresa said she saw.)

                    FATHER DOWD
You mean to say there's more you haven't told
me?

                       SÍLE
                (with sudden energy)
Oh, aye! You know She's been comin' to us two
or three times a week for all this time, and
there's so much She wants to say. . . .

Over the past several nights, I'd begun to feel more comfortable
at Napper Tandy's than I had even at Brona's. It was a nice, relaxed
place to have a drink, and up to this point, everyone had been
very friendly toward me.

But tonight there was a big game on, and the pub was crowded
with raucous men in football jerseys, their eyes fastened to the
television above the bar, cigarettes tucked behind their ears. Most
of them rolled their own. "A rough sort," my grandmother would
have called them. Brona leaned into me and said, "I don't care for
the pub on nights like this."

"We could go somewhere else," I said.

Leo shrugged. "The match will be over soon."

"It's only just started," Paudie pointed out.

"And we've only just started our pints!" Leo cried.

At halftime the soccer fans made for the door to smoke their
cigarettes, but a few of them lingered outside the snug. "Evening,

gentlemen," said one, as another came out with, "How're ya, now?" The first man bobbed his chin in my direction. "Who's the Yank?"

"None of that, now," Paudie said coldly. "We'll have none of that tone here."

"He *is* a Yank, isn't he?"

"*Céad míle fáilte*," sneered the other man from behind the first. "Ireland welcomes you home to her shriveled bosom."

"James Hennessey!" Brona piped up. "Your mam never raised you to speak that way, not to anyone."

Brona's talking-to drew several more men to the table. I could see them staring at me out of the corner of my eye. "Sure, I don't mean to offend ya, Mrs. Tuohy," Hennessey said. "It's just that this one shows up from America, and all he's doin' is askin' questions about things we're better off forgetting."

I leaned forward, eager to defuse this without any more help from a well-meaning widow. "Excuse me," I said, "but I have no idea who you are. I can't see why my presence here should matter to you in the slightest."

From the back of the crowd a shrill voice parroted, "*I can't see why my presence here should matter to you in the slightest!*"

Good grief. How had this pub suddenly turned into middle school all over again? "Pay them no mind, lad," Paudie was saying under his breath. "They're most of them on the dole."

"Ye ought to be ashamed of yerselves." Brona was fierce, and I felt a little explosion of love for her deep in my chest. "Take that nonsense back to the schoolyard, the lot o' ye."

The man in the green jersey flicked me a look—as if to say *we haven't finished with you yet*—but there was no arguing with Brona Tuohy.

"Nearly forty years of age, and would you look at them," Brona sighed as the last of the men filed out the door.

"I'm just glad I didn't meet them when they were twelve," I said. Everyone laughed, and for a while we talked of other things.

When there were thirty seconds left in the match, I excused myself and made for the front door. "You didn't tell us you smoked," Leo called after me. He'd rolled one earlier but hadn't gone out all evening, no doubt because of the company on the sidewalk.

"I don't," I replied from the doorway. "I just need some air. I'll be back in a few."

There was a little grocery shop across the street, open late. I hadn't bought a pack of cigarettes in at least a half a dozen years. In my jacket pocket I had a matchbox I'd picked from a bowl at the bar the evening before.

When I left the shop, the men were outside again. The match was over, their team had lost, and the looks on their faces were even more sour than when I'd first seen them.

I stopped a few feet away, lit a cigarette, and waited for someone to speak to me. They ignored me at first, but I knew they weren't going anywhere. The end of the match never meant the last of the Guinness.

After a few minutes, some of the men heeled out their cigarettes and went back in. Hennessey and his friend remained, silently finishing their smokes and eyeing me warily. They reminded me of wolves who hadn't had anything to eat all winter long, only in this case, they were hungry for an argument.

"What's the crack?" the second man said finally.

"I'm sorry," I said. "I never got your name."

"Yeats," he said as he flicked what was left of his cigarette into a puddle in the road. "Willy B. Yeats."

"Well," I replied as I held out the pack of Player's. "I never thought I'd be offering a cigarette to a dead poet."

He pulled one out, stuck it in his mouth, and spoke through

pursed lips. "Sure, we never stop needin' a bit o' comfort on a cold night," he said in a quavering falsetto, like the voice of an old Irishwoman, and his friend snickered.

"Can we cut the bullshit?" I asked.

Willy arched an eyebrow as he brought his lighter to the end of the cigarette. The spark momentarily threw a red glow over his wolfish features. "Just like a Yank."

"You don't like me asking questions about the apparition? Is that it?"

He took a deep drag. "Now, whatever gave you *that* idea?"

"Sarcasm duly noted," I replied. "I'm going to assume there's a legitimate reason for this hostility, and I'd really like to hear what it is."

"I'll tell ya what it is," Hennessey said. "You come back here in your little Nissan Micra, talkin' all this shite because you think you've a claim to the place."

"A claim to the place," I echoed. "What's that supposed to mean? I only came here to go to a funeral."

"Aye, and look where you've been since then," Willy scoffed. "They say you've been all the way up Benbulben to see the fairy queen."

Smoke streamed out of Hennessey's mouth as he laughed. "Aye! To rescue her!"

"Did anyone ever tell you that you guys gossip like a bunch of old women?"

I was surprised this comment provoked no reaction. Hennessey finished his cigarette, and again I held out my open pack. "See, this here's the trouble with you Yanks," he said. "It's nothing to do with you. Do ya see?"

"But what does it have to do with you either?" I asked. "Is it just because you were born in Ballymorris that you feel like you own whatever happens here?"

For a minute no one spoke. A scowl, apparently, was all I'd get from Hennessey for an answer.

"You know nothin' about anythin'," Willy said finally. "You know feck all."

"You're right," I said. "So why don't you tell me?" I looked at their crow's-feet and the silver at their temples. They could've been friends with Declan, back in the day. Of course they had been. "Was it real?" I asked.

Willy shook his head. "And *I'd* know feck all if I thought I'd an answer to that."

"It was something." Hennessey stared down through the pavement with his arms crossed, cigarette crimped between his lips, breathing the smoke out and in like an automaton. "It was something—whatever it was."

"*It?*" I asked, as the face of the boy on the hill flickered before me.

The man took the cigarette away from his mouth and looked at me as he exhaled. "If you really think it was the Blessed Virgin Mary they saw up there, then you're every bit as daft as we took you for."

My room at the B and B bore a similarity to Brona's spare room—maybe it was the vague whiff of mold—and though I had a full-size bed, it wasn't any more comfortable. The little room was crowded with furniture, a floral armchair blocked the door to the wardrobe, and the faded print of Christ and his crown of thorns above the bureau mirror made me cringe. At least my grandmother couldn't nag me afterward about putting Brona out.

I switched off the light and felt the springs dig into my ribs as I settled onto my side. I thought of listening to Síle's second interview tape, but I was already so riled up that if I did, I'd probably never get to sleep. What had they implied about the apparition—that it was real, but something only pretending to be the Virgin Mary? How had they come to believe that?

As I was finally nodding off, lulled by the analog alarm clock ticking softly at my ear, I suddenly rose with a start. I could have sworn I heard someone, a woman, sigh.

6

NOVEMBER 10

After the listlessness of the day before, I was even more determined to drive back up to Sligo after breakfast. My hostess at the B and B was on the chatty side, but she didn't seem to mind when I put on my headphones once she'd brought out my plate of eggs and black pudding. Síle's second interview tape was dated the third of March—a week after the first tape.

>   FATHER DOWD
>   Did the Blessed Mother reveal herself to you
>   in any way?
>
>   SÍLE
>   (puzzled)
>   How do ya mean, Father?
>
>   FATHER DOWD
>   I'm only attempting to reconcile your account
>   with the others'.

                    SÍLE

But I don't know what you mean by "reveal
Herself."

                 FATHER DOWD
                   (smugly)
You'd know it, if she had.

                    SÍLE

But I might. There are things I'm not supposed to talk about yet.

                 FATHER DOWD

Did she tell you not to speak of them?

                    SÍLE

She said She'd tell me when the time had come
to tell you.

                 FATHER DOWD

Pardon my cynicism, but that's rather conve-
nient.

                    SÍLE

I'm only tellin' ya what She said to me.

                 FATHER DOWD

The Blessed Mother didn't give any sort of
secret knowledge to the others. Tess spoke
of no such thing.

                    SÍLE

It isn't always when we see Her on the hill.
Other times, too.

                FATHER DOWD
                (taken aback)
She doesn't only come to you at the grotto?

                    SÍLE
                (nodding)
There's a voice at my ear, tellin' me things.
It might be Our Lady's voice, but I can't say
for certain.

The priest's brow furrows in concern. This young girl
is even more troubled than he suspected.

                FATHER DOWD
What sort of things?

                    SÍLE
She tells me if someone's about to call by,
or if someone's going to ring, and they always do. Or I'll know somebody's name before
they tell it to me.

                FATHER DOWD
                (scoffing)
And just when d'you ever meet anyone new to
you?

SÍLE

Yesterday there was a girl down at the shop
with her parents. They were only drivin'
through town on their way to Derry. She smiled
at me, and I told her I could guess her name,
and I was right. It was Alice.

FATHER DOWD

It must have been embroidered on her jacket.

SÍLE

It wasn't, Father. I didn't see it anywhere, I
only heard "Alice" in my ear. A whisper, like.
She had dark hair; she didn't even look like
an Alice.

FATHER DOWD

Why do you think Our Lady is telling you
these things? What purpose does it serve?

SÍLE

She's askin' me to trust Her. I told Her I
trusted Her from the very beginning, but She
says every foundation must start from the
ground. If I hear right when it's only the
small things, I know I can trust Her about
the big things when the time comes.

FATHER DOWD
(with the tired air of a skeptic)
And what are these "big things"?

SÍLE

I don't know. But someday I'll know things
that *will* matter, and when that day comes,
I'll tell you straight away.

FATHER DOWD

You confound me, Síle. Every time we sit down
to speak, you confound me. None of the others
have heard what you've heard. No wonder the
bishop is looking on all this as if it were
a Gypsy carnival. So much talk, but too few
answers and precious little sense.

SÍLE

I know it seems that way, Father. She's telling Tess something else altogether. We've
asked Her about it, but the Blessed Mother
says not to fret about it, that it's all part
of loving us equal but different.

FATHER DOWD
(sighs)

Let me put it to you this way, Síle. You can't
say whatever you like and expect the world to
hang on your every word. There's no proof in
anything you've said to me, only imaginings,
or at least that's how the bishop is inclined
to see it. If you've a message for the world—if
Our Lady is truly appearing to you—then I must
have consistency among your accounts, or no
one will heed your story. Do you understand?

Síle's response wasn't audible, whatever it was, and the priest sighed one more time for good measure before he came down on the STOP button.

After a perfunctory pat down, Martin accompanied me up the stairs to Síle's room, and this time she met me at the door. "It's a lovely day," she said. "Let's go for a walk on the strand."

"They really let you out for walks?" I asked.

She cast me a sly look as she shrugged on her jacket. "They let me do more than you think."

I may have imagined the glance that passed between Síle and Martin as we came out of her room. The orderly followed at a discreet distance as we went down a set of service stairs and out the back door. "Tell me the truth," I said quietly as we passed into the garden. "What's it really like, living here? Don't you want out as soon as possible?"

"I don't think much about leaving. Not just yet."

"But you won't live here forever," I prompted. It occurred to me then that it was Saturday, and Dr. Kiely probably had weekends off.

"That's true. But it's where I live today, and where I'll live tomorrow, and probably the day after, too. As for the day after that, now, who's to say?"

We passed through a gate in the high stone wall, onto a narrow concrete path leading through the dunes, and I watched as she pulled off her shoes and socks.

"You sure you want to go barefoot?" I asked as she stowed her sneakers just off the paved walkway. "It's freezing out."

"For you, maybe." She cast a smile over her shoulder as we passed softly onto the sand. "We always talk about me. What have *you* been up to the last twenty-five years?"

I glanced back and saw Martin standing at the gate watching us. "I'm not nearly as interesting as you are."

"I don't believe it," she said. "Tell me something. Something important. Something you'd never tell anyone else."

The beach was at least a mile long, and we were the only people on it. The wind whistled in my ears. "I can't think of anything."

She rolled her eyes and held out her palm. "Give me your hand."

"Not this again."

"No, not that again." She held my hand as if it were an artifact, something to be handled very gently. Slowly, deliberately, she pushed back my sleeve, and her fingertip tickled like a feather across the inscription on the inside of my wrist:

MALLORY

∞

We looked at each other. "You must've noticed it the last time I was here," I said.

Síle shook her head. "I think of her," she said gently. "They brought us up here every summer, but when I walk this strand, I can only remember the day you and Mallory came with us."

I gave her what I hoped she'd take for a grateful look. "Do you have any tattoos?" I asked.

"I do," she laughed. "I've loads of them."

I couldn't help glancing below her neck. She was wearing a rather low-cut T-shirt under her open jacket, but the skin was unmarked. "Where? I don't see any."

She arched an eyebrow. "I don't believe in makin' 'em too easy to spot." She went on walking, and a minute later, she pointed to the rolling green line along the northern horizon. "That's Donegal." She indicated the high, flat hill directly ahead of us, a few miles distant. "And that's Benbulben, as you may recall."

A mocking voice murmured in my ear: *They say you've been all the way up Benbulben to see the fairy queen!* Today it seemed like so much more than a silly insult. She had only to trade her jeans for a moss-green gown to take her rightful place in the folklore.

"It's a magical spot," Síle was saying. "Yeats liked to write about it." Then she aimed her finger at a rocky outcropping maybe a mile beyond the end of the beach. "And you see that castle over there? A German family bought that place not too long ago. How'd you like to live in a castle?"

"Ask me when I'm warmer."

Síle laughed, and laughed again as the wind jostled us together.

"How well do you remember that day?" she asked.

I thought of Tess, how the color of her hair changed whenever the clouds obscured the sun. The day came back to me as if it were still happening all around us: Síle and my sister racing in their bathing suits to the far reaches of the shoreline, snatches of laughter carried back on the wind. The adults in their beach chairs, John and Gran and Paudie and the Gallaghers, passing around a thermos of tea, and then a flask. Tess and Orla in denim cutoffs, whispering between themselves. Tess looking over her shoulder, smiling, drawing me in.

And it hit me then: the woman I'd met here, when I'd wandered away from the others to dig for sand crabs. She must have been a patient at Ardmeen House.

"They told us it was a car accident," Síle was saying. "But you weren't in the car?"

I shook my head. "She was coming home from a basketball tournament." An elderly driver had blown through a red light and rammed the backseat passenger side. Everyone else in her friend's mom's station wagon survived.

"We were fourteen," Síle said softly.

I felt as if something cold and hard had lodged itself in my throat. I couldn't tell her that the infinity symbol had been the tattoo artist's idea, not mine, or of how my mother clung to me and cried when she first saw the name etched on my wrist. Síle saw a lot of things, but she'd never know how false I'd been, getting that tattoo when I didn't feel everything I should have felt.

"She was different with you," I said.

"How was she different?"

"She was happy."

"She wasn't always?"

I hunched my shoulders as if bad posture could get me any warmer. "I don't remember her that way."

"Then it's a good thing *I* do." Síle paused. "When you think of her now," she said slowly, "is she always fourteen?"

I shook my head and kicked at the sand. "She can be other ages. Grown-up. Sometimes I picture her that way." Mallory, twenty-three, weeping on my shoulder after yet another heartbreak; Mallory, twenty-seven, a diamond glittering on her ring finger as she lifted a martini glass to her lips; Mallory, thirty-one, laughing at the horrible things we did to one another when we were small; Mallory, thirty-three, nestling a baby in the crook of a freckled elbow. Picturing her in this impossible future allowed me to forget, however temporarily, that there was precious little similarity between the brother I could have been to her, and the brother I actually was. I lay awake at night trying not to think of how good it had felt to pinch her till she bruised.

"I can see her, grown," Síle said, looking over her shoulder at our footprints in the sand. "She has that wild curly hair—how I wanted her hair!—and she's let it grow long, sort of bohemian-like. She wears fuzzy jumpers and knee-high boots and that American cologne that smells like real smells—like woodsmoke or honeysuckle."

That wasn't how I saw my impossible sister at all, but I wasn't about to say so.

"She lives someplace where it rains," Síle went on. "Like Seattle. Only it isn't the real Seattle—it's a city for everyone who never got the chance to grow up." I didn't say anything, and she asked, "Do you believe in a world beyond this one?"

"I don't know if I do," I said. "I know *you* do."

"I do," she replied, "but I don't often speak of it. If you want them to tell you you're getting better, you have to admit that everything you believe in is probably wrong. Ordinary people don't have to do that," she said, though not bitterly. "They've the luxury of believing whatever they like."

"But people here believe in an afterlife," I said. "Almost everybody's Catholic."

"Sometimes I think people are only trying to convince themselves. Go to Mass, and if you look round, you can tell their hearts aren't in it. They cling to belief, but they're not believers," she said. "Not really."

I thought of the people at morning Mass, all of them droning through their prayers. Comfort, not belief. "You sound like you've lost your religion," I said.

She laughed. "That isn't my religion. It never was. Even when I was small, I knew I had to find my own way to God."

"And have you found it?"

"Sometimes I know I have," she said softly. "And then it goes away again. But at least I know it'll come back, and maybe someday I'll get to keep it."

I turned and found Martin standing maybe fifty yards behind us, his hands thrust in his jacket pockets, staring out at the sea. Maybe he felt my eyes on him, because he turned to look at me. He didn't return my smile, and I thought maybe I hadn't imagined that glance between them after all.

"Tell me what she looked like," I said.

"You want to know what she was like—even if she wasn't real?"

"Tell me," I said.

"She was lovely," Síle said softly. "The loveliest woman I'd ever seen." It gave me an eerie feeling, hearing her say the words I would have used for her. "I wanted to go to Her and hide my face in Her robes, to drink Her in," she was saying, "only I couldn't. I was on my knees, rooted to the spot."

"I read in one of the newspaper articles that you did eventually feel her touch you," I said. "You said it felt like when your mother used to come in to kiss you good night."

Síle smiled into the distance. "I remember that like it happened only last night. She was so lovely. Lovelier than any of the Harry Clarke windows. Lovelier than the Díseart Madonna, or the Inishmaan Madonna, though I do love the Inishmaan Madonna for the babbies peeking out from under her cloak. He came closest with the Terenure Madonna, but it's still the difference between a real woman and a model in a magazine." She smiled again. "In a manner of speaking."

I had no idea what she was talking about, but I was eating it up. "I don't know Harry Clarke," I said.

Síle's eyes lit up. "Ah, he was brilliant. Harry Clarke painted with light."

"That's very poetic, but who was he?" I asked.

"He was Ireland's greatest stained-glass artist. One of those who died young, leaving you wonderin' forever what else he might have done, had he lived."

"I'll have to look him up," I said.

"Silly," she retorted. "You can see his windows all over the place. Will you spend any time in Dublin whilst you're here?"

"Probably not," I said. "I'm flying out of Dublin, but I only have until the sixteenth."

"That's plenty of time."

I smiled slyly. "Maybe I prefer Sligo."

She punched me playfully on the arm. "You should go to Dublin and see the *Eve of Saint Agnes*."

"I'll go when you can come with me."

"Then I'll have to paint it for you with words," she said. "Do you want me to tell you about the eve of Saint Agnes?"

I felt that faintly familiar thrill, the anticipation of a bedtime story I'd never heard before.

"On the eve of Saint Agnes—that's the twentieth of January," she began, "all the starry-eyed maidens of the Middle Ages would perform certain bedtime rituals so they might see their future husbands. Not just in their dreams," she went on in a hush. "In their bedchambers. In the flesh."

I cocked an eyebrow. "Certain bedtime rituals?"

Síle laughed. "She goes to bed without dinner."

"Saints and witchcraft," I said. I wanted to taste the salt on her lips.

"Not witchcraft," she said softly. "Not the way you think of it, anyway."

"Conjuring up a person who isn't really there—that isn't witchcraft?" Too late, I caught myself. I looked at her, afraid of her reaction, but she just gave me half a smile.

"Who said he isn't really there?" Her hair was whipping in the wind, and I watched her smile broaden as I reached to brush a lock out of her eyes. "The legend says he'll come to her," she said. "Not a vision. Not an apparition. Just that he comes." She arched an eyebrow. "Will I go on?"

"Please do."

She turned and kept walking as she spoke. "We begin our tale in the house of Madeline, whose family has mounted a lavish banquet. Madeline cannot partake of it, however. She will go to bed early, for it's the eve of Saint Agnes. The bedesman's in the chapel praying for his master, and you can see his breath in the frosty gloom—"

"What's a bedesman?"

"A poor old man under the lord's protection, whose only task is to pray for his benefactor. Anyway. You see the candles flickering on his solemn face as he counts the beads on his rosary with his pale, cold fingers"—she mimed this as she spoke—"his lantern restin' on the floor at his knee.

"The bedesman prays for the sinners at the banquet, at the dance; he prays so that his master may go on feasting and continue with his merriment—so that someday, when his flesh turns to dust, the rich man will pass his penance in Purgatory instead of Hell."

"Is that how it works?"

"They liked to think so," she said. "I'll go on, will I?" I nodded, and she smiled as she drew her next breath. "The lord wears a suit of brilliant orange, intricately beaded, and his face is fine and cruel. He dances with ladies richly dressed in pink and crimson, with glittering baubles at their throats, as the minstrels play their instruments in the gallery above. As he leaves the chapel, the bedesman hears the sounds of the revelry, and it weighs like a stone on his heart." Síle lifted her arms and did a dainty two-step along the wet sand, and I thought of her unmade bed.

"The noble Porphyro begins a long, cold journey by the light of the waning moon, and an elfin lantern glinting off the sword at his side." She leaned forward, taking her next few steps as if she were bracing herself against even rougher weather, and I wondered why she'd never taken to the stage. "The wind blows the plume in his hat and the cloak on his back, but the chill can hardly touch him, so alight is he with ardor for his beloved. So in love, in fact, that it does not matter that he is the only son of her father's sworn enemy."

"Very *Romeo and Juliet*," I said.

"Now you know where the Bard got it. Meanwhile, fair Madeline prepares herself for bed with the help of her elderly servant, Angela, who looks more like a queen in a blue-and-silver gown with a brilliant red petticoat. Porphyro arrives at the castle gate, finds Angela, and begs her to lead him to Madeline's chamber, and the old woman says, 'Come away from the revelry, lad, lest these stones become thy bier.'" Síle held up a finger, storyteller fashion. "Remember, Madeline's father will kill Porphyro if he sees him. *He's* the one in the dandy orange suit, with the cruel glint in his eye. Angela leads the noble youth up the stairs to Madeline's room, and conceals him there just as Madeline is falling softly to sleep, the light of the moon shining down through stained-glass windows upon her pale breast."

I pictured Síle asleep in a room full of stained glass—saw myself climbing a secret staircase in the dark, coming inside, finding her naked body awash in tinted moonlight.

"Porphyro comes out of the darkness and, as three fairies above their heads dance inside the fair maiden's dreams, he lays out a feast for her, takes out his lute, and begins to play. She awakes to him, does fair Madeline, but believes she's still dreaming. He's come to make her his bride, says Porphyro, but they must flee the house of her father this night." Síle stole a glance and found me looking back. "*Far o'er the southern moors I have a home for thee,*" she said softly.

I swallowed. "That's what he says to her?"

"That's what he says."

An ordinary girl looks at you, and you look *good*—you can see it in her face—but when Síle looked at me, even if she seemed to be teasing or flirting, I couldn't see what she was thinking underneath. I couldn't tell who I was.

She'd stopped, as if she were waiting for me to finish thinking

my thought before resuming the story. "For the last time, Madeline rises from the bed of her childhood and dresses herself
by moonlight. Next we see the lovers tiptoeing down the turret
stairs, dressed in blue robes studded with stars, the anxiety and
the ecstasy plain to see upon their comely faces. Down in the hall,
praise God, the watchman and his dog have fallen asleep. *The key
turns, and the door upon its hinges groans*, and away they flee into
the winter storm."

"Happily ever after?" I asked.

She smiled as she turned to face me and walked backward for
a few steps, moving as gracefully as if she had eyes in the back of
her head. "You know, when my mam used to read us the fairy
tales, that ending never made sense to me. Madeline and Porphyro
could freeze to death, and would it still be a happy end?"

"You can't be too literal about these things, or else you ruin the
whole story," I pointed out.

"But I'm askin' ya. Is it a happy ending even if they die in the
snow?"

I shrugged. "They're going to die eventually anyway."

"Aye," she said, with a sparkle in her eyes. "But they haven't
consummated the marriage, have they?"

How long had it been since she'd been with a man? Probably
not as long as I supposed. I felt Martin's eyes on my back. "You
must've spent hours staring at that window," I said.

"Maybe an hour," she said with a shrug. "Some pictures stay
with you." She glanced over my shoulder, and when I followed her
gaze, I found Martin closer than I'd expected. Síle nodded to
him, and we turned to walk back. "We haven't much time. There's
something I've got to give you." She took my hand, lacing my fingers with hers, and with her other hand, she drew a small leather-
bound notebook out of her pocket. "That's it," she said, placing it
in my open palm. "That's everything. I've left nothing out."

"You told Father Dowd you were keeping a diary," I said, and she nodded. Again I tried to read her face, to see if this meant as much as it seemed to me, but her eyes were too serene.

I shook my head. "I can't take it, Síle."

"Why not?"

"It's too . . ."

She stood in the wet sand, the bitter wind whipping her dark hair over her eyes, but this time I couldn't reach out and touch her. "Say whatever it is you're going to," she said.

"It's too much," I finished lamely.

She looked up at me with no expression on her face. "It isn't," she said. "I wrote it for you."

I turned away from her, shaking my head. "That doesn't make sense," I said.

"It does. You just don't see it yet. She said you would come back someday, and that you would ask me all about Her."

When my skin broke into gooseflesh, it had nothing to do with the November weather: it was as if someone besides Martin were watching us. I crossed my arms tight across my chest, resisting the urge to look over my shoulder. "I don't get it," I said. "We spent one day together—*one day*, twenty-five years ago. Why do I matter?"

Síle just looked at me, smiling as if she'd never tell me, and I felt the full force of Hennessey's words. Maybe it *was* something else—something that had fooled all four of them.

Again she nodded, and we resumed the walk back to Ardmeen House.

"Read to the end of it." Her manner was earnest, even plaintive—there was no trace of teasing now. "You're there. She *told* me."

I looked at Síle and saw my picture of her slipping. Nothing was clear now. Her face shimmered in the cold air like something

I'd traveled thousands of miles to find, something precious that might vanish if I blinked.

I stopped walking and faced her again. "Can you hear yourself?" I asked. "Do you know what you're saying?" She gave me a sad smile and didn't answer. I took her gently by the shoulders. "All this time I thought you didn't belong here," I murmured.

"Ah, but in fairness—I never agreed with you." She averted her eyes, and I released her. "Tell me something. Up to this point, when you read about the visitation or listened to Father Dowd's tapes, did you believe us?"

"I don't know."

"You do know. It's only now you're doubting."

"I was willing to entertain the possibility," I said.

"Why? Why would you, when it all sounds so mad?"

I took a deep breath. "I wanted to know you," I said. "That's the only reason."

This time Síle didn't ask if I'd come again. Martin saw me to the front door, and I stood at the edge of the parking lot looking down at the shoreline. There were no showers or snack stands like we had at American beaches, but one of the grown-ups had set up a tent for us in the dunes so there'd be a place to change into and out of our suits. They called swimsuits "togs," and that confused me.

It was late in the afternoon, after Orla had pulled Tess away, and my sister's giggling drew me to the right place between the dunes. The door was fully unzipped, and I could see Síle and my sister leaning forward as they peeled off their suits. Síle spotted me through the doorway of the tent, threw her wet bathing suit at me and laughed. So I must have seen her naked once, before she'd had much of anything to show.

I unlocked the door, hurried inside, and opened the diary. The wind buffeted the car as I ran my hand over the Celtic design embossed into the leather, opening to the first page and shutting it again before my brain could resolve her teenage scrawl into words. I knew there might be things inside I wouldn't want to know, things that might make me want her less, and once I'd read them, there could be no unknowing any of it.

Still, I began to read. I had to.

First She says I must write about what happened those nights when I was small. Orla and I have always shared the room looking out over St. John's Road, and it's true the room and the house are no different to any other room or any other house anywhere in Ballymorris. Still, this room with its grey gloomy walls, black painted headboards, and plaid duvets will always be special for the world it revealed to me in the middle of the night.

It happened maybe a dozen times across two or three years. I would be fast asleep, and I would wake to the sound of my name in the mouth of someone I'd never seen before, though there was no one else in the room but Orla, who was sleeping still. For a time I rested there, sweetly drowsy. It never occurred to me to fear, not even when I heard my name called a second and third time. Man or woman or child, I couldn't have said who it was; when someone whispers your name it might be anybody. Who is it? I asked. Who's there? And I never did have an answer, only it was as if the air and the stillness and the silence were smiling down at me where I lay. I knew then that there were people there in the darkness, watching me without eyes, and still I didn't fear because I knew they loved me.

Then came a whispering rush of air, the same as when a

summer breeze blows through the bluebell wood, though it was usually winter when the people came in the night. From the front window-corner the ceiling curled up and away, like the lid on a tin of tiny salted fish, and then I could see the sky, black as pitch and crusted with stars. I forgot everything then, and looked up and wondered and my heart clutched with the joy and the thankfulness of it. I even forgot Orla sleeping away in her bed beside me.

I never could have described the feeling, I was too young then, but I suppose it seemed that the world was mine, it would give me anything I asked of it. I still feel that way. Maybe that's why all these marvelous things are happening to me . . . to <u>us</u>. Because I believe.

When John's cell phone rang late that afternoon, it was Paudie inviting me over for a spaghetti dinner. "Nothing fancy," he said. "They've ready-made garlic bread at the SuperValu, you've only to put it in the oven. Brona has some sort of a do on at the parish hall tonight, but Leo will be here."

The stairs leading up to Paudie's apartment were pretty much an extension of the shop itself, stacks of paperbacks on either side of the steps leaving a narrower space to walk. "I'm glad ye could come," Paudie said over his shoulder as Leo and I followed him up. "After all, you can't go to the pub seven nights out of the week."

"Some do," Leo put in.

"Aye," Paudie replied crisply, "and them's the sort who should avoid it altogether."

As we came into the apartment, I spotted the full bed spartanly made with a brown blanket in the back room and, on the left side as we turned toward the front of the house, a tiny kitchen making the sixties-era yellow-enamel range seem even more enormous. The scent of the lazy-man's garlic bread baking in the oven made the whole place feel warm and cozy. Paudie ushered us into a sitting room overlooking the street, the walls lined floor to ceiling with gold-stamped cloth- and leather-bound editions. "These ones have never been for sale," he said with a smile as I surveyed the shelves.

Leo and I sat down on an old leather sofa as Paudie went to stir the sauce. He came back with tumblerfuls of red wine, and as I thanked him, I spotted an old studio portrait of his wife on an end table. With my free hand, I picked it up to admire her. "She was a good-looking woman," I said, and he sighed.

"You said you remembered her? From the last time?"

"I wish I could remember her more clearly." It only occurred to me then that Paudie might know about me and Tess, that one of the adults might have seen us together that day; but if he knew, he hadn't let on.

Paudie took the picture from my hand, kissed the glass, and pressed it to his chest. "She was the best of all women."

"*One* of the best," Leo agreed. At first I thought Paudie might be offended, but one glance satisfied me he wasn't. Your oldest friend should have license to say whatever he's thinking.

We slotted ourselves into chairs around the little kitchen table, and Paudie doled out too-generous platefuls of spaghetti. As we ate, we fell into talking about the bookshop. "It's such a quiet town," I said. "It can't have been easy, staying in business all these years."

"I'd have lost it, surely, if they'd opened an Eason's," Paudie replied. "And thank heaven for the Internet!"

The old men twirled the spaghetti on their forks. "I've no use for it meself," Leo said merrily, "but sure, I'd be buyin' all me own pints without it."

Paudie rolled his eyes. "When you pass from this earth, Leo Canavan, we'll discover every last pence of your pension money stuffed in the wall behind the stove."

It felt good to laugh. I took another sip of cheap wine.

"These days I post books all over the world, that's true," Paudie went on. "America, mostly, though last week I did send *The Demi-Gods* all the way to New Zealand. You'd think no one would care about first editions anymore when they've everything at their fingertips online, but some still do." Paudie sipped at his wine with an earnestly satisfied look on his face. "Enough still do."

"I'd love to own a bookstore," I said. I have no idea what brought me to say it. I'd never once considered it before, having met enough people working in independent bookshops to know how difficult it was to stay in the black.

"Ah," Paudie said. "You're better off writing books than sellin' 'em."

Leo leaned in. "I'll tell you what you can write about, lad. They'll want to hear all about it when you go back to America."

"What's that?" I asked.

Leo grinned as he drew a glass bottle out of his jacket pocket. "I brought ye something you'll never find at the pub."

"Now, that's something else I haven't seen in ten years," Paudie said. "Poteen."

"Moonshine, that's what you Yanks call it," Leo said. "Made by me da's da, in a still hidden up in the Irons, in the year of our Lord nineteen-oh-three."

"Jesus," I said. "It's still drinkable after more than a hundred years?"

"Sure, 'twasn't drinkable to begin with," said Paudie, and the two men doubled over with laughter.

"That old drum's still up there, so far as we know," Leo said. "Tucked among the rocks and stones up by the bluff overlooking

Lough Allen, and my grandda would ride up there on his old mule in the middle of the night to tend the fires. My father, God rest his unhappy soul, told me once where I could find it, but 'twasn't where he'd said; and when I came down again and told him the way I'd gone, he said I'd got it wrong, 'twas somewhere else entirely. I'd gone up in the car, you see, and where it's hidden, there isn't any road."

"Couldn't he draw you a map?" I asked.

"'Twas too late, by that point," Leo replied. "He'd the Parkinson's. And then he passed, and the secret died with him."

"You'll never find it now, sure you won't," Paudie said.

"Ah, the poteen he made was mighty," Leo sighed. "And here's the very last of it."

"Are you sure you want to waste it on me?" I asked, and they chuckled.

"We won't finish it tonight, lad," Paudie replied. "You'll only take a little. Powerful stuff, that poteen."

Leo rose heavily and toddled to the kitchen counter, found a little glass pitcher in the cabinet above the sink, and filled it from the faucet. "We'll cut it with water, so."

"No," I said. "I'll drink it straight." Leo and Paudie traded a look.

"We'll give you only a little, to start," Leo said, and poured a mouthful of hooch into the shot glass.

"It's clear as water, but don't let it fool you," Paudie said.

"Aye, that's why they call it 'the water of life,'" Leo interjected. "*Ish-ka bah-ha.*"

"Don't let it fool you," Paudie said again. "It's mad powerful stuff. The poteen will kill ya if you're not careful."

"I can take it," I said. On Leo's count of three, we tipped our glasses, and the drink tore through me like a chainsaw.

The men dropped their shot glasses and slumped in their seats to recover. "Ah," Leo sighed. "I can taste the air up on Slieve-bawn, and the breath of them lonely pines up along the ridge there. You remember the place I mean?"

"Aye," Paudie said, still shuddering a little. "Aye, I remember the place."

All I could taste was battery acid, but I wasn't about to say so. The old men lined up their shot glasses for a second round, and Leo began to pour. "There'll be no shame in switchin' to Jameson's," Paudie told me, but I waved him off. I wasn't about to be out-drunk by a pair of octogenarians.

The second shot was even worse than the first. The third and fourth and fifth rounds they did cut with water, though, and I guess that's the only thing that saved me.

I don't remember how I got back to the B and B that night, but I do remember the dreams. First I was in a phone booth with Síle in the middle of the night. She was wearing a slinky black dress, and when she pressed herself against me and felt my erection, she laughed in my ear, and her breath on my neck made me even more crazy for her. We started making out, but then she pulled away from me. She lifted her fingers to the corners of her face, tugged off her skin, and turned herself inside out; I tried to get out of the phone booth, but the door was stuck.

I looked back, and it wasn't Síle anymore. It was Mallory, and she was hanging from the roof of the phone booth by her seat belt like we were in the station wagon turned upside down on the side of the highway. My sister opened her mouth, and a trickle of blood, spit and blood, ran down her lip and dripped onto my shirt, and I rammed my shoulder against the door of the phone booth and pounded on the glass, but it wasn't any use. The light of the full moon fell brightly on the rocky ridge outside, and I could see the pine trees bobbing in the wind. Nobody would ever come here. The still was too well hidden.

I woke up, stumbled to the bathroom, and retched until there was nothing left in my stomach, and even then I couldn't stop heaving. I'd been stupid not to stop when they'd told me to.

7

I awoke to the worst hangover of my life, and that was really saying something, given all the late nights in New York City bars over the past fifteen years. I brought Síle's diary down to the breakfast room, ferrying forkfuls of eggs to my mouth and taking no pleasure in it.

Trying to decipher the next entry in the diary only exacerbated my headache. She'd written the first one in an ordinary girlish script, but in this passage the words and lines were tightly packed, overlapping even, as if she were both writing blindfolded and worried about running out of room. I flipped a few pages ahead, finding more of the same impenetrable handwriting, so I gave up and turned to the next normal entry.

How does She speak to us? That's the first thing Father Dowd wanted to know. He even asked if She spoke with an accent. It's like how in a dream someone is speaking to you and you felt their urgency, but afterward you'd never be able to say what they said or which words they used to say it. They could be speaking Swahili, and yet you'd understand them.

Today I asked,—Is it true about Heaven and Hell and Purgatory?

—Very little of what they've told you is the truth. There IS a Heaven, Síle. That is the only essential thing for you to know.

—I've read in books that you've taken the others to all three realms. Hell and Purgatory as well as Heaven. You take them there so that they can come back and tell people about what they've seen, so they'll try to live more virtuous lives.

—You mean the others to whom I have appeared in this way?

I nodded and She said,—Do you believe that if I loved you as well as they, I would bring you to those places?

—No, Mother.

—Then why do you speak of a place called Hell? Is it idle curiosity?

—I don't want to go to those places, Mother. I want you to tell me they don't exist.

—Ah, but what if they do? What if it's you who build that dark and fiery place in your minds as you're in the throes of dying, racked with regret?

—But isn't that why the priest comes to a person when they're dying? Doesn't he give them the Last Rites, and hear their final confession?

—For some of you, confession will bring no relief.

—Is it the ones who've committed the most terrible sins? The murderers?

—The magnitude of the sin itself is of no consequence. The truth is, Síle, it doesn't do any good to ask for forgiveness from an earthly 'father' if you believe, underneath all the Acts of

Contrition, that there is a God who, when you rise to meet Him, will see you only for the stain on your heart.

She reached out to me, took my hand and squeezed it, and She was as real as my own mam.

—In life or after it, She went on,—you'll never see beyond whatever it is you're <u>expecting</u> to see. So whatever it is you're bracing yourself for, you WILL see it. Do you understand?

—I think so, I said, and I was trying.—But there is a Heaven?

—There is.

—A real Heaven? Not just a Heaven inside our minds?

—Aye, She said, smiling.—A <u>real</u> Heaven. With twelve gates, each of them carved of a single pearl, the street beyond it made of gold and transparent as glass.

—It sounds very beautiful, Mother, but doesn't it get boring?

She laughed.—Can you recall the last time you were bored on a bank holiday Monday?

—Never, I said.—There are always too many fun things to do, things there isn't time for in an ordinary week. Books to be read and pictures to be painted. The day to be savoured in the sunshine, if we happen to have any.

—There, She said, and She was satisfied with my answer.— It's only the children who haven't any imagination who complain of boredom. Heaven is no different.

—But a bank holiday passes too quickly, I said.—If I had forever, I don't know what I'd do with it.

—That's not for you to worry about, pet. You've a long life ahead of you, with hundreds of bank holiday Mondays to enjoy.

It's funny how I can't remember the important things when it comes to studying for exams, but when I sit down after one of the Visits to write down everything She said to me, I find I can

recall it perfectly. It's as if there were a tape recorder always run-
ning in my brain, and never running out.

After breakfast I walked up to Shop Street to Mrs. Kettles, a
place with red-and-white-check vinyl tablecloths and a lackluster
cake display Paudie said had the only decent coffee in town. It also
happened to be the only café open on a Sunday. Mrs. Halloran's
discount French-press brew wasn't cutting it, and I needed a bit
more time to figure out my plan for the day. I brought my mug to
a table by the window and opened Síle's diary. By now I had
enough caffeine in my system that I could make out some of the
strange passage I'd skipped earlier.

> *It was a sin not to eat it but you <u>couldn't</u> eat it, how did she not*
> *see that you could barely move with all the weight on you?*
> *Someday she would see and then she could feed the poor hungry*
> *babbies in Africa like she was always harping on. You knew*
> *she'd root through the bin afterwards so you'd hide the rasher*
> *and spuds in your pocket and leave them in a box under the*
> *bed, and then the day came when the shoebox was teeming with*
> *things, crawling white things, and as soon as you looked at them*
> *you felt them under your skin too, eating away at you from the*
> *inside out. . . .*

Was this pure fiction, or had she speculated about the private lives
of her neighbors? There was more—much more—but I couldn't
read on without my brain jangling in my skull, so I flipped ahead to
the next real entry.

> *The first time Our Lady came to us I thought for sure things*
> *would be different between Orla and me. There <u>has</u> been a*
> *change, but it's for the worse. I want to speak to her about Our*

Lady but every time I try I feel farther away from her than ever. I say something and she takes it in a way other than how I meant it, and then I never know how to fix it.

Last night I tried to speak to my sister, and here is what passed between us.

—I look at the sisters we know at school and I want us to be like them, Orla. I want to walk together in the mornings the way the Donaher sisters do, and I want to sit together in the caf, your friends and mine together. I want to laugh with you the way Annie and Maura laugh. I want to hear your secrets, and tell you mine.

—But you already tell me everything, she said, and you never give a thought to whether or not I want or need to hear it.

I felt myself growing smaller and smaller beneath the bedclothes.—I don't tell you everything, I said, and she didn't answer, and then I asked,—Why do you hate me?

Orla just sighed and rolled to face the wall.—I don't hate you.

—You act as if you do.

—You can't help what you are, Síle. She said it wearily, as if she were twice as old as our mam.

—What do you mean by that?

—We're too different. Why can't you see that?

—I don't see how we're that different. And anyhow, Annie reads books and Maura's the silly one, but the things they do like, they do together. I want us to be like that.

—Would you stop moaning about the Donahers already? If you want their lives so badly go and see if they'll have you for a third.

I knew it was hopeless, I felt it cold as a stone on the floor of my stomach, but I couldn't stop the words coming out of my mouth.—I don't want their lives. I want you to love me, Orla.

—And I want you to shut your gob so I can get some sleep.
It is so hard to relax when she speaks to me this way. I can't
feel the peace when Orla's near, there can be no peace so long as
you're yearning for something you know you'll never have.

Someone tapped on the window glass, and I jumped. When I looked up I found Orla already walking into the coffee shop, and I closed the diary and pushed it aside, shivering at the undeniable sense that I'd conjured her out of her sister's teenage handwriting.

She strode to my table in leggings and Ugg boots, carrying an expensive leather purse and a grocery bag weighted with a jug of milk and a block of cheddar, and she looked down at me with an expression so withering I could only respond with blank surprise. "You didn't tell me you were planning a visit to Ardmeen House."

"You didn't ask." I gestured to the empty chair. "Would you like to sit down for a bit? Coffee's on me."

Orla glanced over her shoulder at the counter as she hooked her bags on the back of the chair. She sat down without taking off her coat, and when the waitress looked over, I gestured for her to bring a second mug. "I can't stay. My parents are taking the children to Mass, and I have to be getting back before they leave—for the baby."

I nodded. "Síle mentioned you'd been in touch recently, which struck me as odd," I said, "since you told me you hadn't spoken to her in years."

She rolled her eyes. "As I told you, my sister is not well. If she sees people who aren't there, she can just as easily imagine they're ringing her up."

"How else would you know I'd been to see her?"

"The director rang my dad." Orla thanked the waitress as she brought her coffee. "She's promised to keep him 'apprised' of any developments," she added, with a bitterness I didn't fully understand.

"Do I count as a 'development'?" I asked, and she gave me another scornful look. "Síle doesn't get visitors all that often, then?"

Orla arched her brow as she stirred in two packets of white sugar. "If she told you she does, doesn't that only confirm what I've been tellin' you?"

"She said she has people coming in every so often to buy her paintings. That isn't true?"

She sniffed. "And what *did* ye talk about, besides Síle being the next Michelangelo?"

I smiled to myself. "Anything but the apparition, basically."

Orla frowned. "In the old days she'd speak of nothing else."

"Maybe she's changed."

She brought the coffee mug to her lips, then set it down again. "They've an expression for people like you."

"Oh? What's that?"

Orla smiled grimly. "Relentless optimist."

I looked down at the diary. She couldn't have recognized it. "I guess I should tell you I listened to the tapes," I said.

She stiffened. "Which tapes?"

"The interviews you all did with Father Dowd."

"Jesus," she said. "You *are* relentless."

"That's considered a positive quality in a journalist, you know."

Orla sighed. "There's no story here. When will you see there's no story here?"

"There's always a story," I said quietly.

"You know what? You're right." She slid her untouched coffee mug to the side and leaned so far forward that her nose was inches from mine. "I wasn't going to tell you this," she hissed. "It is *completely* inappropriate for me to be telling you this, and you'll know in a minute why it's none of your bloody business—"

My stomach lurched. I glanced over Orla's shoulder, but the woman behind the counter seemed to be occupied with a bakery order. "Fine," I said under my breath. "You don't have to tell me, Orla. You don't have to tell me anything."

"The apparition," she said. "This is why I can't trust my own memory."

"What do you mean?"

"She *told* me things. Things about my sister." Her face grew darker and darker, and for the first time, I felt afraid of what I might have dredged up. "Things that turned out to be true."

"What do you mean?" I asked. "What did she say?"

"It was Síle," she said. She was shimmering with rage. "She and Declan."

"She and Declan . . . ?"

"She and Declan, aye. Do you need me to draw you a diagram? Settin' aside for the minute that it's the worst thing a girl could do to her sister, I should remind you of her age at the time. She was fourteen. *Fourteen*."

Orla paused for breath, and we regarded each other in silence. I didn't doubt that she was telling me the truth; I just needed some time to figure out whether or not it mattered.

"You're speechless, I see," she said as she slung her handbag over her shoulder. "So was I."

I reached out and laid my hand on hers. "Don't go yet. You haven't had any of your coffee."

She rolled her eyes. "I don't mean to be short with you, but I can't see what else we have to talk about here. Did you want to reminisce about our day by the sea?"

Jesus. No wonder her husband made himself scarce. "Can I just say one thing?" I asked. She nodded reluctantly, and I said,

"You should talk to Tess. I think it would do you both a lot of good."

Orla shook her head, her eyes on the table. "It's much too late for that."

"It's never too late until you're dead . . . right?"

For an interval she looked at me—a strangely blank look, given all the unpleasant ones she'd shot my way over the past ten minutes. Finally she rose from the table and picked up the rest of her bags. "Thank you for the coffee," Orla said, now icily polite. "Enjoy the rest of your holiday in Ballymorris, if I don't see you."

Sometimes when we're meant to be praying I glance over at the others and find Declan looking at me. One day last week Orla didn't come up with us because she was feeling ill, and I knew I had to speak with him.

—Why doesn't Orla love me?

—She loves you, he told me.—She has to, only she doesn't know how to show it.

And I said,—You're telling me what I want to hear.

I watched a sad smile come onto his face.—I'll not deny it. I feel for you, Síle, I really do, but I'm not gettin' involved.

—I don't know what you mean about 'gettin' involved.'

—Orla's the stubbornest person I've ever met. If you think anything I could say would change her mind . . . not just about you, about anything . . . then you don't know either of us as well as you think.

And I said,—I know my own sister.

—You don't, he said.—You think you know her. But sure, we're all strangers in the end, aren't we?

It was well past lunchtime when I went out into the rain and around the corner to Marian Terrace. By the estimation of her elderly neighbor (Parish picnic? Why couldn't I remember that?), Mrs. Keaveney ought to be home from Sunday Mass and up again after her nap.

I rang the bell and heard footsteps shuffling toward the front of the house, and Declan's mother opened the door. She wasn't petite by any means, but up this close, Mrs. Keaveney looked even more fragile—she had wide, colorless eyes, and her nose was brightly patterned with rosacea. She shifted her rosary beads from her right hand to her left so I could shake her hand as I explained that I'd come to town for my uncle Johnny Donegan's funeral. "I was wondering if I might speak to you about Declan for just a few minutes?"

The woman warmed as soon as I spoke the name of her son. She stepped out of the doorway and ushered me in. "I'm only after puttin' the water on for tea. I'll fix you a cuppa, and we'll have a wee chat about Declan."

Her clothing wasn't new, but she'd taken good care of it, and her salt-and-pepper curls were neatly brushed. So far, at least, she seemed much more lucid than Brona and Father Lynch had made her out to be.

"Thank you," I said. "That would be great."

Like nearly every other house I'd been to in Ballymorris, this one was small and lit only by the gloom of another sunless day. The air in the sitting room was almost as cold and damp as it was outside, and with each breath I caught another smell: first bacon, then mildew, then a very faint whiff of cigarette smoke. I didn't see any ashtrays on the end tables, and I wondered if someone, a smoker, had come to visit a decade ago and I was breathing the same air.

I took a seat on a lumpy brown sofa studded with needlepoint cushions as Mrs. Keaveney disappeared into the kitchen. I noted the crucifix above the doorway and a variation of that woeful Christ with his crown of thorns in a cheap metal frame above the mantel. The room was eerily tidy—no stacks of books or newspapers or mail, not a speck of lint on the rug—and the mantel itself was bare apart from a foot-tall statue of the Blessed Virgin that had probably come from Mag O'Grady's tchotchke truck. There was a small television set with old-fashioned dials and only a few framed photographs, Declan in various stages of childhood.

Then I glanced again at the nubby brown chair by the unlit fireplace, and noticed a little spiral-bound notebook open on the armrest. I heard the switch pop on the electric kettle, and the sound of the hot water being poured into the teacups—I had time. I darted forward to read what she'd written and found a list of names.

Donal Ward

Thomas McElway

Mary Louise Carroll

Mallory

I made my way back to the sofa by instinct alone—finely honed after thirty-eight years of covering my tracks—and a few seconds later, Mrs. Keaveney emerged from the kitchen with two mugs of tea on a scuffed plastic tray. "Did you say you were a friend of Declan's?"

What is my sister's name doing in that notebook?

I took a second to gather myself. "I'm afraid I've never had the chance to meet your son, Mrs. Keaveney. No, I'm a friend of Teresa McGowan's. I was here once, a long time ago, and we met each other then."

"A friend of Teresa's," she echoed as she settled herself in the brown armchair. Recalling her occupation before my arrival,

Mrs. Keaveney flipped the cover and laid the notebook and pen on the side table.

"I'm afraid I've interrupted you." The woman regarded me blankly, and I prompted, "You were writing?" *How does she know?*

"Ah, yes." Mrs. Keaveney closed her eyes. "They'll wait. They're always waiting."

The room felt even colder than it had a second before. "Who's always waiting, Mrs. Keaveney?"

She opened her eyes and regarded me benevolently, as if I were five years old. "The holy souls, of course."

"The holy . . . souls?" *Shit,* I thought. *I grew up Catholic. I should know this.*

The woman nodded, and I waited for her to continue. "Teresa McGowan," she said slowly. "Aye. She and Declan were together quite a bit, growing up." She let out a contented sigh, and I hoped she wouldn't notice my impatience. "My son always did have a lot of friends. He was very well liked, indeed."

It's a coincidence. It has to be. There was a film on the surface of the tea, as if she'd used a greasy spoon to stir in the milk and sugar. I forced myself to take a sip, and it was simultaneously too sweet and flavored with bacon fat. "Do you remember Orla?"

"Orla Gallagher." Mrs. Keaveney gave me a beatific smile. "Did you know Orla was Declan's first love?"

Yeah, and how many Mallorys have you met in Ireland so far? I nodded. "I guess you still see her around town sometimes?"

"Around town? No, I can't say I do. I prefer to stay at home, when I can, apart from going to Mass."

"Declan didn't have a girlfriend before Orla?"

"How do you mean?"

He was a good-looking kid, and he would have taken advantage of it—that's what I meant. "Just that I imagine he was popular with the girls at school."

I watched the smile melt from her face. "Declan wasn't the sort of lad to go running around," she said. "He never was. Orla was a good girl. He brought her round for supper nearly every Saturday."

"You like to cook, Mrs. Keaveney?"

"Aye, I always have. There's no greater satisfaction in life than nourishin' your family with a table full of good, fillin' food." She sat there, offering a vague little smile to the wall behind my head. In this house there was no such thing as irony.

"Why did Declan decide to go to Australia?"

"The promise of work," she sighed. "Isn't it always the reason they have to leave us?"

"Have you ever been down to visit?" I asked. *Mallory. What does she know about Mallory?*

"I haven't, no. It's too far. Ballymorris is my home, and I've never felt the need to wander as some do."

"Like Declan did."

"Declan is very like his father," she said softly. "He always was."

"So you knew even when he was young that he'd leave home someday?"

"Aye," she said. "I always knew."

"How often does he come home?"

"Not as often as he'd like to. Declan is a very busy man. He owns a restaurant in a place called Sydney. Gourmet seafood. Very posh."

"Yes, I've heard he owns a restaurant. It sounds like he took after you in that respect."

In her nubby brown chair, the woman seemed to grow taller and brighter with pride. "Aye. Aye, I suppose he did, although we don't eat much in the way of fish here, being so far from the sea."

So far from the sea? She wasn't kidding when she said she didn't go anywhere. But I said, "That makes sense."

"Declan will have a holiday soon, though. A holiday, at last. He'll be home from Australia in two days' time."

"That's wonderful," I said. "You must be excited to see him."

"Tomorrow I'll go to the SuperValu to pick up his favorite cereal, and to Malone's for a leg of lamb, and we'll have Father Lynch over for dinner. 'Twill be just as it was in the old days. Of course, this will be the first time he's met Father Lynch. Father Dowd was here when Declan was home last."

"I wanted to speak to you about Father Dowd, actually—"

"God rest him," she said automatically.

"Er—yes. I understand he spoke with Declan at length about the visitation that occurred back in late 1987 and early 1988, in the months before Declan left for Australia?"

A strangeness settled over Mrs. Keaveney then—a mixture of earnestness and wistfulness, and maybe a dash of regret. "Aye," she said cautiously.

"Do you remember that time?" I asked.

She closed her eyes and leaned back in her seat. "You must forgive me. It gives me a queer sort of pain to think back on that time in our lives." I opened my mouth to apologize, but she continued. "Before it happens to you, you can't imagine how it feels to be so blessed—to have a child who has been so blessed. I've since read of the ecstasies of Saint Teresa, and 'tisn't a feeling reserved only for the holiest among us. Even I have felt it—a poor sinner like me—and after Declan, it has been the greatest blessing of my life."

I couldn't see what a woman like Mrs. Keaveney could possibly have to spill inside the confession box, though I would've bet all the cash in my wallet she went every Saturday morning without fail. *Not to mention the matter of the "holy souls."*

"Did Declan tell you right away about what he'd seen?"

"He didn't say anything at first, but I knew something was

happening. Something had softened in him, you might say. He didn't take me for granted the way he had before—the way children always do, at that age."

"Thanking you for cooking dinner and doing his laundry, things like that?"

"Aye," she said. "'Twas more than that, though. He said the Blessed Mother had asked him to love his poor old mam with all that was in him."

This remark made me squirm. It was obvious to everyone but his mother that if the Virgin Mary had given him any such admonition, Declan had forgotten it long since. I asked, "So would you say the visitations changed your lives for the better?"

"Oh, aye. There's no comparin' it to the life we lived before."

"It strengthened your faith? And Declan's?"

"Oh, aye," she said.

I waited for her to elaborate—*Mallory?*—but she just took a sip of tea and stared at the carpet between our feet.

"Did your life improve in other ways?" I asked.

"Other ways?" She sat up in her chair, eyeing me intently, and I felt somehow that I'd been put on the defensive. "What other ways?"

I knew then that no matter how I prompted her, she'd say nothing more about that notebook. "In, I don't know . . . more practical ways, perhaps? I imagine it must be very difficult, being a single mother."

"I raised Declan with no one's help, that's true," she said. "You may have heard that his father was killed in an automobile accident when Declan was only a wee lad."

"I didn't know that," I replied, and I was pretty sure it wasn't true, given what Father Lynch had told me. "I'm sorry to hear it."

"Sure, Our Lady had Her husband Joseph to support Her, hadn't She?" Mrs. Keaveney glanced up at the statuette on her mantel and crossed herself with a sigh. "But She did say, She told Declan, that my reward in Heaven would be the greater for all the hardships I've borne without complaint."

I wondered just how many mothers made their lives more bearable by telling themselves the same thing. My mother never complained either, and look at her now: every inch of her as frozen as her low-fat TV dinners. I shook my head. "What else did the Blessed Mother say? Did she ever speak to you directly?"

"'Twas an even greater blessing, to hear Her words on the lips of my only son. She and I have that in common, you see. She was always tellin' Declan to remind me of that."

"What sort of messages did she have for Declan himself?"

"Ah, I'll let him tell you that now, when he comes."

I wouldn't hold my breath. "Are you in touch with any of his other friends?" At first she looked at me blankly, and I went on, "From his school days?"

"There are still a few of them in town, but sure, you don't want to be talkin' with the like o' them." She shook her head. "You'll want to speak to Declan himself, when he comes. Didn't you say you were writing a story about him?"

I hadn't said so, in case she wouldn't want to talk to me, but it seemed that even those who kept to themselves were up-to-date on the local gossip. "That's right," I said. "I'm writing a story about the apparition."

"For a newspaper in America?"

"A magazine, yes."

The woman nodded. "I always wondered why the people stopped coming," she said. "Why the miracles seemed only to fade away after those few wonderful months. . . ."

"Miracles?" I asked. "Were there others, besides what happened with Mrs. McGowan?"

"Martina's was a special case, that's true," she admitted. "But they came away changed. Sure, there's more than one way to be healed! Everyone who came left the better for it." She sighed. "I thought my Declan and the others would be known throughout the world for the message they brought. The lives they touched."

"How did Declan react when that didn't happen?"

"Ah, they none of them wanted the limelight—apart from the Gallagher girl, Orla's sister. You could see how she thirsted for it."

"Síle is very theatrical," I said. "I can see how people would confuse that with attention seeking."

Mrs. Keaveney was staring through the carpet again. She hadn't heard me. "Our Lady told him things," she said softly. "Strange things, wonderful things. About how his life would go, and all that he'd do with it."

"He'd come home and tell you what she said to him?"

"Aye," she whispered. "We'd pray together, and afterwards he'd tell me all that She'd said." The woman tilted her head, her eyes losing focus, and I thought back to the boy on the hill. *Listening.*

I shivered. "Did she tell him he should go to Australia?"

At the mention of Australia, Mrs. Keaveney's demeanor changed abruptly. Whoever else she thought was in the room with us, she was no longer paying attention. "I hope you don't mind, but I really must be getting on with making supper. I'm sure Declan can answer the rest of your questions, when he comes."

I was letting myself back into the B and B when I remembered a book on the shelf in the breakfast room I'd only noticed in passing. The hallway smelled of cabbage and onions, and from the kitchen at the back of the house, I could hear Mrs. Halloran humming to herself as she prepared her husband's dinner.

The tables were already set for the following morning, though as far as I knew I was the only guest. I took the worn green cloth-bound copy of *The Catholic Dictionary* off the shelf and flipped to the H section.

> **HOLY SOULS.** *These are souls who have died in a state of grace, but have not yet completed punishment for their venial sins. Their eventual place in Heaven is assured, but first they must suffer in Purgatory in proportion to the magnitude and severity of the sins they committed in life. This term of punishment may be somewhat shortened by the prayers and good works of the Faithful, if performed in the name of a soul in Purgatory.*

It was just a coincidence. The poor deluded woman believed the restless dead were whispering in her ear, writing down the names of people she'd seen interviewed on television a week or two before.

The next few passages in Síle's diary were of the nearly illegible variety, but they weren't making my head ache now that I'd had a bit of practice deciphering them.

> *She was your mother's sister but little warmth there was between you, it was expected that you would do anything that needed doing as if you hadn't a life of your own. One day you were in the shed and you found the jar with the money in it, with her fingerprints in the dust on the lid. You took two punts and waited for her to accuse you. A week went by, you took a fiver, still she said nothing, and then you knew she wasn't counting what she put away. So every week you took from the jar and*

when she died you took all of it and no one ever suspected. You
think of it every time you go to Confession but you never tell and
you never will—

I thought of Mrs. Keaveney's notebook, of my sister's name in a
stranger's handwriting. Síle and Mallory in their pink and purple
bathing suits, holding hands as they cast themselves into the surf.
What *was* this? Why had she wanted so badly for me to read it?

"Terrible news," Paudie said as I slid into the snug that night.
"Terrible. One of Tess's lads."

I passed a fresh pint across the table and he nodded his thanks.
"Tess's lads?" I asked.

"One of the lads she mentors at the youth center." He sighed
and rubbed at his forehead. "The boy went and hanged himself
last night."

"Jesus!" I thought first of the boy at the grotto yesterday.
Chances were it was somebody else, though—Tess did work with
a lot of kids. "I'm so sorry. She must be devastated."

"She is," he replied darkly. "She's gone home to her parents' for
the night, the poor lamb."

The front door swung open, and Leo came in. I hadn't touched
my pint yet, so I gave it to him and got up to buy another.
"Terrible day," I heard him say as I approached the bar. "They say
poor Aileen Gerrity found him in the closet."

I came back with my pint and sat down again, but tonight
there could be no settling in for an easy evening. I thought of
Mrs. Keaveney and that list of names in her little notebook,
and my run-in with Orla at the coffee shop, and of what she'd
said about Síle and Declan. It was just as well the conversation

would go nowhere near any of that tonight. I turned to Paudie. "Is there . . ." Suddenly I felt very foolish. "Is there anything I can . . . do for Tess, do you think?"

"There'll be a vigil for Owen tomorrow night in the park," he replied. "It would do her good to see you there."

"Sure, we'll all go," Leo said, as if we were headed to a ball game.

"They say it's becoming an epidemic in this country," Paudie sighed.

"Suicide, you mean?"

"Aye, particularly among the young people." Paudie took a long drink of Guinness before he went on. "For as long as I've been alive, there's been a hopelessness to living here, and all the days of your life you'd need to be vigilant about keeping clear of it. Day after day, not feeding yourself to it." He looked at me, to see if I understood, and I nodded before he went on. "The feeling may change tenor from one generation to the next, but it's always there. These lads have everything given to them now, but they're no happier than we were."

"We were happier, all right," Leo chimed in. "What you hadn't got didn't matter so much as it does now."

I didn't know what to say when old people started to talk like this—as they invariably did, once you spent enough time with them. I would have bet that back in the day, Leo would've cared quite a bit if he hadn't owned a single pair of shoes, but it did nobody any good to say so. Especially tonight.

"This is the first one she's lost, in her eight years at the center," Paudie said. "And, please God, may he be the last."

We only managed two rounds before calling it a night. I walked back to the B and B in the rain, left my jeans on the radiator and got into bed with the diary.

Last night the Blessed Mother came to me whilst I was sleeping, and we went for a walk along the Rathgar road and through the bluebell wood up to the holy well. She said there was such peace and loveliness to be found in the Irish countryside and that we must go down from the hill we know so well and see more of it together. The Blessed Mother wore Her blue mantle and even when we went up the hill She never got out of breath. Her feet were bare but there was never a spot of mud on them. I knew I was dreaming but still I'd put on my boots and I remember thinking I should wake up before it came time to wipe them off the way Mam's always making us do. Time stretched itself thin, so I couldn't tell if we'd been walking for minutes or hours.

When we came to the end of the bluebells Our Lady took my hand and looked at me, and Her eyes were dark like the deepest part of the ocean. I looked at Her and I felt the truest peace I'd ever known settling around my heart, soft as a kitten. For once I forgot all about Orla. I wanted to stay there with Her like that forever, but She said there was something She must show me at the holy well, so we went on.

As we walked side by side I asked Our Lady if She'd come to the others too but She said no, and it wasn't because She loved the others any less only She hadn't as much to say to them. I asked Her what did She want to say to me that wouldn't also benefit the others, and She said I was a good girl for not wanting anyone else to be left out. And I said,—Father Dowd says I'm not to go making myself into somebody special. He says I hold myself above everyone else, them who haven't seen You.

—When we criticise others, Our Lady said to me,—it's ourselves we should be looking at.

We came to the well and it looked different to the last time I'd seen it. The trees were decorated with all sorts of things, rosaries and Christmas ornaments and bright scraps of fabric and even a baby's tiny white leather shoe, and there was a wrought-iron votive stand under an awning to keep the rain off. The air grew brighter around us, little birds sang their sweet little songs, a gentle breeze blew through the ash trees, and the water came gushing out of the rock like I'd never seen it do in real life.

—You are made of water, the Blessed Mother said to me as She dipped Her fingers into the stream and gently pressed a wet thumb to my forehead in benediction.—You learned that in school, didn't you, Síle?

A tiny trickle went down the side of my nose. I knew I was dreaming but I felt the water on my face, real as waking.—Aye, Mother. We learned it in science class.

—And does it not follow that the water which has given you life will also heal what ails you?

—I don't know, Mother.

—Ah, but you will. Tomorrow afternoon I want you to bring Mrs. McGowan to this well. Have Mr. McGowan drive you in the car along with Tess and the others. When you come to the end of the road Mr. McGowan can carry her the rest of the way. Bring a stool and let her sit beside the spring, and then you must kneel before her. Carry the water in your hands and let it pour down over the knee and leg they've said she must lose.

I started to ask if Tess should do it, it seemed only right since we were talking about giving life, but the Blessed Mother shook Her head and smiled. Then I asked,—Will the water heal her, Mother?

Our Lady smiled.—Do as I have asked, and see. Whilst you are anointing Mrs. McGowan's knee with the water from the well, ask the others to pray for her.

—Will You be with us?

—*My dear child, She said.*—*Whether or not you see Me, know that I am <u>always</u> with you.*

She blessed me once more, the air around us began to shimmer, and then there I was back in my bed with the morning light streaming through the window.

—*You were talking in your sleep, Orla said at breakfast.*

—*I went for a walk with Our Lady. She says we have to take Mrs. McGowan up to the holy well after school today. That the water there will heal her leg.*

Orla just rolled her eyes and took my plate to wash it before I'd finished my toast. I wish the Blessed Mother would come to her that way too, maybe then she'll believe me.

This afternoon we did as She asked. Mrs. McGowan was afraid but tried not to show it, dear lady, and I knew Tess and her dad were willing to try anything if it might spare the leg. Orla and Declan kept themselves apart, sitting on the bench by the gate and praying quietly together whilst Mr. McGowan brought his wife over to the lip of the well and laid her down on the stool we'd brought. The air and the light and the smells weren't like how it was in the dream, the rag tree was gone, it was all very cold and ordinary and the water gurgled like a leaking faucet.

Tess's mam drew a shaky breath as I cupped the water in my hands, and let it trickle over her knee. I laid my hands over the bruised and swollen part and I felt the warmth welling up under the skin. Her rosary beads trembled in her hands and I heard her begin with—*Hail Mary, Full of Grace, the Lord is with Thee* . . .

When she finished the prayer I took my hands away, and we were gobsmacked. She walked back to the car on her own.

It's as if the wee folk came in the night and took the old Mrs. McGowan away, leaving a whole new person, spry and smiling, in *her place. She's been to the doctor and it's true, it's real, they won't be taking her leg after all.*

The McGowans had us over for dinner along with Declan and his mother and Father Dowd. Tess took me into her arms and held me there for ages, and it was the loveliest feeling apart from needing Orla to see it.

—Soon they'll be coming, Father Dowd said, and there was a proud look on his face as he lifted his wineglass.—They'll come to be healed, and we must be ready to serve them just as Our Lord served the poor and downtrodden in His own day.

Funny how you can avoid dealing with something—or get *away* with something—just by saying you can't remember. Even if you take the time to think back over what little you can piece together, you probably can't trust whatever other pieces come up. They do say memory is faulty that way, don't they? That day at the beach my sister threw a pebble at me, it pinged me in the chest and stung for a second, and I know she only did it to impress her new friend; I may have heard her say, "He'll make me pay for that but I don't care," or maybe she never said it and it was just my guilt filling in the gaps. Sometimes I felt like I'd give anything to have her back again, to have the chance to be good to her.

It was some other Mallory in Mrs. Keaveney's notebook. It had to be. I may not have retained a whole lot from my Sunday school days, but I did know this much: not even the God of the Old Testament would stick a child in some gray and comfortless place between life and death, leaving her to repent for somebody else's sins.

8

I was all but dead before the brisk knock on the bedroom door. "Will you be wanting breakfast this morning?" I opened my eyes, glanced at my phone, and sighed. I'd slept through the alarm.

I could picture Mrs. Halloran hovering at the far side of the door, wide-eyed and anxious to please. "I'll just leave something on the table for you, so." I thanked her and fell back onto the pillow as her footsteps receded. Thirty-six hours after the poteen, and I was still recovering.

Midway through a bowl of Weetabix, I thought of calling Tess, but it didn't feel right. We didn't know each other, not really, and it wasn't like I'd know what to say to her anyhow.

There are people beginning to come from far away. Father Dowd said yesterday he met a man who brought his sick daughter all the way down from Waterford. Every day over the past fortnight they've been driving out to the well, they form a queue and Father Dowd dips his fingers in the spring and he anoints them. He says they asked for me, they said wasn't it my hands did the healing, but Father Dowd told them Our Lady blessed the water itself, and anyway I shouldn't be taken out of school. I'm not special, remember.

Yesterday the pilgrims came up to the hill and watched us as we prayed before the grotto, but Our Lady never came. I know the others hate the attention and I would rather we were alone, too. There was one woman who had to be carried out of a van, with everyone round her making a big fuss, and once they'd got her settled she just sat in her wheelchair and stared at us like she was waiting on the show to start. Some of them are ill, truly ill, but the others are only expecting somebody else to fix what's wrong with them, what they've only done to themselves.

On Sundays Father Dowd doesn't want to mention us in his homilies, he says it does no one any good to speak of us as if we're holier than the rest of them. But it doesn't matter. People I've known all my life look at me now like they've never seen me before.

When Mass is over I watch Father Dowd in the church doorway, chatting and laughing with the most ancient ladies of the parish. They're delighted with him, and to me this is a greater mystery than all the Lord's miracles rolled in together. Sometimes when we're in his office speaking of the Visitation I have to hold on tight to the chair to keep from twitching, for it's hard having to trust someone you know is judging you all the while. Those ladies can't see he's a hard man, sharp as glass underneath, and I can say it now that the Blessed Mother has told me I should never let him read this.

Orla and Tess and Declan and I still go up to the hill for a little while after Mass. Sometimes She comes and sometimes She doesn't, but I feel Her there either way.

I got in the Micra and drove out of town. I was itching to head for Sligo, but I had the feeling I might only be let in to see her one more time—if that—and I wanted to keep that visit ahead of me a little while longer.

Instead I took the gravel road up the hill and parked across from Old Mag's little white truck of marvels. "Ahh," the old woman said, with a distinct air of satisfaction. "Didn't I tell ya you'd be back, now? And another foul-weather day it is, too. But sure, we only leave the house to come home again for a cuppa." She nodded vigorously. "And isn't that what it means to be Irish?"

I matched her grin for grin. "I was up here the other day, actually. I came over to say hi, but you were—how do you put it?—'having a kip.'"

"Go on wit'cha! How could a poor old woman like me take any rest with the wind roarin' like it does, and the rain comin' in sideways?"

"It *does* feel like it rains sideways in this country." I laughed, and paused. "The last time I was up here you mentioned something about the miracle with Tess McGowan's mother?"

"Oh, aye. Poor Martina McGowan with the diabetes, and they would have cut off her leg the very next day—did young Teresa tell you that?"

I nodded. "But what did the doctors say, do you know?"

"The family said 'twas the apparition what did it, but the doctors never would. They'll never believe in miracles, so they won't. They only acted as if they'd never told poor Martina she was to lose the leg in the first place."

"Had they ruled out all other possibilities? There'd been no change in her diet, or anything like that?"

"None a'tall," said Mag, bringing a wizened little fist down on the counter for emphasis.

"And it happened at the well?" I asked. The old woman nodded. "When they poured the well water over her knee?"

"Aye. I wasn't there meself, but there were plenty there who say her knee healed right before their eyes. T'would be easy to see the change, with the diabetes—and wouldn't I know, when both me brothers suffered with it?"

"But I hear Mrs. McGowan's health still isn't great," I said.

"'Tis twenty years since the Blessed Mother cured her," Mag replied indignantly. "Sure, none of us can live forever!"

"Except *you*, maybe." I grinned. "They say you're older than you look."

"Sure, none of us will live forever," she said again, not so spirited this time.

"Were there any other miracles?" I asked. "A lot of pilgrims came afterward, didn't they?"

"Aye, they came for six or eight months, steady-like," she replied. "We heard of nothing so dramatic as what happened to poor Martina McGowan, but don't you go round thinkin' there weren't any. The best miracles can't be seen with the eyes."

If the Irish were a most articulate race, they could also go on about a whole lot of nothing. "That's very poetic," I said, "but what sort of 'miracle' are you referring to, exactly? Something psychological?"

The old woman eyed me shrewdly. "What is it you're lookin' for, lad? They say you came back here for a funeral, but that isn't the reason. They say you want to write of the visions, but 'tisn't that, either." She leaned in, breathing the sweet fug of Barry's tea with milk and sugar. "Sometimes folk ask a lot of questions because there are others, other questions they may not want to know the answers to."

I thought of Lucy in the old Peanuts cartoons, dispensing

worthless advice for a nickel a pop, and stifled the impulse to laugh. She was bullshitting—I'd been right about that.

"I'm not sayin' that's you," Mag went on. "Though maybe it is. I'm only sayin' that for an auld one who doesn't travel much, I see more than you'd think."

When I logged on to a public computer at the town library later that morning, I saw Andy was online. hey dude. you get my email?

yeah

I waited for him to elaborate. This wasn't a good sign.

listen, I looked into this thing—

it's pure delusion

the girl who saw it first is in the loony bin.

i've met her, I typed back. she isn't delusional.

then why is she in there?

I fell back on stereotype. she's an artist. her family can't cope with her mood swings. off the top of my head I can name at least a dozen people in New York who belong there more than she does. I was trying way too hard, but I couldn't help it. They were laying off at least five staff writers before the end of the year, and I didn't want to lose my job any more than the next guy.

Andy hadn't answered after five minutes, so I wrote, you're always skeptical, Andy. then i write the story and you love it, or at least you say you do, and you run it and everyone says it's great, and then you act like you were never skeptical.

Finally I could see he was typing. you got a thing for this girl?

I sighed at the screen. you would too. she's extraordinary. trust me—this could be great. the best thing I've done.

just enjoy the rest of your vacation, all right? i'll see you next week.

I signed off without saying good-bye. I should've known all along I'd never get a story out of this.

I got in the car and turned onto the road for Galway, tuning the radio to one of the Irish-language stations hoping the babble would clear my head a bit. I was almost there when it occurred to me that, if I wanted to make it back in time for the vigil, I'd only have an hour in Galway, two tops. Then I wasted ten minutes looking for a spot on one of the narrow streets before giving up and pulling into a garage. I passed a chalkboard sign outside a pub for a traditional Irish music session at 9 P.M., and thought to ask Paudie or Leo if any of the other pubs in Ballymorris offered something similar.

I trudged down the Dock Road and passed the Spanish Arch, crossing the bridge toward the Salthill promenade. Brona had spoken enthusiastically about the invigorating benefits of a long walk on Galway Bay, but I had to turn back when the drizzle intensified into a proper downpour.

So I took refuge in an old pub back on Quay Street, realizing only after I'd ordered a pint that what I'd taken for a quiet local was mobbed with hipster tourists. Why had I bothered to come at all?

I managed to find a stool at the bar and pulled out the diary, flipping ahead to the next real entry.

Father Dowd's wanting to make preparations for the May Day procession and I don't know what to say to him. He's talking like there'll be the four of us there, carrying the statue with her crown of white roses from the church all the way down to Saint Brigid's Well, and from the way he talks you know he's expecting a great big crowd from all over will turn out to listen to him. And I hope they do come, but I can tell you the names of two people who won't.

Something's happening to Orla and Tess. They used to be always together but now Tess hardly ever comes round to our house for dinner like she used to. That used to be the way of it since her mam wasn't often well enough to be cooking, and she cooks now but that's not the reason. Last night Dad asked what was the news with Tess and Orla got this look on her face, incredulous like, and all she said was—Tess is grand, she's always grand.

It isn't only Declan coming between them. It's more than that. I want to shake Orla and say do you know how lucky you are to have her for your best friend? But she doesn't. They've been mates since they were in nappies but she's never seen it. The only friends I've had have come and gone in a matter of days, weeks if I was lucky, and when they change their minds about me they join in the whispering. Once they decided I was queer, everything I said and every which way I moved had to be queer too, because people will think whatever they like so long as they don't have to see they're mistaken. I wish there were someone else at school like me, but there isn't, there never has been. So many times I go back to the day with Mallory at Streedagh and I wonder if she's the best friend I will ever have. Tess is kind to me but since she's not in my year I hardly ever see her. Orla sees her all the time and it's like Tess is slowly fading into the wallpaper. Oh how I long to shake her.

Sometimes Our Lady tells me things, things I'm not supposed to know, and I write them down here but afterwards I don't remember doing it. She says Father Dowd had a twin sister who drowned in a river when they were three years of age. She says Tom Devaney keeps filthy videotapes in a locked box at the back of his shop and all of the men in town know about it. I know Dad and Uncle Jim have lost a great deal of money in a bad investment and they're holding off telling Mam and Aunt Fiona for as long as they can. And She says Tess will become a nun though her heart will never be in it. I asked Her why, why would she do it if she didn't really want to, and Our Lady said she didn't know her own heart well enough to tell the difference. I said we should talk to Tess about it, to keep her from making that mistake with her life, and the Blessed Mother seemed surprised.—Ah, but there won't be any mistake in it, She said.—Haven't you ever done the right thing for the wrong reason?

When I saw Tess the next day I wanted so badly to speak to her, but I didn't know how to bring it up. Finally I said,— What does Our Lady tell you about what we're meant to do with our lives?

—You mean, do we have a vocation?

—I don't know. Maybe.

—You know you'll never be a nun, Síle, she laughed, and I must have had a look on my face because she reacted as if she'd hurt my feelings.—It's only that you're meant to do so many other things. Things a vocation wouldn't allow you. You want to paint, don't you? And travel? I told her she was right, and she said,—See? You're too full of life. Not that the convent isn't its own kind of life, only it isn't the life for you.

—Or you?

She looked down at her hands in her lap.—I don't know yet. It's different for me.

—Don't you see yourself getting married someday, Tess? Don't you see yourself having a husband who'll come home to you each night, and babbies of your own?

She tried to smile.—I don't see anything. Sometimes I lie awake at night trying to picture it, any of it, even a small thing

*like how I'll wear my hair when I'm thirty-five and will there
be any grey in it yet. But I can't.*

—But you don't see yourself in the convent either.

—You're right. I don't.

—Do you ever speak about this with Orla?

Tess laughed.—Not about going into the convent?

*—No, what we're all going to be someday. For a minute or
two we sat in silence, and then I said,—Isn't it strange that
She'd come to the four of us, when none of us belong in the religious life?*

*—But I don't know that the religious life is a higher calling
than any other kind of life, Tess said.—After all, wasn't Our
Lady a wife and mother?*

*I wanted to answer her then, I wanted to say you do think
it's a higher calling, that's the reason you're thinking of it, but I
didn't. I must keep Tess on my side, I don't know what I'd do if
she turned away from me as Orla has.*

*—Wherever you go, whoever you become, Tess told me
then,—there'll always be the potential for temptation as well as
virtue. Even in the convent.*

The rush-hour traffic was heavy coming out of Galway, and when
I got back, I found Brona, Paudie, and Leo already tucked into
their favorite snug.

"I've been meaning to ask you," Brona said once I'd sat
down with my pint. "Did you ever manage to speak with Peggy
Keaveney?"

I gave her a recap of my conversation with Declan's mother the
previous afternoon—everything but the notebook—and Brona
responded with a heavy sigh. "The poor creature, tellin' you her
husband was killed in an accident. What a terrible shame."

"I remember Tommy Keaveney," Paudie said. "I remember him well, and I remember the time when he began to be missed. If there'd been an accident, even as far away as Dublin, we'd have heard of it."

"Surely," Leo chimed in as he licked the paper on a new cigarette. "We'd have heard of it—there'd be no doubt about that." He tucked his handiwork behind one of his dribbly ears.

"Father Lynch told me people seem to think he just left town in the middle of the night and never came back," I said.

"And that's as near to the truth as any of us are ever likely to know," Paudie replied.

"And then Declan takin' after his father like that." Leo drank long from his Guinness before adding, "No wonder the poor woman doesn't see things as they are."

Leo spoke those words, and I knew beyond all doubt that Mrs. Keaveney hadn't gotten those names off her TV set. Who are any of us, to say we *do* see things as they are?

"Life is very cruel sometimes," Brona was saying. "And sure, what can we do but tell her how pleased we are to hear he's coming home at last?"

We finished the round, and at five minutes to eight, we shrugged on our jackets and walked down the road to the town park. It was very square and symmetrical—you could tell the English had laid it out—though at the center there was a memorial to the Irish killed in the Easter Rising and the Civil War. Someone had arranged a row of pillar candles all around the memorial, so that the candlelight flickered on the bronze faces of the figures in the tableau; and for a second it felt like we were gathering here to worship a much older god, not just one but a whole company of them.

Paudie spotted Tess in the gathering crowd, and I hung back while the rest of them clasped her by the shoulder and expressed their condolences. Then, her eyes rimmed in red, she saw me over Leo's shoulder and I wished I hadn't come. I didn't belong here. Yet in the next moment I found her in my arms, and I never would be able to recall which of us had reached for the other; but at least I knew she was glad of my presence.

It seemed like most of the people of Ballymorris had turned out, the elder residents parking themselves on benches along the walkway and the dead boy's friends sitting or squatting on the pavement near the war memorial. I glanced around, but I didn't see the kid from the grotto. "Thank the Lord it's a dry night," Leo said as he and Paudie took a seat.

"For now," Paudie replied as he buttoned his coat to the top and hunched his shoulders to try to preserve the warmth of the pub. Brona had gone off to talk to someone.

I was still searching the faces. "Are Tess's parents here?"

Paudie shook his head. "Martina isn't well, I'm afraid. I told them I'd be here, if Tess should need me."

A teenage boy in a hand-me-down leather jacket stood in front of the memorial, flicking his long hair out of his eyes as he tuned his guitar. A rather chubby girl of about thirteen came over and conferred with him before propping a laminated school portrait against the base of the memorial inside the circle of candles, where several people had already laid bouquets wrapped in cellophane. I took a step closer, shuddering as I recognized the face in the picture.

Shit. Owen *was* the boy on the hill.

The girl who'd brought the picture approached Tess, casting an anxious glance at us as she spoke. "Will you go first, Tess?"

She laid a hand on the girl's arm. "If you like. Are ye ready to begin?"

The girl nodded, and as Tess followed her back to the memorial, a hush settled over the crowd. "Welcome, everyone," Tess said, and her voice carried to the far reaches of the park. "I'm so grateful to see everyone here tonight to celebrate the life of Owen Gerrity." She paused to collect herself, her hands clasped at her heart. She'd never looked more like a saint. "He was a kind boy, bright and caring, and compassionate to those around him, and in time he would have grown into a bright and caring and compassionate man." Tess cleared her throat. "We will none of us have the chance to meet that man, but tonight we'll remember the boy—the dear, sweet boy who was Owen Gerrity—as his spirit reunites with God our ever-loving Father."

I'd talked to this kid only two days before—we'd been drawn to the same place, breathed the same air—yet in another day or two, he'd be lying under six feet of earth. The horrible creeping-crawling came back to me then, the panicked *get it off me get it away from me* feeling that had kept me wide awake, frightened, and guilty every night for months after Mallory's accident. I wondered if Mrs. Keaveney were here, if she'd already written Owen's name in her book.

Tess closed her eyes, and in the candlelight we could see the tears spilling down her cheeks. She wiped them away with trembling fingers before she continued. "As many of you know, music was an important part of Owen's life, and so we have his closest friends here, Rory Farrell and Jim Murray, to play a few of the songs Owen liked best. Then we'll have Owen's sister, Ciara, read a poem she's written for her brother." Tess stepped back into the crowd, and I watched a middle-aged woman rest a hand on her elbow and murmur in her ear as Rory and Jim took their places inside the circle of candles.

"None of this is real to me yet," Rory or Jim began. "I keep thinkin' we're here for some other reason, and Owen's just a little late joinin' us."

"We always talked about gettin' a band together," Jim or Rory went on. "Someday we'd have done it. I feel like we have to do it now—for Owen—y'know?"

The crowd responded with what seemed like compassionate silence. "Anyway, this was Owen's favorite song. He was still workin' on learnin' how to play it."

The boy strummed tunelessly on his guitar; a few chords later the other joined in, and I couldn't help thinking, *Good Lord, this will be tedious.* After the first thirty seconds, I figured out it was Johnny Cash, but I still couldn't make out most of the words. I looked over and saw Paudie with his chin on his palm, wearing a too-intent expression that indicated (to anyone who knew him well enough) that he was zoned out entirely. Leo, of course, made no pretense of listening; the night wasn't warm by any means, but it wasn't too cold to prevent him dozing off on the park bench once he'd finished his cigarette.

But the old men perked up once the boys stopped playing and Ciara began to speak. "My mam and dad decided not to be here tonight," she said, her voice surprisingly clear and steady, "but they asked me to tell ye all how much it means to them that ye've come."

She looked around at the better part of Ballymorris assembled before her, and I was amazed at her air of calm, her self-possession. I couldn't believe a young girl could stand up in front of her neighbors like this only the day after her brother killed himself. "I wrote a poem for Owen," she said. "I only wrote it this morning, so it isn't any good."

"Ah, now," someone said, gently reproving, and Ciara replied with a bashful half smile as she began to read.

You showed me how to move through the world,
and once or twice, when we couldn't sleep,
we talked about what might lie beyond it.

You didn't know any more than I did,
But at least you didn't pretend to.
Other times it felt like there was all of the Atlantic between us
Instead of the kitchen table,
with me always waiting on you to speak.
I can write that you're gone, but I can't believe it.
I will save my memories of you, like the coins we can't use
    anymore,
And try not to think that only one of us is growing up,
That only one of us will leave the home we've known.
But you know what lies beyond us now,
And someday
I expect you will tell me everything.

The crowd responded to the girl's reading with a different kind of silence. No one clapped, but you knew they would have given her a warm ovation under happier circumstances. I'd never felt so apart from anyone, anywhere, as I did then. *Was it that pure and simple between them, really? Had he always been that good to her? Or has she already forgotten all the times when he wasn't?*

Ciara's friends surrounded her, hugging her and murmuring their admiration for what she'd written, and it looked as though the vigil might be over already. "We'll leave you go before anyone gets wet," called Rory or Jim, "Only Tess would like us to play 'Amazing Grace,' and have everyone join in, if ye are willing."

The boys' rendition of the old hymn wasn't any clearer than their Johnny Cash, but this time Tess's voice held everyone's attention. Hearing that voice, you knew that back in the day she'd sung every solo in the children's choir. No one joined in. I felt goose bumps all over as she sang the last verse: *Yea, when this flesh and heart shall fail, and mortal life shall cease, I shall possess within the veil, a life of joy and peace.*

I looked over and saw tears in the corners of Paudie's eyes. "She sings so beautifully. She never lets on how beautifully she can sing."

"The voice of an angel, the heart of a saint," Leo confirmed, and put his arm around his old friend's shoulder as if they'd had three times as much to drink.

The song ended, and Tess was met with another interlude of admiring silence. She cleared her throat. "And now we'll have some refreshments over at the youth center. I doubt ye can all fit in the house, but we'll try our best."

The rain started, softly at first, and when we got to the little row house on Milk Lane, it looked like most of the people who'd been at the park weren't coming for the "afters." In the sitting room where Owen had passed his school days playing video games, a girl was slumped on the black vinyl sofa, openly weeping as her friends attempted to comfort her. Down the corridor another bevy of teenagers crowded the kitchen table, tearing into the packages of cookies and chocolate Tess had laid out earlier that evening.

A young man with a receding hairline was standing by the kitchen doorway eyeing the chaos, and as Tess came in, he gave her a hug that might have lasted a beat too long. She turned back to me and introduced us. "Liam is one of our after-school literacy tutors," she said as I shook his hand.

"Pleased to meet you," he said, though he didn't much look it. "Can I make you a cuppa, Tess?"

"I'm all right, thanks, Liam."

Paudie and Leo stood in the kitchen doorway, clearly ill at ease. "I think they'd rather go back to the pub for their refreshments," I said wryly, and when Liam glanced at me then, I felt as if I'd said the wrong thing, or at least said it the wrong way.

The young man turned to Tess, touched her shoulder, and

said, "You're knackered. Why don't you go home and get some rest? Your friends can walk you back, and Mairéad and I can tidy up here when everyone's finished."

Paudie and Leo each offered her an arm, and they walked that way down Shop Street: two old men escorting a handsome russet-haired girl, the one person I knew who'd offered up her life to something beyond herself. I walked a few paces behind, feeling a fondness for all three of them unwarranted by our brief acquaintance. Twenty-five years ago didn't really count.

"Where are we headed?" I heard her ask.

"Where do ya think?" Leo replied.

"Not to the pub. I won't, thanks, Leo."

"C'mon, Tess," Paudie said gently, as Leo declared, "You'll not go home to your own four walls tonight!" I could see from behind her how Tess seemed to melt with relief at his rumbling confidence. After a day like this one, an early night was the last thing anybody needed or wanted. "Not yet," Leo blustered as they quickened their steps. "Not yet."

We ducked into Napper Tandy's and found our usual snug occupied. Paudie and I went for the first round while Leo and Tess found us a booth in the back. There was a hurling match on the television, the bar crowded with the same obnoxious men in green jerseys. Hennessey and "Yeats" were among them, but if they looked my way, they didn't let on.

"Do nuns drink?" I asked as Paudie waved the bartender over.

"She does tonight," he answered. "She'll have a hot whiskey with lemon and sugar. Sure, we must all take our comfort where we can find it."

I shook my head a little, trying to remember where I'd heard that sentiment before. We carried the drinks to the booth, and I inched in beside Tess. "It was terribly good of you to come out tonight," she said as I delivered the hot toddy.

Paudie raised his pint and nodded to his niece. "For Tess," he said. "There never was a dearer girl, or a kinder heart."

"*Sláinte*," said Leo, and tipped his glass.

The old men soon fell into conversation between themselves. "I don't know what to talk about," I said to Tess. "I know it's been really hard for you, and I don't want to say anything to upset you."

"You're all right," she said. "We can talk about the vigil, if you want to."

"I only wanted to say that I think you did an amazing job."

She deflected my compliment with half a smile. "What did you think of Owen's sister, Ciara?"

"She's very talented. And remarkably self-possessed for any age, but to be that young, and able to write and speak that way after what's happened to her?" I shook my head.

"And she's only fourteen. He made a poet out of her, didn't he?" She sighed. "They do say that's the way it happens. You turn your grief into something bigger than yourself."

I didn't know how to answer that. "Did you mind being an only child?"

"Only in that it pained my mother not to have the brood she'd always imagined for herself. I felt it, growing up, you know?" I nodded, and she continued. "She became very ill while she was expecting me, and the birth was difficult. There was never any question of her having another child."

"I've been wanting to ask you about that."

She waited for me to go on, but I let her finish my thought. "The healing, is it?" I nodded. "She *was* cured of the diabetes, thank Heaven, but even so, she's never been in the best of health. It wouldn't do her any good to speak of it now." Tess looked me in the eye once she'd gotten that out. "I'm sorry," she said.

I gave her half a shrug and half a smile. "That's all right. I understand," I replied, though I was already mulling over how I might change her mind. Maybe part of me was still hoping I could write this story and publish it somewhere else. "How did your parents take it when you told them you were becoming a nun?"

"They were more or less expecting it."

"So they didn't give you a hard time?"

"How do you mean?"

"Parents can get pretty ornery when they find out you're not giving them any grandkids."

She looked at me wryly. "Speaking from experience, are you?" Then she softened. "I'm so sorry. It must have been hard for you, being there tonight."

Yet again I didn't know what to say, and Tess gazed at me with her clear gray eyes. If Mallory were here, they'd be talking about medieval mystics and the Celtic stone carvings at Newgrange. They'd forget I was even here.

"After it happened," I said, "when I'd meet someone for the first time and they'd ask if I had any brothers or sisters, I didn't know what to say. Even now, I don't know how to answer."

"I don't suppose you ever will." Tess let her hand rest near mine on the table. "I pray for Mallory. I always have, since they told me what happened to her."

I felt her name twitching beneath my shirt, begging for a good hard scratch, as if I'd gotten the tattoo only yesterday. Maybe Tess kept a notebook of her own. "Forgive me," I said, "but I don't see what good that does her now."

"It does," she said. "However far away they are from us now, it still matters."

Who is it who gets to decide what matters and what's pointless? It was all so preposterously arbitrary. "Can I ask you something?"

Tess regarded me warmly. "Of course."

"How do you know where someone's gone to? After they've died?"

"Well, you don't," she sighed. "But oftentimes they'll ask for prayers, and that's how you know they're waiting. Perhaps you can hear them, if you sit quietly for a while."

I suppressed a shiver. Was it something in the water here, or what? "You really believe in Purgatory?" I asked.

"It isn't a matter of my believing in it," she replied, and I knew then that there were more than four of us in the booth. Leo and Paudie were busy arguing about something involving a postal truck and a series of road signs pointing the wrong way. The crow twitching on the highway, the relentless rain, the white of her eye. Tess was looking at me, earnest and maybe a little concerned. This had nothing to do with religion, hers or anyone else's.

Finally I said, "To me, it *is* a matter of belief. I want to know what you really think about this stuff."

Tess smiled at my reducing her entire worldview into *this stuff*. "You already know what I believe."

"You believe all of it, though? You don't take issue with anything the Church teaches?"

"Let me answer you this way. What is it *you* take issue with?"

I gave her all the usual arguments—the sex abuse scandals, the Church's stance on abortion and contraception, that women should be allowed to be priests, that homosexuality isn't a sin. "Most of all, though," I said, "I can hardly ever find anything with real-life relevance in the readings. If it's there, they've done too good a job of hiding it."

Tess cast me a tolerant smile. "Are you finished?"

I chuckled. "For now, anyway."

"Right, then. When I have this sort of conversation, I certainly don't expect anyone to fall into line with my own way of looking at the world and what lies beyond it," she said. "But I do take exception when people try to argue there's nothing a'tall behind any of it. It's easy for a person to scoff at something when they haven't taken the time to understand it." She read my face and rushed to add, "Oh, I'm not saying anything about yourself, necessarily, I'm only trying to make the point that there's nothing simple about theology. Some things, the big questions, they're much too important to be distilled any further, and there's something essential that's lost whenever you try."

"Can I just ask you one more thing about this?" I asked, and Tess answered with a nod and half a smile. "Do *you* hear them? The souls in Purgatory?"

"Not their voices, as such," she conceded. "It's more of a feeling. A knowing."

"But how is that different from ordinary grief?" I knew I was pressing too hard, but this had nothing to do with either writing the story or scoring a point for rational thought. "How can you tell the difference?"

"It's easy to tell when you hardly knew the person." She was staring through the table again, and part of me wanted to grab her hand and hold it tight. "You know you wouldn't be thinking so much of them otherwise. But when it's someone you loved . . ." Tess swallowed before she continued. "There's a sort of steadiness to your thoughts about them. It's like they're waiting in the hall, there whether or not you'll allow yourself to think of them. That's how you know it's not only the grief." She glanced up at me. "Or the regret."

Waiting in the hall, I thought. *Or the backseat.* "Thank you," I said. "That helps." She gave me another half smile as she ran a Kleenex under her eyes.

True to form, Leo headed for "the jacks" as soon as someone mentioned getting the next round. Paudie rose heavily out of the booth, his hand rough and red on the polished wood. "Will you have another, Tess?"

"I won't, thanks, Paudie."

"I'll bring you a glass of water, so," he said, and shuffled away.

"You're a cheap date," I said, and she laughed, or tried to. "I'm sorry. I shouldn't be making jokes on a night like this."

Tess shook her head. "It doesn't matter. None of it feels real to me anyway."

"Not yet," I said. "Not yet."

She slid me a quiet smile of understanding.

"Is there anything I can do?"

Tess patted my hand, and the gesture felt almost sisterly. "You've already done it." But when she took her hand away, I felt something else. "You know, I keep thinking about our conversation the other day. It was hard for me, speaking round it like that. Not because I didn't want to talk, but because I wanted to tell you everything. *That* was what frightened me."

"You can talk to me now, if you want." I tried to smile reassuringly. "You'll notice I left the recorder at home."

Tess glanced over my shoulder toward her uncle waiting at the bar. "We'll save it for another time," she said. "Sometime when it's just the two of us."

"Of course," I said. "What would you like to talk about now?"

"Oh, anything. Anything but the week I've had." She sighed. "Tell me about yourself, for once. What your life in New York is like."

I didn't want to talk about my life in New York. "It's a good life," I said. "Not many people get to write for a living, you know? I have good friends, a nice apartment in Brooklyn. Have you ever been to the U.S.?"

"I haven't, no."

"But you've traveled quite a bit, haven't you? You said you volunteered."

"At children's homes, mainly," she replied.

"I read an article once about a Romanian orphanage during the revolution," I said. "They interviewed a volunteer there who said there were babies traded for television sets."

"I'm sure it wasn't an exaggeration," she said darkly.

"Remind me where you were?"

"Kenya and Nepal. Kenya first. An orphanage in Nairobi."

"How long did you volunteer there?"

"Only eight months, that time. I was meant to stay at least a year, but . . ."

"Did you get burnt out? I know I would have."

She gave me a haunted look. "I didn't want to see it that way at the time, but I was. I'm sure I was. You need to feel that you're making a difference, and if you can't see it—and in my experience, you rarely can—then it wears on you very quickly."

"We can talk about something else, if you want."

"I don't want there to be this many things I shouldn't speak of," she said, more to herself than to me. "No. It's fine. I'll be glad to speak of it."

"Okay," I replied. "Tell me what it was like. How big was it, and how many children were there, and were they really orphans, or . . . ?"

"Most of the children in the home still had living parents, or at least we could assume that to be the case. You know that scene at the beginning of a fillum, where a desperate woman leaves a baby in a basket on the front steps of an orphanage in the middle of the night? That happened more often than not."

"That *is* what they say about clichés," I murmured into my pint glass as Paudie and Leo came back to the booth.

"Go on, then," Paudie said. "Tell us about that place in Kenya."

Tess sighed. "You've heard all this before, Paw."

Paudie jabbed his thumb in my direction. "Ah, but *he* hasn't."

"How old were the kids there?" I asked. "What were they like?"

"Oh, all ages. Young teens to the tiniest babbies, only weeks old." She stared into her toddy glass, shaking the wilted lemon slice. "There were so many children and so few people to mind them that sometimes the babbies would be sittin' in their dirty nappies for hours before anybody could notice. There were never enough hands to bathe or feed them as often as they should've been, and what toys they had to play with were even filthier than the linens. I tried to wash them, but I could never seem to get them clean enough." She sighed. "What do you do when you arrive into a situation like that? What can you do, apart from your best?" Tess glanced at me, and I nodded for her to go on. "But my best wasn't good enough. Not by half. It didn't matter how I held them or what I said to them, they'd lie slack in my arms like a bundle of curtains—as if I weren't holding them a'tall." She leaned back against the old red upholstery. Just talking about it had exhausted her. "They'd been left, and they *knew* they'd been left."

"Even the really little ones knew?"

She looked at me and nodded. "You could see it. They always knew."

"What did you do?" I asked. "I mean . . . how did you cope?"

Tess took a long drink of water before she answered me. "I suppose I had to pretend I didn't see it—didn't see what would happen to each of them in the future, what their lives would become. You can't grow into a loving and purposeful member of society in a place like that. You just can't. Nobody could.

"There was one wee lad," she said softly. "Daniel. He was the only child I found on the front steps—it was usually the housekeeper who found them first thing in the morning. I couldn't sleep that night, the night Daniel came to us. I was sitting by the window just looking down over the street as the moon went down. I saw a woman hurrying up with something in her arms, and I knew what she was about. She was gone before I got to the door, and there was Daniel tucked inside a shipping crate. They let me name him."

"Didn't it get cold at night?" I asked. "Even in Africa. I mean, didn't the mothers ever knock?"

Tess shook her head. "I imagine most of them waited until just before sunrise, the way Daniel's mother did that night. They'd be bundled up tight and out there no more than an hour. They were warm enough to live.

"Something happened to me that morning, as I took Daniel into my arms. He looked up at me with these dark, fathomless eyes, and it felt like how, in a dream, you might meet a loved one with a stranger's face but all along you know who it is underneath. I don't know, maybe that was why I thought I could reach him. It tore at my heart every time I saw him in the crib with the others." She laid a pale hand on her chest, as if she meant it literally. "It always tore at me, but with Daniel it was even harder. I made sure I was always the one to feed him, but it wasn't enough. I wanted to lie down with him to sleep—to soothe him the way I'd been soothed as a baby—but there wasn't room apart from my own bed in the volunteers' dormitory. I suppose I knew by that point that I wouldn't be a mother myself, but I felt that instinct all the same, the instinct to nurture."

"Ah, Tess," Paudie said softly, so as not to interrupt her. "You've a heart of gold."

She did cut herself off, though, giving him that look I was beginning to know all too well—the look that said *I'm not who you think.* "One afternoon," she continued, "I brought him into the dorm and when the director came in and found us, she was very angry with me. She didn't see what I was trying to do, she didn't care enough to see it, and it drove me mad." Tess closed her eyes as if to protect herself from the memory. "She'd a thankless job all right, but she treated it like a license to drink." She opened her eyes and sighed as she reached for her water glass. "But they weren't all like that, in fairness."

"Is that when you left?"

"Aye," she said. "Only it wasn't by choice. They asked me to leave." She cast a glance at Paudie, and he reached across the table and squeezed her hand. "Not many people know about that."

"Just because of what happened with Daniel?" I asked.

She nodded. "I'm not ashamed of it, mind. I'd do it again if I could. It's just easier not to explain the whole thing."

"I'm sorry," I said.

"Everything's for the best," Leo said, and excused himself for a cigarette.

"Aye," Paudie sighed as he inched his way out of the booth. "It's only we can't see it, for all our hopes."

"Paudie, wait." I drew out a twenty-euro bill, and he accepted it with a smile of thanks.

Tess picked something up off the table and looked it over before handing it to me. *Save a dozen souls in the time it takes to boil an egg.* "Looks like you knew about the holy souls after all," she said.

I looked at the text on the card as if I'd never seen it before. "I didn't realize that's what it meant."

"Let me guess. You bought it from Mag O'Grady, just for novelty's sake?"

It's easy for a person to scoff at something when they haven't taken the time to understand it. "Touché," I replied, and tucked the card back in my wallet.

"If you say that prayer sometimes . . . whenever you think of it . . ."

"Yeah?"

"It *will* help," she said.

She meant Mallory, but I couldn't think or talk about Mallory any more tonight. We looked at our hands, the table, the crowd at the bar. Neither of us wanted to go back to talking about dirty forgotten children. *What happened when you went up to the hill on your own?* I wanted to ask her. *Do you know some people think the apparition wasn't Mary at all?*

Then Tess turned to me and said, "Has anyone told you about the fairies?"

This swerve in the conversation left me stumped. "Fairies? Like folklore, you mean?"

Tess gave me a radiant smile, even more remarkable given what she'd been through over the past forty-eight hours. Her eyes glittered, and for a second she reminded me of Síle. "You can call it folklore, if you like," she said.

I was going to say something about a belief in fairies maybe being incompatible with Catholicism, but I thought better of it. If I'd learned anything over the past week, it was that the Irish had their own brand of logic.

"You never heard any of the old rules?" she was asking. "That you should never speak to them, or eat their food or drink their wine, or you'd be lost to our world forever?"

"Nope."

"None of the old stories? Not even from your gran?"

"My grandmother isn't much of a storyteller," I said. "Not like Leo. She's very practical."

"I wasn't aware of the impracticality of storytelling," she replied dryly.

"You know what I mean." I finished my pint and sat back with a sigh. "So what made you think of the fairies?"

"Oh, I don't know. I suppose there's been a certain feeling of unreality to life lately. It's strange to be here with you like this." She traced a finger around the condensation left on the table by my pint glass, and I hoped she wasn't thinking of Streedagh. "I couldn't tell you the last time I was inside Napper Tandy's. I may have been a teenager."

"Tell me your favorite story about the fairies," I said.

"I'd have to think on that, now." She bit her lip in a manner I found appealing. "There are so many of them."

"Pick one," I said. "Whichever comes to mind first."

Tess took a breath. "All right. I have it. Now, there was a tragic series of episodes in our history among the ordinary people, who believed that sometimes the fairies might steal away a newborn child and leave a changeling in its place. The changeling would howl and grimace, taking no nourishment at the breast of the woman meant to be its mother. 'Twas plain, or at least the people thought so, that the real babe had been taken away. There were some who believed that if they cast the changeling into the fire, the fairy child would vanish and the true child would reappear in its cradle, though who knows how many mothers and fathers steeled themselves for the deed. We know it happened more than once. It must have." As Tess spoke, I marveled at the change in her demeanor. Storytelling had given her new energy. "On other occasions, the parents might carry the changeling out into the night, up to some dark and boggy place in the lee of a fairy mound, and leave him there for the fairies to reclaim."

I waited a beat before saying, "That's some story."

"That wasn't the story. Sure, I was only givin' you a bit of background." Tess smiled. "You wonder, don't you, what happened to the child left on the hillside in the wind and rain?"

Paudie came back with the pints. "It died," I said, "and if the parents ever went back they'd've found the bones."

"Ah, but what if it didn't?"

"What if there really were fairies?" She nodded, and I said, "But there aren't. The babies died of exposure, just like they would've died of third-degree burns."

Leo came in, stinking of smoke, and Paudie made more room for him in the booth. I watched Leo look tenderly upon his fresh pint as he brought it to his lips—as if it were the face of a woman he'd loved all his life, his first drink instead of his sixth.

"It won't do to think on it too literally," Tess was saying, which brought to mind Síle and our talk of happy endings. "When you're listening to a story, any story a'tall, you've got to believe in it with all you've got as it's being told, or else there's little pleasure to be found in it."

I took my first drink and licked the head off my lip. "Okay," I said. "I'll stop butting in. Continue."

Once more Tess settled herself into a posture for storytelling. "Now, there once was a young woman in the west of Ireland who had the dreadful ill luck to discover a changeling in the cradle one gloomy morning. The sweet rosy face and twinklin' blue eyes of her baby boy were gone, and in their place a gaze blacker than coal and the scowl of a man who'd lived twice as long and twice as hard as he was meant to. The poor woman had gone through all the usual charms to protect her firstborn, as the mothers of her parish used to do. But there was no human magic strong enough to keep the fairies away from her wee boy, and now he was gone from her forever.

"She called her husband in from the fields, and together they decided what they must do. That night they walked five miles to the nearest *Shee*—the fairy mound, wreathed in whitethorn trees— and they left the changeling on a bed of sedge. From the first breath of dawn to the time they laid it down in the heather, the thing had not ceased to wail for an instant, and even as they left it miles behind them, they could still hear the echoes of its cries in the whistlin' wind of the night. In the silent cottage, they climbed into their bed, weary and heartbroken."

Leo and Paudie were listening intently. "She's a beautiful sto-ryteller, so she is," Leo whispered. Paudie looked as proud as if she were his own child instead of his brother's.

"For a year or more, the couple mourned their loss," Tess was saying, "and it was often whispered of in the village pub. In time, though, they had another child, and another, and another until there were six altogether, and as the years passed, the couple thanked God the fairies left them well enough alone. The loss of their firstborn still weighed like a stone on their hearts, but most days they managed to forget, so that the dull ache seemed to have no source that they could tell of.

"Each of their children grew tall and strong, and one after another, it came time for them to go out into the wider world to seek their fortunes. The eldest boy promised to return and care for the family acre when the time came, but until then, the man and the woman were as they'd been at the beginning: just the two of them, and the quiet hope between them. In this way the years passed, their joints stiffened and their hair lost all color, until one morning the woman awoke to find her husband lying too still beside her.

"The children could not come home again to share in the loss. They'd lives of their own now, in Dublin and abroad. One day her eldest son would return to till his father's land as he'd promised, but in the meantime, his mother rose and toiled and cooked and ate and slept alone—as no one is ever meant to."

This was an odd thing to say coming from a nun, and I looked at her closely. Tess was so wrapped up in her story that she never paused to consider what she'd said, how the truth she'd just told reflected on her own life.

"It seemed to her that all the comfort had gone out of her snug little house," she went on, "with her husband lyin' cold in the ground, and the widow began to pray that her eldest would return to her of his own choice, and live with her always.

"One day not long after, as afternoon settled into evening, the widow stood on the threshold and caught sight of a figure walking across the fields towards her cottage. Her heart leapt with joy, for who could it be but her eldest son come home to grant her wish at last?

"But as the figure drew closer, a sense of confusion settled upon her, for he did not carry himself in the way she knew, and his shirt caught the light as if the linen were woven through with silver. Now he was at the edge of her own land, holding up a hand to greet her, and yet this young man was not, could not be, her eldest son.

"At last the man reached the edge of the farmyard. He stopped at the gate and took off his hat. The stranger said, 'Do you know me, Mother?'

"And the woman gazed up at him, her confusion giving way to fear. The sun was behind him, so that his face was cast in shadow, and his skin seemed to glow with the quiet radiance of the full moon. She began to understand.

"He spoke again, and his speech was unlike any she had heard before: 'I am hungry from the journey, Mother, and I smell something simmering on the fire. What have you made for supper?'

"The widow could not bring herself to speak; it was all she could do to lift a hand and invite him inside. He bent his head so that he might enter the little cottage where he was born, and, leaving his boots at the door as his father used to do—though there wasn't a speck of mud upon them—he took a seat at the table laid for one.

"With trembling fingers, the woman ladled out the fragrant stew. She set the bowl before him on the table fashioned by the capable hands of his dead father, and once she'd sat down beside him, the young man bent his head and clasped his hands to utter a prayer, if prayer it was, for the words he used belonged to no human language.

"Then, with a grateful glance at her, he began to eat, and the way he did this too was fearsome and wonderful to her. Each spoonful delighted him, each bite of meat or potato brought another smile to his lips. There was a queerness to his every movement, too, as if the fairies had taught him a different set of manners. Even so, the widow once caught a glimpse of her husband inside the face of her strange guest, and such a terrible thrill it gave her.

"'Ahh,' the young man said at last, drawing a fine handkerchief from his pocket to wipe his mouth. 'Had you kept me, this stew would have been my favorite. I have never known such nourishment—not since the last time I fed from your breast, dear Mother.'

"'How can that be,' she asked plaintively, 'when you have grown so tall and strong?'

"'They filled my belly with other things,' he said, and because she was afraid then to ask any more questions, there came a silence between them. Finally the young man laid his kerchief on his knee and spoke as he began neatly to fold it. 'It did not take them long to come for me, but even now I remember how cold it was, and how wet, up there on the hill. That shiver,' he said quietly. 'It will never leave me.'

"As he spoke these words, it was as if the old chill spread from his heart into hers, though she could not understand this sympathy, for the babe she'd left wasn't her babe a'tall. 'They'd already taken you away from me,' she said, and in her voice there was a note of pleading. 'All that I brought to the hill was the changeling they left in your place.'

"The young man shook his head, but his attitude was one of

sorrow, not of reproach. 'The fairies did come in the night,' he said, 'but they did not steal me away. They haven't the power for that, though they'll have us believe they do, and in the end that's nearly the same. They could only cast a spell on me through a chink in the shutter, drawing all the warmth and joy out of my tiny heart so that I would seem to you a different babe altogether. They knew then that you would take me up to the hill and leave me there in the darkness, and then truly I would be theirs.'

"The widow clutched at her breast, as if her heart were giving out with the grief of it. 'How was I to know?' she whispered. 'How could I be wise to such a trick, and we such simple folk?'

"'I have never blamed you, Mother,' the man said gently, and when he reached across the table to reassure her, she felt a hum beneath the skin of her work-worn hand.

"'You must tell me,' she said, her voice choked with emotions she had not known she could feel. 'I must know. Was it a good life you led with them? What did they teach you, and did you sleep warm at night, and did they raise you with love, as I would have done?'

"The man rose from the table to stand by the hearth and stoke the fire, staring into the flames just as his father used to do. And like his father, he seemed to be lost in his own thoughts.

"For the first time, she uttered the name she had given him, and the young man looked up from the fire. 'You must not call me by that name,' he said, and a sharp note had entered into his silvery voice. 'It was lost to me when they took me from the hill.' Another silence settled between them, and the woman felt a kind of shame for all the things she did not know. 'I shall answer your questions as best I can,' he said at last, 'though there are certain things I may never speak of.'

"'I had a fairy mother,' he began, 'and in the beginning she loved me, in her way, almost as well as you did. Even among the

Shee there are womenfolk who cannot bear children of their own, and it is this want which leads them to steal away the offspring of humankind. She kept me in a cradle of moonwood carved with scenes of desert caravans, marching elephants, chariots, and epic battles, so that night by night I might dream myself into a future of greatness.

"'I was schooled in the ways of the *Shee,* but I always knew I was set apart, and I asked many questions that went unanswered. As I grew, a great restlessness came upon me, so that at last my fairy mother was compelled to show me a vision of you in this very room: surrounded by the brothers and sisters I would never know, and my father quietly stoking the fire just as I have done tonight. And I grieved for the life I should have had as your eldest son. She told me I could never go above, that once a human child is taken, there can be no taking him back, but this too was a falsehood. It was a long time before I began to see that the fairy folk hold no reverence for truth—and how can they? For even before they've spoken the lie, they've convinced themselves it is so.' He sighed. 'After that my fairy mother grew cold to me. I was told I had no further need of schooling, and I became a servant of the *Shee.*'

"The woman was surprised at this, for it seemed to her that this young man was dressed like the son of a lord, with his fine linen shirt all shot through with silver, and his soft leather boots with their shining buckles.

"'The fairies are, as you have guessed, an immoderate race,' he went on. 'There is hardly an end to their balls and banquets, so that as they sleep, we must tidy up the remains of one feast only to prepare for the next. Even my schooling was executed in the most languid fashion, my tutor more fond of wine and games and noonday slumbers than any book or map.

"'In all that they left unsaid, however, and in their eternal pursuit of pleasure, they showed me how to betray them. I learned for myself that I might return someday to the world of men, that all that was necessary was for someone, even one person, to remember me.' He gazed into her eyes with a look of the most ferocious love, and again he frightened her. 'I heard your prayers, Mother, and I was restored.'

"The woman knew she should feel joyful, but unqualified happiness was beyond her. She had prayed not for the return of this lost son, but for the young man she had thought of as her eldest; and she began to be afraid that perhaps this man, her son, knew this, and harbored a resentment he had yet to show her. 'They won't come lookin' for you?' she said at last.

"'They cannot reach me,' he replied. 'I have come home to you, to till my father's land and to care for the animals, and to be a help and a comfort to you all the days of your life.'

"Oh, how she trembled at this! 'Forgive me,' the widow said, 'but I fear what my neighbors will say, for they will not know you. What shall we tell them when they come to call, or if they should meet you down in the village?'

"'You need only remind them that I am your eldest son,' he said, as if these extraordinary circumstances warranted hardly any explanation a'tall.

"She yearned to make clear to him that the village knew another son for her eldest, that enough time had passed that folk seldom spoke or thought of her old tragedy and they wouldn't believe her if she told the truth, but fear held her tongue.

"'I'll sleep up above,' he went on. 'That was always my rightful place, wasn't it, Mother?'

"'Aye,' said she. 'That is where you would have slept, once you'd outgrown your cradle.'

"She cleared the table and swept the hearth, watching him as he rinsed his face and hands at the washstand in the firelight.

There was still a bit of a glow about him, and she wondered if it would fade with time or if the fairy sheen would always be about him, and if others could see it, too, and if so what would they think of him and how would they treat him. They would set him apart—after all even a man from three miles up the road would always be an outsider to them—but somehow she knew that no matter what looks or words he met with, he'd always have his dignity about him, his quiet confidence. The fairies had been cruel to him, but at least they'd given him that.

"He came to her then, and put his strong arms about her, and kissed her softly on the cheek before climbin' up to the loft. When she said her prayers, she thanked the Holy Father that her eldest, the true eldest, had been restored to her; though in her secret heart she was more than a little afraid that the Holy Father had had nothing to do with it, for the fairy lands lie well beyond the Christian realm, and her child would not answer to the name she had given him.

"In the morning she woke to find her little house still as ever, and her heart seized at the thought that the miracle of the previous evening had been nothing more than a dream. But when she dressed and went to the door, she found her lost son down in the field, mending an old stone wall in poor condition since before the passing of her husband; and when she looked back at her table, she found there a basket of eggs and a jug of fresh milk.

"The widow knew there was magic about him still, for as hard as he worked, he never tired. Whatever he did he made appear the easiest task in the world, even the hoeing and turf cutting that had all but broken her husband's back on the longest days. He'd the fairy airs about him, but unlike the fairies, he would labor cheerfully for hours. He sought no one's company but hers, and he never went down to the pub. But every so often, she would wake to find him comin' quietly down the ladder in the middle of the night, stealing out of the house only to return with the dawn, and she wondered if he'd left behind him a fairy wife.

"The months passed, and the woman received no word from her eldest son—her *second* son—on when he might be returning to take over the farm. This was both a relief and a worry. Her son sometimes referred to her other children, but he never wished aloud that he might meet them, and she wondered if he'd laid down some new piece of magic to prevent them returning.

"At last she received a letter, and another, and another. They were off in Dublin and London and America, busy livin' their lives. One or two sent her money, and her fairy son gazed coldly at the paper in her hand as if she had offended him. These moods of his soon passed, however, and he grew warm and affectionate towards her once again."

I glanced over and saw Paudie and Leo still hanging on her every word. "And in this way the widow lived out her life," Tess said, "her joy tempered by an uneasiness of which she could never speak."

She leaned back on the worn red upholstery and took a breath, just as Leo had done on my first night here. She'd finished her story, and I didn't know what to say, because any compliment I could have given her would have been inadequate.

"Tess, you're a marvel," Paudie declared, and Leo rushed to add, "She's the finest storyteller of the rising generation, so she is!"

Tess laughed. "Leo still thinks I'm sixteen years of age, instead of thirty-six."

Finally I said, "I thought he was going to suffocate her in her sleep, or something," and Tess gave me a weary glance as she lifted the water glass to her lips.

"It's the quiet drama I like best," she said. "No sword fights or shouting matches. There's greater tension just waitin' on the second shoe to drop. The vague unease, the waiting and wondering."

Well, I thought. *You've certainly lived it.*

Outside the rain had stopped, and the air was cold and fresh. Leo stumbled out the door of the pub, and Paudie held out a hand to steady him.

Of all the money that e'er I had, Leo sang in an astonishingly decent baritone, *I spent it in good company. And all the harm I've ever done, alas! it was to none but me. . . .*

For an awkward pause, Tess and I waited behind them, until they began to lumber together down the rain-slicked street. "You'll see her home, won't you?" Paudie called to me over his shoulder. "Good night, and God be with ye both."

Tess began walking in the other direction, and I fell into step beside her. "Where do you live, anyway?"

"Just around the corner from the youth center," she said. "We've a house in Ravens Row."

The walk passed much more quickly than I wanted it to. She stopped outside another whitewashed row house and reached into her bag for her keys. "So this is where you live," I said.

Tess nodded. "You'd better leave me here," she said. "It's late. Otherwise I'd invite you in for tea." She saw me looking up at the darkened windows and said, "The others will have gone to bed long before now."

"Did they come to the vigil?"

She was sorry I'd reminded her. "Everyone came," she said as she turned the key in the lock and the door swung open. "Thank you for seeing me home. What if I ring you tomorrow and we'll make a plan?"

"That would be great," I said, and I watched her weary smile recede into the darkness of the hallway before the door clicked shut.

On the walk back to the B and B, I forgot all about the dead boy, the dying blackbird, the name in Mrs. Keaveney's notebook. I saw Tess taking off her boots and arranging them neatly on a shoe rack beside the radiator, mounting the stairs and treading softly down the hall past the rooms of her sleeping housemates, the other Sisters of Compassion. I saw her closing her bedroom door behind her, taking off that shapeless gray sweater and folding it for another wear. I thought of her shrugging off her bra, her breasts round and lovely in the lamplight, and what a pity it was no one had ever touched them.

9

Dr. Kiely greeted me with a tight-lipped *I've-got-your-number* sort of look on her face. I'd been right to think this was the last time Síle and I would meet. Martin showed me to her room and shot me a wary look as he closed the door behind us.

Síle was standing at the window looking out at the rain. "I love it when it's squallin' like this," she said without turning around. "I wish we were out in it."

"Why would you want to be outside right now?" I asked as I propped my umbrella against the radiator and shrugged off my jacket. "I've just come out of it. It's awful."

She turned from the window then and smiled. "You didn't get wet enough. If you're out a while, there comes a point where it doesn't matter anymore how wet you are. You're soaked to your knickers and you're squelchin' in your boots and you turn your face up to the sky and you laugh and laugh because for once you feel at home in the world. Then you come in again, peel off all your sodden clothes, and put the kettle on. That's the most satisfying moment of the day, even better than the first sip of tea." She moved to the sink. "Speaking of which?"

I was looking around at the walls. She'd pinned a fresh series of drawings over the older ones. "Yes, please."

She dipped a spoon into a rusty tin of loose tea. We didn't speak as the kettle came to a boil. Síle just stood there looking at me, smiling that smile, as if she had something wonderful to surprise me with and she was holding out as long as she could. I thought back to our conversation on the beach, of the diary and everything she'd said. I didn't care if she was certifiably insane. I wanted her either way.

"What?" I said finally.

She reached for the kettle and poured the water into the teapot. "Have you ever been to India?"

I shook my head.

"You really should go."

"I will someday, if you think I'd like it." I took a seat on the unmade bed. "It just feels like such a cliché, going to India to do yoga and 'find yourself' and all that stuff."

"'Finding yourself,'" she said pensively. "I never understood that. Losing yourself, now, that's much more sensible."

"What do you mean?"

"Everything you *think* you are," she replied. "All your trappings. I went to India to forget all that."

"You sound like a guru." I laughed.

She glanced at me as she reached for the sugar bowl. "But I suppose you haven't come to that part in the diary yet."

"I haven't, no." I cleared my throat. "I wanted to ask you about those . . . passages . . . in between the actual entries."

She arched a brow, waiting for me to go on.

"Do you still believe the apparition told you those things? About other people?"

She sighed. "We can talk about all that once you've read it through."

I opened my mouth to tell her I probably wouldn't finish it in time, and to ask if I should mail it back, but something kept me from it. I wanted to give it back to her in person. I took the first sip of tea. "Is this from India?"

"It's chai," she said as she sat down beside me and brought the steaming mug to her lips. "The last of the stash I brought home with me."

"You'll just have to go back and get more."

Again we didn't speak. I inched closer, and she ran the back of her hand along the outside of my thigh. "Oh," she said, turning away from me, "I wanted to show you something." She picked up a heavy black book from her bedside table. "Do you remember how I was telling you about the Eve of Saint Agnes?"

I wanted to say *how could I forget?*, but I nodded.

"There's another window of Harry Clarke's I'd like to see someday. It's in Florida, believe it or not." Síle flipped toward the back of the book and pointed to the picture. "It's called the Geneva Window. It was meant to go into the International Labor Building at the League of Nations, but the Irish government decided not to send it." I breathed her in as she pointed to an illustration of a naked blonde dancing for a repulsive older man slobbing in an armchair. "The window reminded them that their parents had been obliged to fuck each other in order for them to be born, and no one was having *that*." She handed me the book so I could take a closer look at the pictures. "All the beautiful things we ever make," she sighed. "All that we make, they take it away from us."

"Who are you talking about?" I asked. "Your country, or yourself?"

She sighed as she took another sip of tea. "Both, maybe."

"You've got all your art around you here."

"Not for much longer, I'm afraid." She rose from the bed and paced toward her easel, as if she might have to physically defend it. "I told you I've been selling it, but I shouldn't be holding on to the money when Mam and Dad can't afford to keep me here."

"They don't *have* to keep you here," I said. "It's their choice to spend the money."

"Look." She pointed to the windows, where the sky was shifting like a sheet of mercury. "It's passing."

A shaft of sunlight cut a bright line along the dusty hardwood floor. "There's a girl here, Áine, who makes a game of swallowing things," she said. "Dr. Kiely doesn't know she still does it. She thinks Áine's given it up."

"What kind of things?"

"Buttons. Safety pins. Bits of blue yarn—always blue. She'll measure them before she swallows." Síle stood in the center of the room, looking pensively into her mug as if she were reading the dregs. "Nothing too sharp, of course. She isn't as mad as that," Síle said softly. "We're none of us here mad as that."

I put down my tea and went to her. "I wish you wouldn't talk about yourself that way."

"I heard of a girl once who chewed on glass," she said.

I laid my hands on her arms, my arms like a set of parentheses, making her the exception. You'd think I'd want someone "normal," someone who offered everything expected of her, but I'd *had* that. I'd had it and left it more times than I could count. "I don't believe it," I said.

"You'd believe a lot of things, if you'd seen some of what I've seen," she answered, and we just looked at each other. A thought surfaced, of her and Declan, and I brushed it aside. I would never ask her about that.

In another minute, the whole room was flooded with light.

That dreaminess came over her again, and I watched her lie down on the floor, close her eyes against the sunshine, and hold out her hand to me.

I got down beside her, brushing away a few dust bunnies before I let my head rest on the scuffed old floorboards.

"Now," she said, "tell me all that you've been up to in Ballymorris."

I folded my arm behind my head and looked at a crack in the ceiling. "Not a whole lot."

"Whom have you met?"

"Well, Tess, of course. And I've been spending most evenings with Paudie and Leo."

"Ah, they're right auld gents. Who else?"

"Do you remember the old woman who owns the truck of religious knickknacks up on the hill? I saw her again yesterday."

"Mag O'Grady?" Síle laughed. "She's the best crack you'll find in Ballymorris. She bought that truck whilst we were still havin' the visions. She must be near on a hundred by now. I remember people talking years ago about what she was like when she was young. They said she was the prettiest girl in the county."

"Who's 'they'? I can't imagine she has any contemporaries left."

"You'd still find one or two. They said if we'd a pageant like they have down in Kerry, she'd have won it."

"There's something else," I said. "A boy committed suicide the other day. They held a vigil in the park last night."

"A boy Tess knew?"

"Yes. She worked with him. And I . . . I met him, briefly, up on the hill."

She gave me a sideways look. "What was he doing up there, did he say?"

"He didn't, no." I cleared my throat. "Something wasn't right, but what could I do?" It only hit me then: I *should* have said something to Tess. The boy was obviously troubled, and even sending her a short text message would've been more useful than brushing it off. How many people had I ever known who were better off for knowing *me*?

No one. Certainly not Mallory.

"I'm sorry," Síle said after a while, like she was giving me time again to let my thoughts play out. "Will you tell Tess I was askin' for her?"

"I'll tell her." I paused. "Síle? Can I ask you something?"

She smiled as if her name in my mouth gave her physical pleasure. "Course you can."

"You said you saw her—the apparition—in a dream, and that you heard her voice in your head other times, telling you things you couldn't have known otherwise." Something in me didn't want to ask, but I knew I had to. "Did you ever see her—actually see her, I mean, not like that time you dreamed about walking down to the holy well—did you see her anywhere else apart from the grotto?" What if you ran into the Blessed Virgin Mary somewhere—like trying on a blue silk scarf at a department store, or giving her seat to a white-haired man with a cane on a crowded subway car—and she was dressed like an ordinary woman, and you never knew it was her?

"I did see Her other places," she said quietly, and I couldn't tell what she was feeling. "You'll come to that part."

I didn't know what more to say. I watched Síle's eyes trace that crack in the ceiling as if she'd never seen it before. "How long before you leave?" she asked.

I tried to laugh. "Do you want to get rid of me?"

She closed her eyes and smiled. The light was still perfect. "I never want to be rid of you," she said, and when I felt the thrill, I couldn't give in to it.

"You don't know me," I said quietly.

She glanced at me. "You haven't killed anybody, have you?"

I looked back at the ceiling. "No."

"Then it isn't as bad as you think."

I believed her. I wanted her to be right.

Afterward I couldn't say if I'd reached for her hand, or she'd reached for mine, but we lay like that for what felt like an hour, until a cloud came along and blotted out the light again. She ran her forefinger up and down the inside of my arm and murmured, "This will be the last time I see you."

"It won't be. I promise."

"Aren't you going home soon?"

"I can stay longer."

"They won't let you come again. You know they won't."

"Síle," I said gently, "you can leave. You just have to tell them what they want to hear—pretend to be their idea of 'normal.' You said so yourself."

She shook her head, but she spoke breathlessly and her eyes were shining. "It isn't as easy as that."

I propped myself up on my elbow. "Says who?"

I watched her smile fade by degrees. "You don't really want me," she said. "You'd see soon enough, if you could see me out of here."

I sat up and reached for her. "That's not true, Síle!" I should have kept talking, said something reassuring, but I'd never been any good at that sort of thing.

She didn't respond to my touch, and I could tell from how she stared at the ceiling that she was somewhere else. "The drugs they put me on left me so sleepy, and one day I remember waking up to their voices down in the sitting room. My sister was there. I went to the head of the stairs and listened. 'You haven't a choice,' Orla said. 'She hasn't left you any choice.'

"'Ah, now,' our dad said to her. 'She can't help it, poor lamb.'

"'You *always* say that, Dad,' she said. No one said anything for a minute, and then she went on: 'You say it, and she feeds on it. You won't admit it to yourselves, but you know she does. She's even sicker than you think.' They didn't say anything to that, but I knew that if they'd thought she was only bein' hurtful, they'd have told her so." Síle closed her eyes. This was the saddest I'd ever seen her. "She said one thing more. She said, 'It's *us* who've had to suffer through this all these years. Not her.'"

"You aren't sick," I told her, and she gave me a wan smile in place of an answer.

We were interrupted by a timid tapping from the hallway. I rose from the floor with a grunt. "You're wrong, in what you said before," I said as Martin opened the door. "You're right about a lot of things, Síle—but you're wrong about that."

She sprang to her feet, lithe as a cat, but we didn't touch or speak. The attendant stood in the doorway, silent and awkward, as I shrugged on my jacket and stepped into my boots.

"Careful, now," Síle said, smiling again, as the attendant drew the door shut between us. "I'll make you prove it."

I was almost out the front door when the girl appeared, and I recognized her from the charcoal sketches as soon as I saw her eyes. Síle hadn't accentuated their prominence, she'd *captured* it, and I thought again of how unfair was Orla's assessment of her talent.

"Now, Áine," Martin said in a firm and mildly patronizing tone I hadn't heard him use before, "you know you're not to be out wandering the halls at this time of the afternoon."

The girl didn't acknowledge Martin in any way; she just kept looking at me with her pale frog eyes, and though I tried not to look, I couldn't help noticing her nipples poking through the thin fabric of her blouse. The top buttons were undone past the point of decency, and she definitely wasn't wearing a bra. There was a strange smell about her, too, floral but stale, like a bowl of pot-pourri left to gather dust.

"Áine?" Martin was saying. "What have you got there?" He reached for her fist and pried gently at her fingers. "Sorry, but it'd be better if you left now," he said over his shoulder. "She forgets what she's meant to be doing if someone new happens to be about. Isn't that so, Áine?"

I turned to go, but the girl opened her hand and offered me what she'd been hiding. It was a tiny ball of turquoise-colored yarn, the end trailing between her long white fingers. A smile spread slowly across her face, soft and sinister at the same time, and when she spoke her voice was low and honeyed. "You liked it, didn't you?"

I stiffened. "What is she talking about?"

Martin sighed as he tucked the yarn in the pocket of his scrubs. "Even she couldn't tell you what she's on about most of the time." He opened the door wide and waved me out. "Safe travels, mate."

You'd hardly notice from one visit to the next, but when I think back on it now I see how Her looks have changed. When She'd first appeared to us there'd never be any mistaking Her for an ordinary woman. There wasn't the mark of any earthly care about Her, and the glow on Her would've lit up the night for miles.

Then, slowly, She became real to me. When She took my hand I could feel it was chapped, there were faint lines around Her eyes and when She took off Her mantle I saw Her long dark hair was lightly threaded with grey.

Finally I said,—You look different, Mother, and She smiled as if She'd been expecting me to say so.

—As we've listened and shared with one another over these past months, I have become a friend to you, have I not?

—Aye, Mother. You've been a truer friend to me than anyone else ever has.

She smiled.—Someday you will have friends who will see you for all that you are. Shall I answer your question?

—Please, Mother.

—My Son did not come into this world to be worshipped as a god, She said.—That is the old way. He came to bring pure love and joy to the world, and to show the people a path to peace even if they chose at first not to follow it. This is My work here, Síle—to correct the mistakes and misapprehensions of the men who have called themselves Christians. At other times, in other places, be it near to here or on the far side of the world, I have walked among the people. I have seen their greed, watched them rage at their Creator when the consequences were made manifest. I have trod their streets, cold and hungry and alone, and I have begged for aid. I heard all of their prayers but they gave Me nothing in return.

—No one? I asked. I couldn't believe it.

—They have forgotten the message and the mission of My only Son. There is so little compassion and love left in this world, Síle! Do you not see it?

—I see it, Mother. How can I help You? How will I know what to say?

—You need only open your mouth, my dear child. The Holy Spirit will take care of the rest.

Then I asked Our Lady if the Devil was real.—When you were small, She said,—and you went down in the night for a drink of water, did you ever fear something was behind you as you went up the stairs again in the dark?

I told her I had.

—And do you believe there was anyone there?

I said no, I didn't really think so.

—When you've done wrong, She said,—isn't it easier to say that someone else put the idea in your head? That you were tempted to it?

—Then where do the bad thoughts come from, Mother?

—They need not belong to you. Do you see?

I told her I was trying to.

—Always you must live by the Word. Not as men have written it, for not everything they have written was put down rightly, but as it is written on your heart.

And I said,—How can I trust what's written on my heart, when Yours is the only heart that's pure?

She didn't answer me, and I can't remember how She took Her leave; only that I was sitting alone on the bench overlooking the town as if She'd never been there at all.

I showered and called Leo to make plans for the evening, and he asked if I'd been to the local chipper yet. "Ya can't go home to America without having a meal at McGrory's takeaway," he said. "It's a . . . whaddaya call it . . . an *institution*. Get us some fried cod with chips, and we'll have a nice quiet night, maybe find something good on the telly. Paudie's right, y'know—we've been spending too much time at the pub. If I'm not careful, I'll be drinkin' away me pension." I hadn't seen him pay for a single round in the week we'd been meeting at Napper Tandy's, but I humored him.

I passed the grocery store on my way to McGrory's, eyes on

the sidewalk, replaying the best parts of my afternoon with Síle. I shook myself out of it when I heard someone call my name, and again, and then a third time. I turned and found a middle-aged woman hurrying up the sidewalk in the twilight. "It *is* you, isn't it?"

I nodded. "And you're Mrs. Gallagher?"

She blinked. "How did you know?"

"You look like Síle," I replied. You could see that Mrs. Gallagher had been very pretty once. I wondered if Síle would let her hair go silver someday, instead of dyeing it. "Or, rather, Síle looks like you."

She wore a brown duffel coat and a pink knit hat. "Aye, well," she replied, clasping her chapped and chubby hands in front of her as if she didn't know what else to do with them. "That's very kind of you to say." She hesitated. "We've met before, of course. You were only a lad."

I cleared my throat. "I take it you've been talking to Orla?"

"Oh? Oh, yes, right, well." I saw now where Orla got her nervous energy. "I was wondering if I might ask you a favor," she said, "only it isn't easy for me to come right out and say these things sometimes . . ."

No need to make this conversation any more awkward than it already was. "You don't want me to speak to Síle again, is that it?"

She nodded, relieved I'd made it easier for her. "Oh, I hope you won't take offense. You seem like a very nice young man, and Orla has spoken highly of you, but you do see that it isn't good for Síle to be having visitors like you."

"What do you mean by 'visitors like me'?"

"Ardmeen is the best place for her," Mrs. Gallagher went on. "Perhaps someday she'll be well enough, but for now, it's the only place for her. You *do* see that, don't you?"

"I'm not sure I do," I replied, as gently as I could. "You go to visit her, and you see your sick daughter. I go there, and I see a woman who is capable of moving through the world on her own."

She shook her head sadly. "That's only how it seems to someone who doesn't know her. But, oh, how I wish that were true. Oh, how I wish you were right."

I was tired and longing for dinner, and the sooner I got to McGrory's, the quicker Leo and I could sit down to eat. There wasn't any sense arguing with the woman. "I'm running out of time in my vacation," I said. "I don't know that I would've been able to see Síle again at any rate."

"Ah," she said, pleased by my answer but trying not to show it. "I see. And you . . . you won't write that article, will you? It's only that it's so far in the past now, and none of us can see what good could come of it."

"No," I said tiredly. "I won't write the article."

Mrs. Gallagher leaned forward and clasped my hand. "Thank you. Thank you, and God bless you."

I wished her good night and turned for McGrory's takeaway. I'd told her everything she'd wanted to hear, intending none of it, but with the way things were going, I'd be keeping my word on every point.

When the old man came to the door, his eyes lit up at the sight of the takeout. A grease stain was already spreading across the bottom of the brown paper bag.

"Are Brona and Paudie coming over?" I asked as Leo showed me through the darkened hallway into his sitting room, where the television was already tuned to a sitcom with a bunch of priests in it. "I can go back for more if need be."

Eagerly Leo drew the food cartons out of the bag, breathing in the scent of hot battered cod with eyes rolled heavenward. "Paudie might. But Brona has agreed never to set foot in this house again."

I sat down in the armchair beside him, laughing as I popped open a can of Coke. "That's rather melodramatic, wouldn't you say?"

Leo was already tucking into his meal, the grease glistening along his lower lip. "Not a'tall," he said through a mouthful of cod. "She used to come in here and fret about all the dust gatherin' in the corners. She'd go round the house brandishin' me mother's broom instead of sittin' down for a cuppa tea like a good guest, so one day I said to her, 'Listen, Brona, let's just meet at the pub from now on. 'Twill be pleasanter for the both of us.' Some people need a tidy house, but I was never one o' them."

I could see where Brona was coming from. The smell of mildew was more pronounced in this dark little house than anyplace else I'd been. It was everywhere, so they never smelled it. "You're the quintessential Irish bachelor, Leo. You really don't miss having a woman around? Not having to wash your own dishes is worth getting nagged sometimes. Especially after you've left a big pile of them sitting in the sink for a week."

Leo shot me a sly look as he dipped a french fry into a little plastic container of mayonnaise. "Speakin' from experience, are ya?"

I stared at the dirty carpet, a piece of steaming battered cod falling apart between my fingers, and nodded. "It's like the difference between a home-cooked meal and going without dinner. When she's there, you're warm and full. When she's not, it's still your home, but it's a lot less homelike."

Leo licked his lips as he bent for another bite. "Well, me lad, when you've gone to bed without supper all the days of your life, you can't say you miss it."

I thought of the night I knew I couldn't marry Laurel. *You get a little bit smug,* she'd said. *When you meet men your age who are going bald. I can see it on your face, and I have to hope they can't see it, too.* She was right, of course. But the prospect of waking up next to that much honesty every morning for the next fifty years left me limp as a noodle. I wanted to spend every night from now on in front of Leo's television in this Podunk town three thousand miles from home—anything to avoid going back to that empty apartment.

For a while, we absorbed ourselves in the television. Three priests were playing cards at a table, and another priest, wild haired and decrepit, sat in the corner shouting "WHAT?" every time someone asked him a question. Leo finished his fish and chips, drew out his pouch of Drum, pushed the takeout cartons and crumpled grease paper out of the way on the TV tray, and began to roll a cigarette. *He gets a kind of waxy buildup in his ears, and then we have to syringe them. It's not very nice.*

It's great, though, in a way, said the second priest. *We're never short of candles.*

Laurel would be gone, but everything she'd felt would linger there, as if her anger and her disappointment could gather itself inside the walls and press them closer, inch by inch. Finally I spoke, but only because I thought it might ease the feeling: "She won't be there when I get back."

I watched the corner of the old man's mouth twist into a smirk. "Ah," he said as he licked the paper, "and this time the dishes will."

I shook my head. "No. She'll do them before she leaves, knowing her."

Leo clucked his tongue and lit his cigarette. "And you'd let a woman like that go?"

I studied one of his dribbly discolored earlobes, and found it quite impossible to imagine someone sucking on it. How could a man like Leo get by without sex? Brona had told me he'd never married. I knew he didn't have a computer, it seemed just as unlikely there were any porn channels on Irish television, and it wasn't as if there were any twinkly-eyed widows "calling round" to cook for him. The women in this town looked every bit as sexless as the Blessed Virgin herself.

"Maybe I'm like you, Leo. Maybe I'm built for the solitary life."

He must have managed somehow. People take their comfort where they can find it, after all, and you can have no idea of the source. *Sure, we're all strangers in the end.*

"The solitary life has its consolations," the old man replied as he sighed out a stream of smoke into the dank and drafty air. "But that being said, I'd never recommend it."

Today felt like an ordinary Saturday, to start with. This time no one told me otherwise, no one whispered in my ear—and how I wish She had.

I was on my bed reading a book. Orla had been out for hours but I wasn't thinking about her, I was reading about Padre Pio and the one time when his student was reading a letter he'd sent her, and how the wind carried it out of her hands and she ran chasing it for miles; and finally it landed flat on a rock as if someone had pinned it there. Then the next day he said to her, "Be careful of the wind, if I hadn't put my foot on that letter you'd have lost it."

I wanted to sit and drink in the magic of that story. But the door banged on its hinges as my sister came into the room we shared, eyes blazing, and grabbed me off the bed by the collar. She turned me to face her and hit me clean across the face.—You fucked him, didn't you! You laid down on the ground and let him put his prick in you!

At first I didn't even think to deny it, I just stared at her because it was all too mad, but she took my silence for an admission of guilt, and raised her hand to me and brought it down again and again.

—No, I said, or tried to.—I didn't. I didn't, and from somewhere miles away I heard Mam calling,—Orla! Orla, please!

—You did! You did! Orla screamed, and hit me again. Her fury had turned her into someone else, someone with a splotched red face and wild soulless eyes and a murderous voice I hope I never again hear the like of.—He fucked you, and you let him. You . . . miserable . . . little . . . HOOR . . . always . . . taking . . . what's . . . mine . . . everything! . . . everything!

—I didn't! I said again, and it stung when she struck me, but I knew she'd have to stop soon, and I'd feel better then. All I could think was Why, why, why would he say it when it wasn't true?

At last Dad and Mam came into the room and they pulled her off of me, and for a time we each of us lay crumpled on the beds or the chair or the floor, spent and panting and heartbroken.—Are you hurt? Dad asked finally, and Mam fell into tears. I told him I was fine but Orla went on raging at me with her eyes. Her words hung over our heads in the silence. She'd never take them back, they'd haunt us all forever.

The next day was May Day, the procession from the hill before Father Dowd's special Mass at the holy well. I told Mam and Dad I didn't want to go, and they didn't press me. They told Father Dowd I was sick and Tess led the procession by herself.

I laid in bed awhile trying to listen through the silence, but no one was there. Then I dressed and went up to the hill. When I looked down toward Rathgar I could see them shuffling down the boreen through Jim Boyne's pastures, people I knew and people I didn't, though I couldn't tell them apart from that distance. There were two hundred at least.

It was a beautiful day, but how could I enjoy it? I needed to be alone but Declan was there sitting on the bench where he'd carved their initials, smoking a cigarette, looking out over the town.

I sat down beside him.—Why did you tell her . . . why'd you tell her we'd . . .

—I didn't tell her anything, Síle, Declan said wearily.—She got it into her head that we'd done it, and after that there was no tellin' her otherwise.

—What did you say to make her think it?

—Nothing, he said.—Nothing. We had a row and she leapt to the worst.

—It isn't fair, I said.—She'll never believe us.

—I'm sorry, Síle. I wish it hadn't happened.

He laid his arm round my shoulders and for a minute we sat there on the bench, not saying anything.

—It's over now, he said finally.—Orla and me, we're finished. He kicked at pebbles in the dirt.—It's for the best though.

—Since you're leaving?

He nodded.—I leave this Thursday week.

I wanted to ask him how he'd got the money for his ticket, but I didn't.—Will you be in Australia for a long time?

—I will, he said, and let out a mad laugh.—I'm never coming back.

—What about your mam?

—When I get settled in a good job I'll send for her and she can come and live with me. Declan got this hard look on his face, the way he did whenever Father Dowd was there.—I'm never comin' back here, Síle. Never.

—You hate it that much? Living in Ballymorris?

—*Your sister was never going to leave. She'll find a husband and have a litter of kids. She'll live out her life in this horrible place.*

—*It's not so bad, I said.*—*Maybe you'll see it differently if you come back to visit.*

Declan turned to me then, and it was like he was seeing me for the first time.—*Sweet Síle, he said, and he began to stroke my hair back from my forehead.*—*I won't miss much about this place, but I will miss you.*

—*And I'll miss you sharing your chocs with me, I said.*

He kept touching me.—*You're a lovely girl, you know that?*

—*You make me feel as if I were, looking at me like that. I felt something strange welling up in the pit of my stomach.*

—*You are, he whispered.*—*You are.*

That's how we came to do the thing we were accused of, on the hill above the grotto where no one could see. He took me by the hand and led me up, laid me down, and pulled off my knickers, and it happened just as Orla said. And Our Lady's words rang out in my mind . . . I'm always with you, Síle, even when you can't see Me . . . and I felt sick all over as Declan found a new place inside me, dark and deep. He fell onto me and wept into my hair,—*I wanted this, I wanted this, God help me, I wanted it, and all I could think was why didn't he tell me it would hurt?*

Afterwards he said we should each go down alone, so he left me in the grass, and I lay there in a daze for a long time looking up at the blue sky and the bright clouds. I wasn't pure anymore. Our Lady would never come to me again.

10

NOVEMBER 14

In the morning I texted Tess to remind her I'd be leaving in two days, and she replied within seconds. *We can go for a walk if you like. Have you been to Saint Brigid's Well? Then maybe we can come back by the pilgrims' route, up to the grotto.*

I told her I was up for it, and turned to my breakfast. I'd reached the point in Síle's diary where I didn't really want to read any farther, but it wasn't as if putting it away had ever been an option. Another of those nearly impenetrable passages went on for a dozen pages—this one about a son who fantasized about suffocating his mother with a pillow, as best I could make out—and then I came to the next entry.

> *I hadn't gone up to the hill in a full week. It was over, all the wondrous mystery of it had finished forever through our own stupidity.*
>
> *I was in our room reading when She came to me. Orla had*

gone out with her new friends. The Blessed Mother was so bright
and I was so full of shame that I couldn't bear to look at Her.

—Why do you turn away from Me, child?

—I'm ashamed, I said through my hands.—Ashamed of
what I've done.

—I know what you've done, She said, but Her voice was
gentle and sweet.

—I've sinned, I said, and I hid my face in my hands.—I've
sinned and she'll never forgive me. You'll never forgive me.

She lifted my chin with Her finger and my hands fell away
again as I rose to face Her.—Have you, now? She said softly.—
Show Me. Show Me what you'd do, if you had it all to do over
again.

In a flash She was gone and I was back on the hill in the
warm spring sunshine, Declan sitting beside me on the bench,
and this part of me sat quietly inside of myself whilst the rest of
me went on saying the words just as I'd spoken them the first
time. Why did you tell her. She'll never believe us.

Inside I waited and listened, waited until Declan said the
words you're a lovely girl, you are, you are. It was like moving
through honey to draw back when he touched me, to rise from that
bench, but I did rise.—No, I said.—It isn't right, and I turned
from him and ran down the hill, and I heard the crunch of my
runners on the gravel echoing in the space between then and
now, done and undone.

The day melted away again, I was back at home on my bed,
and there She was before me.—Good girl, Síle. I knew you'd
make it right.

I opened my mouth, but at first I didn't know how to ask
what I was so desperate to know.

The way Our Lady smiled then, it reminded me of the beginning, only there was just myself and Tess left now.—You were

made by God to wander the world, high and low, bright and dark, and bring the Light, God's light, to every man, woman, and child you encounter. To walk in the joy of Creation, and to share in that joy.

And I said,—That's lovely, Mother. Thank you. I . . .

—What is it, child?

—Have I . . . I hardly dared to ask.—Have I undone it?

The Blessed Mother nodded and kissed me on my forehead. She'd never kissed me before, and how it thrilled me. And the relief of it, I'd never in a million years be able to describe the relief.

A half hour later I knocked on the door of the youth center, and Tess emerged in a slouchy hat, a crimson rain jacket and well-worn hiking boots. "This way," she said, and a couple minutes later, we were walking down a muddy lane between two hedge-rows, as if the town were even smaller than I'd thought.

"How are you feeling today?" I asked.

"It's becoming more real to me," she sighed. "It felt so good to sit and chat with you the other night—to forget for a while." She hopped nimbly over a puddle in the lane. "I wish you had more time. I'm afraid I'm bound to be terrible company today, but it wouldn't have felt right not to see you before you go."

"Well, I'm glad we're doing this. It's good to see you." I watched her cast half a smile into the gloomy sky. "Besides, I haven't gotten any exercise all week."

"You'll have it today," she replied. "It's just under ten miles to the well and back."

We walked in silence for a minute or two. There weren't any houses beyond the hedgerows now, just cows grazing in green fields. I waited for Tess to speak again.

"I wasn't sure I was going to tell you any more," she said finally.

"Did you listen to the tapes? I was going to ask you the other night, and then I didn't." She glanced over at me, and I nodded. "I don't remember what I said."

"Way more than you told *me*," I said teasingly.

She hesitated. "Tell me what I said."

"You told Father Dowd the apparition showed you her heart."

For the next few paces, Tess closed her eyes. "There's a bluebell wood not far from here," she said as we kept walking. "If you'd come in the spring, I'd have taken you there."

"Maybe next time," I said.

She opened her eyes and smiled a little. "Just don't let it be another twenty-five years, all right?"

I smiled back. "I promise."

"Orla and I used to spend all afternoon there in the summer holidays sometimes, when the weather was nice."

"All afternoon?"

"All afternoon," she sighed. "Just talking and making flower chains."

"What did you talk about?"

She smiled sadly. "Boys, mostly."

"You don't miss it?"

"What?" Tess gave me the closest thing to a laugh. "Talking about boys?"

"I've always been curious about the whole celibacy thing."

She seemed amused. "Why?"

"I could never go the rest of my life without . . ." I remembered who I was talking to, and fell silent.

"You don't understand it because it's not your calling," Tess replied.

"You never wanted a partner, though? Kids?"

"Everyone wants those things at some point in their lives. The younger priests, they'll even admit as much to the congregation because they understand it's important for people to see we're as human as they are."

"If you want marriage and children, though, how does that jive with being 'called'?"

Tess paused to formulate her answer. "It's like going to a place on holiday, falling in love with it and wishing you could live there for always," she said gently. "But you come home again because it's where you belong."

"I don't believe that," I said. "I think we can 'belong' wherever we want to be."

Tess looked at me. "So you'd say you belong in New York?"

I could tell by her face that my face had betrayed me. I'd lived there all my adult life—traveled to warmer, greener, sunnier places I hadn't wanted to leave—and yet I'd never truly given it any thought.

We came to a turnoff. A wooden signpost for ST. BRIGID'S HOLY WELL pointed right, and I followed her onto a track even muddier than the first. Tess took a breath, looked as if she were about to speak, and closed her mouth again. I waited. Finally she said, "You said you'd spoken to Orla."

"Yes. I've talked with her a couple of times now."

"And she said she didn't believe she saw it. That she only convinced herself to hide Síle's illness."

"It doesn't make sense," I said. "If you all saw it, then how come only one of you is in a home?"

Tess gave me an unreadable look—or, rather, there were so many emotions vying for control of her face that I couldn't tell which would win. "That might be the one thing you came here to find out." It was the only thing she'd ever said that didn't ring true.

Lightly she ran her fingertips along the dull green leaves in the hedge. "There's loads of fuchsia here in the summertime," she murmured, and again we walked in silence for a bit. "Seeing as we're headed to her well, would you like to hear about Saint Brigid?"

"Sure," I said.

"There's a legend says that when she was a child, a host of angels carried her, asleep and dreaming, over the sea and back in time to witness the birth of Christ."

"That's a nice story."

"Isn't it? There's such a depth and richness to the history of our Church that most people never explore," she said. "So many nooks and corridors that lead you to something obscure and wonderful."

"I never looked at it that way." I smiled. "But you know what I think of the Church. Dusty and humorless and completely out of touch."

"Aye," she said earnestly, "but it doesn't have to be that. There's a beautiful painting in the National Gallery of Scotland by an artist called John Duncan. He painted two angels carrying Saint Brigid across the sea, with seagulls and seals bobbing in their wake. The angels have wings colored like the sunset, and if you look closely you can see their robes are embroidered with scenes from the Old Testament." She sighed. "I went to Edinburgh when I was nineteen, and I just stood and looked at that painting for what felt like all afternoon."

"You sound like Síle," I said. "Painting pictures with words."

Beyond the hedge, sheep were nibbling on weeds growing among the ruins of an old stone farmhouse. "You've been spending a lot of time with her," Tess remarked.

"I wouldn't say 'a lot.'"

"But you've been to see her several times."

I nodded. "She said to tell you she was asking for you."

"And you said she's doing well?"

"Very well," I said. "She draws and paints all day and goes for walks by the sea."

"That sounds like a good life," Tess replied. If anyone else had said so, it would've sounded sarcastic.

"If you forget she isn't allowed to leave."

Tess glanced at me sidewise. "She's bewitched you."

I laughed a bit too merrily. I didn't want her thinking of that fossil on the beach. "Síle bewitches everybody, doesn't she?"

"I liked her," she said. "I always liked her, even when Orla didn't want me to."

At first I didn't reply—*what if she shuts down on me?*—but in the end, my curiosity won out. "She told me you used to go up to the grotto alone, without telling anyone."

Tess looked at me. She didn't answer; she didn't have to.

The hedge had given way to a low wall, the rough stones mottled with lichen. "You never told that to Father Dowd, did you?"

"I *couldn't* tell him, because then he'd have to know what was said, and if I'd told him the truth . . ." She drew a shaky breath. "I've never told anyone what she said to me those days I went up alone."

"You can tell me."

She gave me a weary smile. "Confidin' in a journalist? Even I'm not as foolish as that."

"I'm not a journalist right now. I even left my recorder at the B and B." I reached out and squeezed her shoulder. "Look, Tess: I know we don't know each other as well as it maybe feels like we do, but I'm not going to spend the rest of my time here driving around looking at castles and drinking in pubs. Not if I thought I might be of some use to you."

I watched her blush. "That's very kind of you."

"Are you sure you're okay?"

This time she didn't answer right away, as if this were the first time she'd actually stopped to consider how she felt. "I failed him," she said at last, and when she turned to me, her eyes were glistening with unshed tears.

"C'mere," I said, and we stopped walking. I put my arms around her, and she laid her cheek on my chest. "It's okay, Tess. You didn't fail anybody."

"You don't know," she said as she wept. "You don't know."

I could have texted you. I could have told you I'd met the kid and something wasn't right. "That's it," I said softly, and stroked her head through her woolen cap. Her hair smelled clean, the scent something sweet and unidentifiable. "Do you want to talk about Owen?"

She shook her head against my chest.

"Tell me," I said. "Let me listen." *He was definitely listening to something. But you won't tell her that, will you?*

For a while Tess could only cry. "He was in so much pain," she murmured. "It didn't matter that he'd family and friends. He was completely alone. He wasn't really, but he felt it, and it got to the point it was all he knew. I told his parents he needed to see someone, and they wouldn't have it, they didn't listen. I went to them again and again, and it did no good. Now I don't even know how to speak to them. I can't *look* at them. I'm so . . . I'm so . . ."

"You can tell me," I said.

She broke from me, gently, and looked me in the eye. "I'm so *angry*. But it . . . it goes beyond anger."

"You did everything you could. You know that, right?" *I could have told you.*

Tess hesitated for a second before unzipping her jacket and pulling something out of the inside pocket: a piece of notebook paper, folded and crumpled. Silently she offered it to me, and I unfolded it to find a hasty boyish scrawl in red ink.

Dear Tess

I don't have a choice, I don't really. They tell us we always have one, that we can grow up to be who-ever we like, but you know as well as I do what a lie that is.

I'm writing this not only to say I'm sorry but be-cause She told me to. She says to say She'll go on waiting for however long you need.

When Ciara comes to see you tell her I love her and I'm sorry I never said it.

Thank you for all you've done for me, Tess. You're the best of everyone.

Owen.

Her cheeks were blotchy, her eyes desolate. "He left it on my desk."

"Did you show this to his parents?"

She sighed. "How could I?"

"I don't know what to say," I said, because there was no way I was going to share what I was actually thinking: *I'm off the hook.* And then: *You won't show it to his parents and you showed it to me.* "Do you think he really saw her?"

She looked down, staring through the muddy ground. "I don't know."

"It isn't your fault, Tess. No matter what, you did your best." It hit me then, that when people talked of her impossible goodness, it wasn't idle flattery. They called her a saint because they expected so much more of her than they could anyone else, and in turn she demanded it of herself. Or maybe it was the other way around. "Those kids know they can come to you when they've got something on their minds. Who do *you* go to?"

We walked in silence for a minute. "I don't," she said finally. "I can't."

"You can. You *have* to. You're no good to anyone else if you don't take care of yourself first."

She gave me another sideways look. "Who do *you* talk to?"

I didn't answer right away. "I have a few good friends."

"In New York?"

I nodded, but it didn't sit easy with me—having to lie to her, to leave so many things out. Andy didn't get why I wanted to write this story, I hadn't talked to my best friend from college in nearly four years, and I fully expected every friend Laurel and I had in common to side with her. Did I know *anyone* who would hear about my going for a hike with a nun—not to mention *kissing* a nun, albeit long before she became a nun—and not laugh?

"And you . . . tell them everything?" she asked.

"Define 'everything,'" I said, and she smiled. A bit later, she lifted a finger to indicate the next turnoff. Tess hopped up onto a stile beside a rusty gate, sat on the old stone wall, and swung her legs over. "We're almost there," she said as I climbed over after her. I looked behind us and saw a small parking lot at the end of a gravel track. All along we'd been closer to the main road than I'd thought.

A minute or two later, we arrived at the well, set into a hillock and flanked by thorny trees with bits of faded cloth tied to the branches. A circular ledge enclosed the well itself, and different kinds of ferns and mosses grew out of the old masonry. The water was thick with algae, and from the dimmest corner came the listless gurgling of the old spring.

"Here it is," Tess said softly. "The water that worked the only miracle I've ever seen with my own two eyes."

"It's a charming spot," I replied, and we stood there quietly as if we were back in the church.

"I'm ready," she said finally. I let her words hang between us for a minute, in case they didn't mean what I wanted them to mean. "I need this," she murmured, almost to herself. "All along, I've needed this. And it might as well be here."

"Okay," I said.

Tess took a seat on the ledge and drew a deep breath as I sat down beside her. "When you hear talk of other apparitions, at Knock or Medjugorje," she began, "the people who've seen it believe they've been blessed. We weren't blessed. I wasn't blessed. That much I know for certain."

"I don't understand. I thought you *were* blessed. I thought that was why you became a nun."

"No," she said. "No."

I don't know why it hadn't occurred to me sooner: "When you spoke of the apparition, you said *it*, not *she*." *If you really think it was the Blessed Virgin Mary they saw up there, then you're every bit as daft as we took you for.*

Tess gave me one of those eloquent looks.

"Start at the beginning," I said. "Tell me the little things—the details. Tell me how you felt when she showed you her heart."

When Tess regarded me then, her gaze bright and penetrating despite her sadness, I marveled that she couldn't see clear through me. "This isn't about the story anymore, is it?" she asked.

I smiled a little. "I don't know if it was ever about the story."

She nodded, as if she'd suspected as much from the very start.

"You told Father Dowd she said it was easier for you to show compassion to people on the other side of the world than to the people you saw every day."

Tess sighed. "And every time she came and spoke to me, aye, it was a variation on that."

"How did you feel?" I asked. "When she came and you realized what was happening, and she spoke to you, how did she make you feel?"

"It was queer. Very queer. I've never known a feeling like it before or since. I felt weightless, almost like I was becoming a part of the light that shone out of her and through her. Almost as if there wasn't any 'me' anymore."

"And how did you feel then? Did you panic?"

She smiled. "Not at all. It was the loveliest feeling I'd ever known."

"To feel like you were dissolving? Really?"

"I felt pure. For the first time in my life, I knew what that meant."

"Wow," I said. What she'd said was either inspiring or insane. I put off deciding which.

"In those first few weeks, it was very difficult to go back to ordinary life—what I'd begun to see as the impurity all around me. The filthy world—the filthy relations between men and women— all the filthy thoughts in my own head."

"Tess," I said, "I've never known anyone so hard on herself." *You've never had a filthy thought in all your life.*

She gave me a helpless look. "I don't know any other way. But I . . . let me go on, please. I need to tell you everything."

"All right," I said. "What did she say when she went away? Did she say she'd come again? And physically—did she just kind of . . . fade out?"

"She didn't fade, exactly. She was there and then she wasn't, and all the light winked out with her. It was very disorientating at first, but over time, we got used to it." Tess turned in her seat and ran her hand along the ferns growing inside the well. "She did say good-bye, in a sense—she'd raise her hand in a blessing. She didn't have to tell us she'd come back. We just knew we'd see her again."

"So that's the way it went, the first few times you saw her?"

"That's the way it went."

"But you didn't tell Father Dowd right away."

"Once she'd left us, we didn't know how to articulate it, even to each other. It won't surprise you to hear that Síle was the only one who felt sure of what we'd seen. We saw a difference in her right away—before the apparition she was as changeable as the weather, and no wonder it put people on edge—but afterwards there was a calm, a deep calm, I'd never seen in her before. It was obvious to me it was a change for the better, but that new serenity seemed to aggravate Orla more than ever."

"One of the newspaper articles said you felt the experience had brought you all closer together."

"It felt that way, at first."

"And then?"

"Then, after Christmas, the apparition told us it was time to tell Father Dowd." She bit her lip. "Things were never the same between any of us after that."

"Did you like Father Dowd?"

She raised her eyebrows. "It never would've occurred to me not to."

"But looking back on everything. Did you feel he was sympathetic?"

"Oh, sure," she replied. "Only . . ."

"Only what?"

"He wanted so badly for it all to be true," she said softly. "Sometimes I wonder if it would've been better if we'd . . ."

"If you'd kept it secret?"

She nodded. "It's madness to think of it, and yet I can't see that we did all that much good in the end."

"Talking about it did a lot of good for your neighbors," I pointed out.

"Still, that wasn't much comfort once the money dried up. The shops closed, the restaurants closed, the ladies stopped doing B and B. Then everything was the same as it was before."

"But *you* were different," I said. "Did you ever listen to the other interview tapes?" She shook her head. "Declan sounded as if he'd been locked inside the parish office against his will."

Tess almost laughed. "And Orla spent all her time defending him, no doubt."

"Whenever she wasn't saying she saw the apparition only because she didn't want to admit that her sister was sick—yes."

"See, she never told me she was having doubts. Not even at the end. I knew she was having them, but she never said."

"In her interview she said that you were the most honest person she knew." Tess glanced at me then, with her pale gray eyes, and I felt suddenly unsteady—as if I were two different people inhabiting the same body and I'd only just noticed the discrepancy. "It seems to me she didn't want to disappoint you," I said quietly.

She gave me another grim half smile. "You think you know someone."

"Tell me exactly when things began to turn," I said.

"*Turn,*" she echoed. "Now that's the best way to put it. It happened by degrees. I couldn't see it until it was too late."

"That's always the way it happens," I said. "That's the way it happens when it really matters."

Tess nodded. "As I said, the apparition told me I needed to feel and show love to the people I *professed* to love. But over time the message began to shift. It was the same on the surface, I suppose, but with less and less love as it went along. I know that doesn't make any sense, but there it is. Every time . . ." Tess's voice began to shake, and she took a breath to steady herself. "Every time she grew colder and more repetitive."

"How so?"

She halted as if listening to another old recording, this one only in her head. "I remember her saying, *I see no love in your heart, Teresa. I look into your heart, and I see no love there.* And she'd go on like that until she went away."

I stared at her. I didn't know how to respond. "That—" I stopped short. "Forgive me, but that doesn't sound like something the Virgin Mary would say." Those layabouts down at the pub—how had they known? Tess said she'd never spoken of it, and I believed her.

"There's nothin' to forgive," she said quietly. "Not when I've wondered the same thing a thousand times."

"So that was when you began to doubt?"

She nodded.

"Did you tell the others what she was saying to you? If you were each getting different messages, wouldn't they have heard something just as disturbing?"

A rough wind swept down the muddy lane, and Tess brought her reddened hands to her mouth to blow some warmth into them. "None of us admitted it. I don't know, maybe if I'd come out with the truth, they would have told me something similar, but I never got up the nerve."

"What do you think she was saying to Orla?"

"It's better for me not to think on that," she replied. "In time we began to dread going up to the hill—no one else ever said so, but I could see it—and yet we always found ourselves up there at least two or three afternoons a week, so long as it wasn't raining. Some days nothing happened, and we talked of film stars and exams and walking the Great Wall of China as if she'd never come to us at all. We'd take out our beads, say a few decades, and go down again for dinner.

"When she did come, though, Síle always saw her first. I

wouldn't have minded, except for people whispering about her always embellishing the story, cravin' the attention. I didn't see her that way, but it still mattered." She paused. "I always liked her, but it made me uneasy."

"At what point did you start going up by yourself?"

"It was a few weeks into the new year," she said. "On the wet days, when the others went straight home from school."

"You didn't tell them you were going?"

"I didn't, no."

"Was it because of Síle?"

"Partly because of Síle. But I couldn't seem to keep myself from going. I felt drawn there, like I couldn't have stayed away no matter how much I wanted to."

"You kept going, even though she only said the same thing over and over."

She drew an unsteady breath. "Then one day, she said something new, and I wished with my whole heart I'd never come."

"Tell me," I said gently. "But only if you want to."

Tess nodded. "She said, *Orla has been hiding things.* And I said, 'What sort of things?'

"She laughed then, and it made me shiver. *Can't you guess?* 'Orla is allowed to have her own life.'

"*She's afraid of what you'll say. She's afraid you'll think she's a hoor.* 'I wouldn't say that. I wouldn't think it.' *You may as well speak the truth, Teresa. You can't ever hide it from me. You do think it. You can think a thought without putting words to it.*

"'Why are you saying all this? Orla is my best friend.'

"*If it was between you and Declan, you know she'd give you up. She's already beginning to.*

"'You told me there was no love in my heart—you told me to love my friends—and now this?'

"*Orla is a liar and a hoor. She doesn't deserve your love.*

"'You're testing me,' I said. 'You must be.' But she was gone, and I found myself talking to the statue." She drew up her jacket collar and shivered. What little sun we'd had was gone. "For days I struggled with what the apparition had told me, and in time I began to believe it. The things she'd said . . . none of it surprised me, in a sense. Most of the time, I thought I loved Orla like a sister, that I'd do anything for her; but even when we were small, sometimes I would feel a tiny spark of delight when something unfortunate happened to her—if she fell off her bicycle or failed an exam. And when good things came to her, there was always that tiny part of me that felt as if she didn't entirely deserve it." Tess drew a shuddering breath and turned to me with wide eyes. "I never wanted to feel this. I thought I could hide it and it would all be as if I'd never felt it in the first place."

You and me both, I thought. "Would you say you were jealous of her?"

She stopped to consider this. "Perhaps I was. In any event, it was plain to me that I needed to put some distance between us. I wanted to shrug her off before she could shrug *me*. Oh, it's horrible to look back and see it now, see how I treated her. I'd convinced myself of her falseness when *I* was the false one, through and through."

"Don't say that, Tess. We all have stories like this." I suppressed the urge to scratch at the name written on my arm. "We all have regrets." And as soon as I said it, I felt something even stranger creeping over me: as if someone had begun to pick apart the seams that held me together.

"No," Tess said. "I thought I was better than that."

I laid my arm across her shoulders. "Looking back on it, knowing you'd do it differently—that's the only thing you can do."

"Why did you come back here, really?" she said, stepping out from under my arm to face me. "First it was for Johnny's funeral.

Then you wanted to write the article. You're past that now, and yet you're still here."

It hit me then, the absurdity of saying you're sorry for something you did—or didn't do—a quarter of a century ago, but it wouldn't have felt right to leave it. "I've been wanting to apologize for the way I treated you that day," I said. "In the car, on the way back." I watched my ~~words~~ transform her face. "I don't know what got into me."

For a second, just a second, I could read everything she was feeling—the hope, the elation—but a second later, she was striving to master herself, to suppress whatever it was I'd dredged up. "I thought I'd done something—said something—"

"You didn't," I said. "I was a jerk, that's all."

Tess took a deep breath and sighed it out. "Sure, we're all of us impossible to manage at that age."

"You would know," I replied. She made a small sound, not quite a chuckle, and for a minute or two, neither of us said anything more.

"I've gone back to that day in my mind so many times over the years," she said slowly. "We had everything going for us then. Things were still easy between Orla and me. Declan—we saw him at school, but none of us had ever spoken to him. There was no confusion among us, we saw what was real and no more. My mam was sick, but I could see how she gave my dad a real sense of himself—that he cared for her not out of duty, but love. That it gave him pleasure to look after her while Paudie and Joan brought me on the beach outing." She closed her eyes, smiling a little. "Síle was happier with your sister than I've ever seen her. And you," she said. "You gave me something that day, too, even if it's taken me all these years to see it."

Right then I finally had to admit to myself that I found her attractive—tearstained face, cross pendant, dowdy sweater, and all—but her reciprocal feeling was all the more reason not to speak of what had happened in the dunes.

But I couldn't not ask. "What do you mean?"

"You gave me a sense of the world," Tess replied. "A sense of myself beyond this gloomy little town, this gloomy little country. That was the day I first knew I would leave."

How could it be that I hadn't thought of that day in years, yet she believed it had changed her? *She doesn't know,* I thought. *She'll never know this isn't the thing I should regret most.* "You go to confession, right? Every week?"

She nodded.

"Isn't that awkward? Telling your innermost thoughts to Father Lynch when you have to see him all the time in the course of your work?"

Tess gave me a small brief smile. "It isn't like that, really. Or if he *does* think of the things I've confided to him, he does a sound job of hiding it."

I wanted to ask, but I couldn't bring myself to it: *Is there any way to be forgiven for the things you can't confess?* Instead I said, "I'd like to hear the rest of your story. About Orla. If you still want to talk about it."

Tess pulled a handkerchief out of her pocket to wipe her nose and nodded. "I was telling you how it all came apart between us. I found little ways of doing it. I was busy with family outings whenever she wanted to make plans for the weekend; I led her to a new table in the caf, and let her eat in silence as I made friends with the other girls; and when we saw the apparition, I wouldn't tell her what had been said to me. She was hurt, of course, but she tried not to show it. She and Declan were closer than ever. I heard from someone at school that she was planning to join him in Australia after the leaving cert, that she was going through with it. Then he left without her, and I changed my mind and wanted to mend things, but it was too late. We've hardly spoken from that day to this."

We looked at each other. "I told Orla she should talk to you," I said finally. "Twenty years is long enough, don't you think?"

Tess folded her hands. "She said no, did she?"

"I'm hoping she'll change her mind," I said. "I hope you will, too."

"Why?" she asked. "Why does it matter so much to you?" She studied my face. "It isn't to do with me," she said softly. "It's partly to do with Síle, but that's not the whole of it, either."

We looked at each other. "It's Mallory," I said at last, and it was like I'd opened my mouth and waited to hear what would come out. "You say you want to go back to that day at the beach, and I do, too, only it's for a different reason." Her name in that notebook—her name under my skin. It was happening now, stitch by stitch.

Tess gazed at me with that sweet look of compassion I remembered from the night of the vigil. It was a relief to see she'd misunderstood me.

"You sure you want to go up there?" I asked. We looked at each other, both of us thinking of the suicide note.

"We'll go," Tess said finally, and we continued up the hill. "He was a good boy, but he was troubled. I won't be haunted by it."

I gave her a look.

"Not anymore," she said.

As usual, the little white tchotchke truck was the only vehicle in the parking lot. Mag let out a warm greeting, as if she'd been expecting us. "Cuppa tea?" she called. We came closer, and by the look on Mag's face, I saw she'd taken me for someone else.

Tess reacted with a different kind of surprise. "You've a kettle in there?"

Mag tucked away the wary look she'd been giving me and chuckled. "Oh, aye, I've a power point."

Tess laughed. "You've been holding out on me, Mag!"

The old woman flashed her an impish smile. "Will you have a cuppa?"

"No, thanks. I won't bother you."

"Sure, it's no bother a'tall!"

They went back and forth a few more times, with Tess finally acquiescing as the button popped on the electric kettle. Mag poured water into three brown seventies-era mugs and added the milk before taking out the tea bags.

As Tess and Mag chatted over their tea, I turned back to the parking lot and noticed something odd. There was nothing in the water-stained niche besides a couple of empty cider cans. "What happened to the statue?" I asked.

"The statue of the Blessed Virgin?" Mag stuck a wizened finger in her mouth to readjust her teeth. "'Twas taken down years ago."

"That can't be right," I said. "It's been there whenever I've come up here. Just like in the old newspaper photos." Owen had seen it too; I'd *seen* him looking at her.

"No one can say who it 'twas that took it," the old woman went on, and I realized she was trying not to look at me. "'Twas thieves in the night!"

I opened my mouth again to protest, and Tess regarded me curiously. "Mag's right," she said. "The statue hasn't been there going on ten years now. You must've imagined it."

I carried my tea to the edge of the parking lot and sat down on the scarred green bench overlooking the town, hoping to clear my head. Tess had told the priest she hadn't seen the statue when the apparition came—that the statue had gone away, leaving bright white light and a flesh-and-blood woman in its place.

A minute or two later, Tess came over and sat down on the other side of the bench, and we looked out over Ballymorris in silence. Then she turned to me with a sad smile. "There," she said, pointing to a set of initials scratched into the seat: *OG + DK*. "I remember the day he carved it. It was one of the days when the pilgrims came up here to wait, but she never came."

"You know what you said to Father Dowd in that interview?" I asked. "About everything else in the world falling away whenever she came to you? And there being no more time?"

Tess shivered. "Aye. I remember."

"It reminded me of something. Did you ever hear that thing they say, about time happening all at once?"

She shot me a curious look. "Who's 'they'?"

Johnny's phone beeped before I could come up with a reply. It was a message from Brona. *Leo having chest pains, in hospital now. Let us know if you'd like to come along once he's able for visitors.*

Tess's phone vibrated as I was reading Brona's text. "It's probably from Paudie," I said. "Leo's having heart trouble. They've taken him to the hospital."

Late that afternoon, Brona drove Paudie and me to the county hospital, one endless corridor of gray linoleum and fluorescent lights. Leo was asleep when we arrived, and we took seats around the bed and waited for him to wake up. I hadn't spent much time in hospitals, but I knew that a visit only counted if your friend in the bed knew you were there. "This is the last place I expected to find you, Leo," I said when he opened his eyes. "We've been waiting for you at Napper Tandy's for hours."

He gave me a weak smile. "It's a lie," he said. "You haven't the smell of the pub on you."

"How're ya now, old man?" Paudie asked.

Leo struggled to sit up, giving the IV drip an impatient tug. "Not too sure I'm long for this world, to be honest wit'cha. Just look at the job they did on me arm." He pointed to a dark ugly bruise on the inside of his elbow. "Man or pincushion, she couldn't tell which."

"Have they given you anything to eat?" Brona asked.

"Ehh, they brought me a bit o' soup. I can't even think to be hungry with all the squeezin' in me chest."

Brona took his hand in hers and stroked the rough dry skin on the back of his palm. "It'll get better," she soothed. "Just do as they tell you, and you'll be out of here in no time."

"Sure, isn't that what you said to Colum the last time he was here? And he *did* come out again, only not the way you meant!"

Brona stiffened and withdrew her hand, and for once Leo caught himself right away. "Jaysus, Brona. I'm sorry. I ought not to have said that."

"No." It was rare to see Brona less than perfectly cheerful, so the look on her face stunned me into an embarrassed silence. "No, Leo Canavan, you shouldn't have."

Paudie stepped into damage-control mode. "I think Brona and I had better go down to the canteen for a bite. We forgot our lunch in all the excitement. We'll see you in a while, Leo, all right?" Brona strode out of the room, and Paudie turned in the doorway and looked to me. "Can we get you anything?"

"No, thanks."

"You'll be all right?"

I nodded and smiled. Leo tried to laugh, to smooth it over, as his friends took their leave. "They don't envy you, lad." He smacked his forehead with his palm. "It's not me heart that'll do me in," he sighed. "It's me tongue."

"It's fine," I said. "We all say the wrong thing sometimes."

Leo gave me a wry look. "Sure, she'll forgive me once she's had a bite to eat."

"Is there anything I can do for you?" I asked. "Anything I can get you? Do you want a newspaper or something?"

"No, thank you, lad. I only read the paper at the bookmaker's."

"Nothing I can do for you at all?"

"Just sit with me a while," he said. "Help me take my mind off the divil in me chest."

"Sure," I said. "What would you like to talk about?"

"There *is* the one thing I've been wantin' to ask you," he replied hoarsely. "Tell me, now. Didja ever think about gettin' married?"

"In general?" I asked.

"Aye. Or to anyone in particular."

"In the most abstract sense, I guess." It was my turn to attempt a laugh. "What about you? Brona told me you never married."

"Aye, and lived to regret it, which is why I'm askin' ya now. Don't go makin' that mistake."

"Which mistake?"

Leo sighed. "Lookin' beyond what's right in front'a ya."

I listened to his labored breathing. "And who *was* right in front of you?" I asked finally.

"Wouldya like to know, or are you just humorin' an old man?"

If I were, I'd never admit it. "Go on, Leo. I really want to know."

The old man fiddled with the hem of his sterile white blanket. "Your gran," he said at last. "I don't suppose she ever toldya."

"Wait . . . you mean you and my grandmother were . . . you mean you went out?"

"We did," he said, and glanced up at me sheepishly.

"You old rascal!" I laughed. "I should have guessed, from all the questions you were asking about her."

"I wish she'd have come back wit'cha," he said quietly. "I wish I could see her one last time."

"Why didn't you ever come to the States?"

"John could go, but how could I go with him? I'd come home from England, and if he'd been to Philadelphia, I'd ask him about your gran till he ran out of patience. 'You had your chance,' he'd say. Then we wouldn't speak of her again till the next time he went."

"What happened?"

"Between the two of us?" He sighed. "We were young, and I was an eejit. She wanted to get married and go to America together, and I kept thinkin' she'd change her mind."

"You wanted to stay?"

The old man shook his head. "But I was afraid to go. I was afraid we'd land in America and I wouldn't find a good job and she'd be ashamed of me. Sure, I never made much of myself in England, either, but at least I knew I could come home again." He looked at me intently. "It's that feelin', the feelin' trapped, that gives a man funny notions of the right thing to do. I loved your gran, but I thought maybe there was someone else I could love even better. Someone who wouldn't ask me to leave."

"I take it you never found her."

Leo shook his head. "And your gran got tired of waiting. I never doubted she'd go, but even so, it came as a shock when she told me she was takin' the train to Cork in the morning. 'Twas the longest night of my life."

"But you let her go," I said.

He gave me a tortured look. "How could I ask her to stay?"

It occurred to me then that the man in the hospital bed might have been my grandfather. It was a useless line of thought, and yet it was oddly comforting to think back over how he'd advised me since the night of John's wake. It felt like so much longer than a week ago.

Leo squirmed beneath the stark white sheet. "So here's what I'm tryin' to say to ya. That lass you left in New York. Maybe you'll go back to her. Maybe you've just let all the shite they sell you in the fillums get in the way of somethin' true."

I shook my head. "I don't think so. She deserves better than what I can give her."

Leo shot me a sharp look. I'd never seen him so deadly serious. "And just who is it you're savin' yer best for?"

I sighed. "I wish I knew, Leo." Síle's face flashed before me, laughing on the beach, but I couldn't give in to that. I couldn't have her.

The old man shook his head. "That's the trouble with you young ones."

"What's that?"

"You shrug and throw up yer hands as if you don't know."

I smiled. "And you used to be one of us."

He let out a growl of frustration, then clutched at his chest and cringed. "That's why I'm tellin' ya, lad," he managed to say. "Take it where you can find it."

"What's *it*?" I asked. "Love? Sex?"

"All of it," he sighed. "Just take it. Take it from whoever you can, and know then that you're among the lucky ones."

Brona drove us back to her house, and Paudie and I watched the Irish news while she defrosted a container of beef stew. "I'd hoped to make a big lovely meal for your last night in Ballymorris, but some things there can be no planning for," she said as she ladled out our dinner. None of us felt like going to the pub afterward.

I woke sometime past midnight. I wasn't alone in the room, and this time I knew it was real. A shadow rose from the armchair in the corner and crept toward where I lay in the bed. I caught a flutter of silk as she came into the light from the window, the gleam of an eye—no, not this time, this time it was real—and her dark hair loose and lustrous over her shoulders. She wore a robe, and nothing else.

"How did you get here?" I asked. "How did you know where—"

"Hush," she answered. "No questions."

I cast off the covers and made room for her in the bed, and she settled herself in beside me, the springs protesting beneath our weight. "It would be so easy to fall asleep beside you like this," she said. "Feeling your pulse against my cheek. Ah," she sighed. "It's lovely."

With an unsteady hand, I followed her waist down to where the sash was tied, undid the knot, and drew the silk off her shoulder. I ran my fingers up and down along the soft valley between hip and breast, pressing my face into her neck to drink in her scent. "You can't stay?"

"They'll be after me," she said. "And you'll be the first person they look to."

She was right. "As long as you're here now," I said. I pressed my erection against her bottom and she arched and purred like a cat. The moon illuminated the little room, making a jewel of every knickknack on the bureau. From his frame above the mirror, miserable Jesus, bleeding forever from his crown of thorns, looked down at us as if to say, *I died for this?*

She turned to face me, and I put my lips to her mouth. It didn't matter now who came looking for her, I'd never let her out of my sight.

"Did you want me, then?" she asked.

I ran my fingers through her hair, my tongue along the curve of her throat, and when I took a breath I caught the scent from under her arms, ripe and rousing. "Want you . . . when?"

"*Then*," she said. "That summer."

I shuddered. "*Jesus,* Síle! You were eight years old!"

"And you were twelve." At first I couldn't tell if she was teasing. "We grow up, and we forget just how far back we felt the need."

I kissed her again to keep her quiet. I'd known all along that she'd wanted this, but even so, a voice at the back of my head kept saying, *This can't be real, she's too perfect, it can't be.* How did she get here, she came in barefoot, how did she travel forty miles in nothing but a silk robe? "No more thinking," she whispered. "Only love."

Her robe fell away as she mounted me, and I stared at the vivid green tendrils winding up out of her pubic hair to frame her navel. "So that's why you wouldn't show me your tattoo on the beach," I said, and she laughed. "It's beautiful. I've never seen anything like it." I ran my fingers up the smooth flesh of her belly to cup her breasts, and as she eased me inside her I was afraid at first that I wouldn't last more than a few seconds. She rocked and moaned, rearing up so that she reminded me of a figurehead on an old sailing ship, and with every stroke she cut through a moonlit sea.

She looked down, smiled, and bent to kiss me, and I knew then that she was drawing something out of me, something that up till now I'd never been willing to give. I moved my thumb across the place where we were joined, and I watched her eyes roll back as she quaked and cried. Some narrow little part of me wanted to whisper, *Síle, not so loud, or they'll hear you,* but the better part knew it didn't matter. I wanted to hear her shriek like this every night for the rest of our lives.

I came soon after she did, and afterward we clung to each other in the tangled bedclothes. I licked the curve of her breast and took her nipple in my teeth. I could taste her sweat for hours.

"What's your plan?"

She yawned, and I let go. "You can't ask me that. I don't know yet."

"I have to ask. I'm driving back to Dublin tomorrow, and I want you to come with me."

In the darkness I couldn't see her face, but I knew she was smiling. "I can't think," she whispered. "You've worn me out."

Síle nestled her cheek against my shoulder and laid a hand on my chest. I thought of Tess, and it hit me like a crosstown bus: what if that kiss had been the *only* kiss? *Soft but callused, and smelling of Pond's. . . .*

"I told you a lie," Síle murmured, and I started.

"What?"

"When I told you about Mallory living in Seattle—or a city just like it. When I said she has a garden flat and two tabby kittens, Sigmund and Ralph, and a boyfriend called Dave who plays bass guitar in a band, and they go to your grandfather's house at holidays."

It was like she was speaking every other word in a made-up language. "You never told me any of those things."

"Still," she replied. "I told you she was there, but she isn't. I said it because I wanted it to be true."

I kissed her forehead. "You're dreaming," I said. "It's okay. Everything will make sense again in the morning."

"If you're right . . . if she isn't real . . ." She pressed herself into me, as if we could be closer than we already were. "Then it doesn't matter, sure it doesn't. We can do anything we like."

Everything made sense again, my pieces fitting together in a way they never had before. I fell asleep, satisfied with the promise of another round of lovemaking at first light, Jesus Christ still glowering from his place above the mirror. No one else was watching, and this time I was sure of it.

II

In the morning I was alone. The room was awash in gray light, the sun as reluctant to shine as ever. I lay in the bed for a long time, feeling her absence so acutely it might've been more bearable if she'd never come at all.

There was no way Mrs. Halloran hadn't heard the noise Síle had made in the night. I put off breakfast as long as I could—spent a good few minutes poring over the little room hoping for any sign of her, her panties crumpled forgotten on the carpet, or a strand of dark hair on the pillow beside me—but there wasn't anything to prove she'd ever been here.

Finally I had to go down, and I braced myself for a talking-to. I pretty much expected the landlady to ask me to leave without breakfast, so I was shocked when she greeted me as brightly as she always had.

"And how's our intrepid young reporter this morning?" she asked as she delivered the French press and toast rack. "Did you sleep well?"

I could hardly get the words out. "I slept great, thanks."

"It's today you'll be leaving Ballymorris, is it?" Mrs. Halloran replied as she hurried back into the kitchen for my eggs. "Will you miss us, when you're home again in New York City? I was there once, years ago." The woman shuddered as she laid down my plate. "Give me the pace of this small-town life any day. Most of the time I can do without all the excitement, and when I feel up to it, I go to Dublin for the weekend."

"I *will* miss it," I conceded, but apart from that, there seemed to be nothing else to say. I brought the fork to my lips, but I hardly tasted the food. I wondered where Síle was now, and if she'd be able to get in touch with me later in the morning.

Where had she gone? Why hadn't she left a note? I found it impossible to believe she'd gone to her parents' house—they'd only drive her straight back to Ardmeen. I had no idea where she could be, and as I finished my breakfast, I felt a coil of anxiety tightening in my gut. Why hadn't I found any sign of her?

I packed my bag and shook hands with Mrs. Halloran, waiting until I was in the car to make the phone call. Dr. Kiely didn't even begin with a perfunctory hello. "Now," she said, "it's my understanding that Síle's family wishes you to have no further contact with her."

"Is she there? I don't need to speak with her," I said hurriedly. "I just want to know if she's there."

The doctor didn't answer right away. "And why wouldn't Síle be here?"

"Have you checked?" I asked. "Have you seen her yet this morning?" In that second before the doctor replied, I felt certain that what had happened last night was as real as anything else. Síle would contact me soon, and that evening we'd drive together to Dublin.

"I have, indeed," said Dr. Kiely, "and she is just where I expected to find her."

Yeah, right. "And where is that?"

"At her easel. Now, if you'll excuse me, I've patients to attend to." She paused. "I would greatly appreciate it if you would refrain from attempting to contact Síle in the future. It's the best thing for everyone involved."

The doctor was lying, that much was obvious. I got out of the car and turned the corner for the youth center. Tess was surprised to see me, but she seemed pleased.

"Síle's left Ardmeen House," I said.

"You sound like that's a good thing," Tess replied cautiously. "Did she get in touch with you?"

I nodded. "She came to the B and B last night."

Tess averted her eyes, an automatic reaction. "Ah," she said, and I thought of everything we'd talked about the day before and everything we hadn't.

"But I don't know where she went. If she gets ahold of you, you'll tell her how to reach me?"

"She wouldn't be likely to come to me. I haven't spoken with her in years."

"She'd be even less likely to talk to her family," I said. "So will you give her my contact info, if you talk to her?"

"I'll tell her," Tess replied. "But sure, you must be all over the Internet. She'll have no trouble finding you."

I gave her a hug in farewell, and she stood in the doorway and watched me as I walked to the end of the narrow street.

After our row Orla stopped coming up to the hill, and Declan's leaving for Australia today. It's only me and Tess now, but we haven't seen Her in days.

At first I thought Tess was just sad about the others, but today she said she didn't want to come any more. I asked her why and she said—Whatever it is, it isn't the Blessed Mother.

I looked at her and it was like I was waiting for her face to change, waiting for her to turn into someone else, because I couldn't believe the Tess I knew would say what she'd just said.

—You're wrong, I said.—What could make you say a thing like that?

—It's how She speaks of everyone else. The pilgrims. Father Dowd. Declan. Orla especially. Our Lady would never say such things, she said.—Never.

I was afraid to ask but I took a deep breath and went for the truth.—And me? What does She say about me, Tess?

—She never speaks ill of you, Tess said, and it pricked my heart to hear the resentment she was trying to hide in it.—You're Her pet.

—But She doesn't have favourites, I said.—She's always said God loves us different but equally. Everyone loved in equal measure, that's how She said it once.

—That's what She says. But She doesn't mean it. I read something in a book once about having a friend with two faces. That one could be smiling but you'd never know what might be coming out her other mouth. I keep thinking about that story.

—That isn't fair, I said.—It isn't fair to speak of Her like that. We have to trust Her.

—You don't understand, Síle. If you heard Her talk that way, you'd see why I'm saying this. But She doesn't talk to you like that—talking against everyone else—because you're Her favourite.

God forgive me, but when she said it that time, that I was the favourite, I wanted very badly to believe it. Everyone wants to think they've been chosen, that they've been set apart for some-

thing grander. But what I said was,—I know you're upset, Tess, and I'm very sorry for it. But whatever She said about Orla or Declan or Father Dowd, surely it must have been true?

She sighed.—I suppose it's all true, in a way. But if an ordinary person said those things you'd say 'she's not being kind.' And who is the Mother of God without kindness?

—Tell me what She said, I said.—You're saying She was unkind but you have to tell me what was said.

—Think of all the unkind things you <u>could</u> say about Father Dowd, or Declan, or your sister. Whatever occurs to you, She's already said it.

—Tell me what She said about Orla.

Tess sighed.—I can't. It's disgusting.

—Tell me, I said.

—She says that they've . . . that they've sinned together. She called Orla a hoor.

As she said it I felt the cold worming up out of my belly, out of the place Declan had made. It was then I knew the Blessed Mother would never have given Orla or even Tess the chance to take back their sins. Tess was right. But I shook my head and said,—I don't believe it.

Tess looked at me.—Which part?

—No matter what they did together, She'd never call Orla a hoor. Never.

—You know I haven't imagined it, Síle. Suddenly Tess seemed very tired.—You <u>know</u> I'm not telling tales. I didn't answer, so she went on.—She has said things no good Christian would ever say, let alone the Blessed Virgin. So it can't be Her. It can't be. Tess covered her face with her hands, and I could see she was trembling.—It's something else. Something deceiving us.

She'd said it. The words were too sharp not to cut through everything that was, all that we'd known and trusted in before. We looked at each other and knew there was no going back.

—Are you saying it's the Devil? I asked.—The Devil appearing to us, pretending to be the Blessed Mother?

—I've been reading about other apparitions, Tess said.— They do say the Devil can disguise himself so well even the Pope would be fooled.

I saw the sense behind her words, but something was hardening inside of me. I knew Tess would never make things up and yet I knew she was mistaken.

—What will you do? I asked.—What will you say to Her, the next time She comes to us?

—There'll be nothing left to say, she replied.—You said it yourself that She's always with us. She's overheard every word we've said.

I thought I'd caught her then.—But if She's only a demon, how could She know our secret thoughts? How could She heal your mother's leg?

—Now, that I haven't an answer for, Tess sighed.—But it keeps me awake nights, remembering how my mam was healed, and to think I might have the Devil to thank for it.

I don't know what Our Lady will have to say to Tess after all this. But for my part, I believe in Her and I always will.

At half past ten I drove down Shop Street to the bookstore, and found Paudie already waiting for me outside. Brona was doing an hors d'oeuvres demo at the supermarket, and said she'd pay Leo a visit later in the day. "It's good of you to bring me," Paudie sighed as he settled into the passenger's seat. "I don't drive if I can help it, and at my age, isn't it a public service?"

Johnny's phone rang as we were walking up the hospital steps, and I hung back to answer it. "I hear you had a chat with my mother the other night," Orla said.

"Don't worry," I replied. "She made herself perfectly clear."

"Have you had any contact with Síle since then?"

I almost laughed. "No." She didn't say anything more, so I asked, "Is that the only reason you called?"

"No," she said. "There's something else. Something I'd forgotten about, and if you're going to write your story, I want you to include it."

I probably didn't want to hear this, but still I said, "Fire away."

"There was a crack in the wall beside her bed," Orla began, "and she used to put her lips to it and whisper, like there was somebody listening on the other side. It went on like that every night for months."

"That sounds like Síle."

"No," Orla said. "You don't get it. There was nothing endearing in it. It wasn't 'cute.' Sometimes I knew she was waiting until I was asleep, and other times she couldn't wait, she was whisperin' away—urgent, like. Those were the nights I'd go down to the sitting room and fall asleep on the sofa."

"It bothered you that much?"

"I was so ill at ease lying in that bed, listening to her whisperin' like that. There was no way I could sleep. I couldn't. I asked our dad to patch up the crack, but he gave in when Síle begged him not to." She added softly, "I'd almost forgotten that."

"Why did it make you uneasy? Lots of kids have imaginary friends. I don't see how it's any different."

"It *was* different. I couldn't tell you why, except that it frightened me. And nobody cared that it frightened me."

I waited for her to continue. Why did she want me to write about this?

"After a few months, she finally stopped," Orla said. "When I asked her why, she said they'd gone away, only she'd never say who 'they' were."

"She never said who she thought she was talking to?"

"No. She never said." I could hear Orla's baby crying in the background. "I've got to go now. I suppose I was only calling to ask you . . . if you're going to write about Síle . . . to show her for who she is, not just who she likes to think she is."

"We're all guilty of that," I replied, and my own words came back on me like the final slug of moonshine.

"You say that, but how many of us believe we've Mother Mary on the line?" Orla sighed. "It isn't harmless. She isn't any sort of 'chosen one.' I suppose that's what I've been trying to say to you all along."

I let the pause go on a beat too long. Finally I said, "Can I ask you something?"

"You can *ask,*" Orla replied.

"Was there another reason you wanted Síle put away? Something besides what you've told me?"

I'd never known a telephone silence could feel so oppressive. Finally she said, "Why would I tell you, when I've said far too much already?" She hung up then, and I stood there in the hospital foyer just looking at the phone in my hand.

When I went in, I found Leo looking considerably worse. A nurse was changing his IV bag, and he asked her irritably when that bloody tube was coming out of his arm. "You'll get used to it," she replied with equanimity, and gave me a look—*he's all yours*—as she passed from the room.

Paudie seemed almost at home as he took the electric kettle off the table by the window and refilled it at the sink. "I'm makin' myself a cuppa," he said over his shoulder. "Would either of ye like one?"

"No, thanks," I said. I was sick of tea. "How do you feel today, Leo?"

He groaned. "Like I flew all night on a tour of Hell on the back of a winged monkey."

"At least your tongue's still working," said Paudie as he stirred a packet of sugar into his white cafeteria teacup.

"Go away wit'cha, if you've only come here to hound me," Leo sighed. "I'd like to see *you* in this bed, Padraic McGowan. We'd all see then if you'd suffer it any better than I can."

"I'm very thankful not to be in your place," Paudie replied, soberly this time. "If you were me, you'd say the same, and I'd not begrudge you for it."

"I'm not begrudging," Leo murmured, more to himself than in reply. "I'm not begrudging." Then he looked up at me and asked, "Did I ever tell you how Jack Brennan came to dance at his own wake?"

"No," I said. The phone call with Orla had unsteadied me, so that I'd much rather listen than talk—and anyway it was too good a story not to hear a second time.

Leo's irritable mood vanished in a wink. "Now, I was only a boy when it happened, but I would have passed Jack Brennan in the street on occasion, and seen him at Mass on the Sunday. We all knew the man."

"I remember him," said Paudie as the electric kettle began to rumble. "Not well, but I do remember him. He was so tall he had to duck through most of the doorways in town."

"And a fine-looking man, too, so all the ladies said. Jack was married to a lass called Mary, and though they'd no children they seemed to be very much in love. He tilled his own plot of land and Mary kept the house, and for a time all was right in their world." Leo sighed. "Then came the sad day. He wasn't a very young man, but sure, he wasn't near old enough to be droppin' dead in the field."

"Not a day past forty, if even that," Paudie put in.

"Nearer to thirty-five," Leo said. "In any case, someone sent for the doctor, but the doctor could do nothing for him. And so his wife and sisters washed the body and laid him out, and the priest came, too, and the next night everyone turned up for the wake.

"Now, you've been to Johnny's wake, but you'll never know how 'twas done in the old days. Everyone stayed up all night, dancin' and drinkin' and carryin' on, till they took the dearly departed to the church in the morning, said all the prayers and laid him to rest in the graveyard. Jack had a good many friends and family, and soon his cottage was packed to the rafters with all those in mourning.

"Night had fallen, and the only light there was to be had came from the candles and the peat fire, and so you might well find yourself dancing with a person when you couldn't quite make out his face. Jack's widow Mary had been sitting in a corner just starin' into the fire, until someone came up to her in the gloom, swept her up and made her dance, payin' no heed to her protests. And for a time the young widow forgot her grief.

"A whileen later, someone else—'twas one of Jack's sisters, if I remember—went into the bedroom to keep vigil with the corpse, and found the bed empty. She came boundin' back into the crowded front room, roarin' with panic because she feared he'd been snatched, though for what purpose she never could have told. When she cried out, the fiddler stopped his fiddlin', and the piper laid down his pipes, and the dancers stopped their dancin', and then another cry rose up from the crowd: it was poor Mary Brennan, who found herself in the arms of her dead husband.

"As soon as he was discovered, Jack gave a moan and crumpled to the floor, and they found this time that he was well and truly dead. And that," Leo said, as his eyelids grew heavy, "is how Jack Brennan came to dance at his own wake."

For a minute or two, we watched him doze. "I suppose you'd better be heading on to Dublin," Paudie said finally. "But I'll tell you this—we'll miss you at the pub."

I drew the unfinished pack of Player's out of my jacket pocket and left them on the bedside table. It would be a treat for Leo not to have to roll his own for once. Paudie watched me do it, but he made no comment.

"You'll miss me for a few nights," I said. "After that, you'll hardly remember I was here."

"Ah, now," Paudie replied. "You're too young yet to be talkin' like that."

The rain was coming down in sheets as I dropped Paudie off at the bookshop. He shook my hand and said he hoped I'd be back in a year or two, but as he eased himself out of the car, I felt the sinking certainty I'd never drink another pint with any of them.

I drove slowly toward Napper Tandy's on my way out of town, the wipers set to frantic, and through the rain I could make out a group of men huddled at the entrance smoking their cigarettes. I saw Hennessey there, and "Yeats," they and all their friends wearing the same green football jersey. They hadn't come to the pub on their lunch break.

A dark-haired man took a step toward the curb as I passed them, the end of his cigarette glowing as he took one last, hungry suck. It wasn't a face I'd seen among the pack that night, but it was a face I knew, albeit with twenty more years on it. Declan Keaveney met my eye through the windshield, smiling insolently as he flicked his used-up cigarette into the road ahead of my car. Home at last? Really?

Another beat and I was past them, though for most of the way to Dublin I wanted very badly to punch something. For the first few miles, I thought of turning around—to see if it was really him or if I was seeing things—but if I did, I knew I'd regret it either way.

There isn't any point setting down the chain of encounters that led me to Kerala, nor can I say why I feel pressed to write again after all these years. I could have left this diary in the box under my bed at home; but then, I do know why. I packed it because She told me to.

I'd been in India nearly nine months when things began to unravel, as I ought to have known they would. At first the night trains and the rickshaws were exciting and new to me, and I felt that sense of adventure everywhere I went, saw the magic in everything I laid my eyes on; all the colours! And the colours were new, and hadn't they been invented especially for me? And aye, I'll admit there was a man, and for a while he made me feel as if no one in all the world had ever experienced any of these things before. We were like Shiva and Parvati, Shiva the god who never blinked and Parvati his consort who playfully showed her love by pressing her palms to his eyes, only to find the Universe plunged into darkness, no stars, no suns, as Shiva's sight was broken. Shiva, the god who could never sleep.

My love brought me to the ashram and I was welcomed, as he'd promised I would be, and within a day I'd settled into my place as if I'd always been there. There were friends there I felt as if I'd never not known. But my favourite place, my favourite time, was in the little temple the community had formed and grown up around. Before they arrived no one had tended it for a thousand years.

In the high heat of the afternoon when the others laid down to rest, I went to the temple, sat down on the cool stone and let my tired eyes rest upon the icons until the colours ran together *and I was refreshed. Indians believe that the divine is not hidden from us, that it is to be seen everywhere we look, and that when they gaze into the painted eyes of the idol the god, the <u>real</u> god, gazes back.*

But sure, the people put so much love and care into the painting and dressing of the icons—they treat them like precious dolls, or living babbies—that you'd almost wonder if it's the lavishing of the attention that brings the deity to life. I never felt as if anyone were looking out of the eyes of <u>our</u> statues, not in the church and certainly not on the hill. When the Light would go away and She took Her leave I'd look up at the statue in the grotto and wonder how they could have gotten Her so wrong.

I often thought of Our Lady on those sweltering afternoons, though I can't say I prayed to Her. I told myself that if She ever came to me again I'd ask Her about the gods of the Hindus, about Shiva and Parvati, and was there any truth in them at all.

And yet . . . and yet I knew for myself that there was, and I'll tell you how I knew. In the hut where we took our meals there was a statue of Hanuman. I'd been partial to him since that afternoon in Bangalore, when my love had taken me to his temple. There the priest's apprentice (a boy of nine) offered me a piece of coconut candy, and the monkey-god watched me from his perch on the roof as the sweetness filled my mouth. I'd never tasted anything so delicious in all my life.

On the evening before I left the community, I saw the statue as if for the first time. Hanuman was tearing his chest open, showing the gods Rama and Sita inside his heart, to prove the love he bore for them, and all I could think was I've seen this, I've seen this already, I've seen this somewhere before. That's when I knew I had to leave.

In the hour before sunrise the next morning I packed my things and walked the five miles to the nearest village, where I caught the bus to Madurai, and from there another bus to Munnar, though that bus never arrived. When it broke down none of the Indians were at all put out, and I watched from the roadside as they set off on foot. When another bus came along in an hour or two, someone said, they'd be picked up; and others were near enough to their homes that they could walk the rest of the way.

The road which eventually led to Munnar wound along a cliff, the tea plantations laid out below, lush and gleaming in the sunshine. I knew I shouldn't have set out that way, not on foot at least, and I can't say what propelled me, only that I was drawn by something, or someone. By the end of the first hour there was no one but me left on the road and I was down to my last sip of water, but sure, the next bus would come along any minute.

At some point I came upon a little shrine, and it was Kali, the goddess of destruction, dressed in blue, forever in the midst of devouring her own baby. The statue seemed to writhe in the heat, and I fell to my knees without intending to, and She came to me there, in that unfamiliar place.

—Blessed Mother, I said, and I noticed I was trembling, as if I weren't quite inside my own body.—How I've missed you!

—It isn't so long as it feels, She said.—And have you forgotten that I'm always with you? She bent over me, Her face hovering inches above mine, and I smelled that same sweet scent of Her, coconut candy and every other good thing I ever ate or breathed.—I bless you, child, She whispered, and I felt Her sweep the damp hair away from my face as the light around us grew dim.—I'll see you safe. No harm can ever come to you, not so long as I'm near.

That was the last thing I can recall before I woke up in hospital.

Orla has come all the way to Madurai to collect me. If I ever thought in years past that she would come round someday, if not to love me then at least to make her peace with my existence, well I know better now. She fumes at the doctor and I can see the nurses cringe whenever she walks in. I thanked her the day she arrived and she only said,—I'll never be free of you, will I?

December

I came home to an empty apartment, and just as I'd predicted, Laurel hadn't left a single dish in the sink. It had been my place to start with, she'd only moved in a couple years before, and yet the air in these four rooms was intolerable to me now—I'd lost something that hadn't felt essential until it was subtracted. It was all so ordinary and lonely that every time I thought of Síle, she seemed farther and farther away from me, remote and impossible. Where was she now? How could she have let me leave without her?

I'd told Andy about the poteen, and he wanted me to write about that instead. Secret histories of any sort of alcoholic beverage were a golden-ticket circulation booster. So the rest of November passed in a fog of late nights at the magazine, Chinese takeout, and catch-up drinks with college friends that wore on twice as long as I wanted them to. I just sat there and kept on drinking, laughing at the appropriate times, wishing I could slink quietly out of their lives. Sometimes I'd catch a glimpse of myself in a darkened mirror, my skin looking like a puddle of weather-worn cloth fallen from the rag tree, and I was afraid that if I looked any closer, I'd see that I was holding myself together with a length of blue yarn.

In early December, I got an e-mail from Tess. *I've decided to give up my place at the youth centre and do a bit of travelling. Not to volunteer, just to see more of the world and try to figure out my true place in it.* She said she hadn't heard anything from Síle.

So Ballymorris wasn't where you belonged after all, I wrote back. *I wish you the very best, Tess. Let me know if you're ever in New York.* She didn't reply, not that I expected her to.

After Christmas I went down to Fort Lauderdale for a few days to visit my grandmother. It was the first time I'd seen her since my trip to Ireland, and she wanted to hear all the details of John's funeral I hadn't already told her over the phone, and how Brona was doing, and how had I liked the little town where she'd grown up. I told her I'd spent a good bit of time with Paudie and his niece, but I didn't mention the apparition or that I'd ever wanted to write about it. I did tell her every funny story about Leo that I could think of, but she never asked any more than I offered, not even when I told her I'd last seen him in the hospital. If there had been some great romance between them, I wondered if it had happened mostly in Leo's head.

My grandmother lived a little under an hour from Miami Beach. One afternoon I drove down to the museum with the Harry Clarke window Síle had told me about, taking her diary with me. I bought a ticket and rode the elevator to the fifth floor, walking past Art Deco posters and furniture until I came to the stained glass.

"The Geneva Window" was an awkward title for it, seeing as it was never installed there, but the window was still impressive enough to warrant the name. It deserved better than this concrete floor, the flimsy white partitions, and metal heating ducts overhead, but on the other hand, they'd never let you get this close to anything at the Met. You could go right up to it and examine every scene, each minuscule brushstroke adding depth to the flat planes of color. You could get near enough to fog the glass with your breath, and no one would say anything to you. I read the information panel putting the window in historical context, rubbing at the letters etched on my forearm. Mallory would have loved this.

Síle was right: the panels weren't that big, but there was a lot to look at inside each one, and even though I didn't know the stories behind them, it was easy to imagine what was going on. There was something lewd happening in almost every one. A yellow-haired girl, fireflies pulsing under her purple dress, danced with her elfin lover, who pressed her hand against his bare crotch as tiny green goblins danced on a hill above their heads; another blonde, this one naked, danced with a purple veil like Salome for a horrible fat old man, a cigar in one hand and a brandy glass in the other. That one I remembered from Síle's book.

Yet the erotic scenes weren't even the most interesting ones. In a panel on the right, a trio of angels appeared to a man and his daughter, who shrank from them in fear and awe. Each of the heavenly figures wore a fiery crown, and each had splendid wings of orange and green and blue. The glances of the angels, stern and withering, fell not on the man and girl but on the viewer—as if to say you could hide nothing from them, there was no use trying. We live all our lives waiting for that one moment of supernatural intervention, the pivotal flash at which your life finally starts to mean something; but the people so transfigured are people alive only between the pages of a book.

I went a few paces into an adjoining room and sat on a bench so I could still see the window through the doorway. I took the diary out of my knapsack and turned to the last page. For weeks I'd been telling myself it wasn't legible, that I couldn't possibly read it without giving myself another headache. Yet another lie.

> *To begin with you only pinched her in places she would've hurt herself anyway—her elbows, her knees—but it didn't satisfy. You told her she was ugly and she believed you. She hid herself, she wouldn't even let your mam see her in her knickers, and then you went for her softer parts.*
>
> *Your gran knew. She knew but she couldn't let herself believe it. You saw how she looked at you, at bedtime, after the day at Streedagh. She closed the door on you and she and Mallory shared the big bed, and in the room down the hall, in the dark, you shook with a rage you could not understand.*
>
> *You'd seen her, in the dunes. You saw between her legs and it didn't matter that you'd seen her in the bath a thousand times, it was different now, after this you could only do worse. Home again, parents sleeping. It doesn't matter, sure it doesn't. That's what She told you. She said you could do whatever you liked because it was already done.*
>
> *So you crept in, pressed your hand on your sister's mouth and pulled back the covers. You made the place inside her, you made the place, but no one else could ever go there.*

I snapped the diary shut as a pair of chatty old women came by. One of them shot me a look, half suspicious and half I-don't-know-what-else.

It was wrong. I *wanted* to hate myself. But after the first time, there could be no undoing it—not for an ordinary mortal like me, anyway—and it felt too good to stop. Some nights, when my sister and I met eyes across the dinner table, I looked back at her as if she were just some girl sitting near me at the Burger King.

And on the day when that old woman plowed into the side of that station wagon, the first thing I thought was *now no one will ever know.*

But this is what religion is for, isn't it? No one's irredeemable, not even me. Síle knew everything, she'd seen "the stain on my heart," and it made no difference. She still wanted me.

For a long time, I sat on that bench looking at the figures dancing inside the glass, running my fingers over the embossed leather cover on the diary, checking the time on my iPhone as if I were waiting for someone.

I *was* waiting, wasn't I? I waited for a dark-haired woman to round that corner, look at me and smile; I waited for a glimpse of a woman too serene, too lovely to be of this earth, a woman who couldn't possibly be there. And when she came, I rose to greet her.